A I S L I N N
H U N T E R

Stay

POLESTAR
An Imprint of Raincoast Books

Raincoast Books acknowledges the ongoing financial support of the Government of Canada through The Canada Council for the Arts and the Book Publishing Industry Development Program (BPIDP); and the Government of British Columbia through the BC Arts Council.

Edited by Lynn Henry
Typeset by Teresa Bubela

NATIONAL LIBRARY OF CANADA CATALOGUING IN PUBLICATION DATA
Hunter, Aislinn, 1969–
  Stay

  ISBN 1-55192-568-0

  I. Title.
PS8565.U5766 S72 2002   C813'.6   C2002-910545-5
PR9199.4.H86S72 2002

LIBRARY OF CONGRESS CONTROL NUMBER: 2002105289

Raincoast Books   *In the United States:*
9050 Shaughnessy Street   Publishers Group West
Vancouver, British Columbia   1700 Fourth Street
Canada V6P 6E5   Berkeley, California
www.raincoast.com   94710

At Raincoast Books we are committed to protecting the environment and to the responsible use of natural resources. We are acting on this commitment by working with suppliers and printers to phase out our use of paper produced from ancient forests. This book is one step towards that goal. It is printed on 100% ancient-forest-free paper (100% post-consumer recycled), processed chlorine- and acid-free, and supplied by New Leaf paper. It is printed with vegetable-based inks. For further information, visit our website at www.raincoast.com. We are working with Markets Initiative (www.oldgrowthfree.com) on this project.

Printed in Canada by Houghton Boston Printers

10 9 8 7 6 5 4 3 2

For Glenn and for Kerry,
and in memory of Stella Laidlaw Shaw

"What would the living do
If they had not the dead to see to?"
— Dermot Healy

"mo ghrá thú*

With me, so you call me man.
Stay: winter is harsh to us ..."
— Michael Hartnett

* "I love you," in Gaelic

CONTENTS

Prologue

ALL EYES were on the church. The door had just closed and Father Whelan, two officers from the Garda, and a young man sent over from the *Independent* were safely in. Workmen on their way up the coast had pulled over; they sat behind their steering wheels in a row of cars that lined the near side of the road. They'd heard about the whole production last night on their tour of the pubs, the barman in Rossaveel relaying the news as he'd handed over their pints. So now they waited, arms hanging out their driver-side windows, stereos on RTE, music trailing over the grass to where twenty or so people had gathered in front of the building, their heads angled sideways, ears perked as if waiting for an explosion.

For a long time, no one moved. The church stood with its back to the bay and did nothing. Above, the gulls swung tight circles, one eye to the ground. A cleft in the clouds opened and the stained glass window over the main entrance winked, illuminated for an instant by the sun. At the front of the crowd a mobile phone rang, and Mrs. Keating pulled it from the depths of her shoulder bag, put it to her ear, whispered into it,

"No, nothing yet, Maeve. Nothing's happened." By the iron gate, a group from Spiddal had gathered. Conneely stood quietly with the rest of them, chewing his bottom lip and stuffing his hands farther into his back pockets. He was already telling the story in his head. Next to him Dermot Fay snorted through his nose at the tension.

Over the next hour more people arrived and cars filled the parking lot. Murmurs gave way to full-blown conversations. A good half of the crowd was running late for work. A general air of impatience welled up; people considered moving on. The Bord na Móna lads in their cars by the road grew restless. One of them eyed his side mirror repeatedly, waiting for the foreman to signal that it was time to go. Dermot checked his watch. It was nearly ten.

Overhead, the clouds that had been pinned over the bay started to move in from the water. The sky turned a dull shade of blue. People bundled themselves farther into their coats, scanned the throng for their spouses and children. Over by the gate: a girl wearing bunny ears and a boy with a wand. Eventually the sun passed behind the clouds and some of the crowd took this for a sign. Then the bells, a slow belaboured series of gongs. The church door opened and one of the garda, Charley from Oranmore, stepped out, the walkie talkie at his hip giving off static. He stopped on the top step, stunned by the size of the gathering, although crowds had been known to appear when reporters came around — something about news in the making and having been there. Coming down the walk, he eyed the motley group, tipped his hat.

"How's it?" one of the locals asked.

Charley lifted his chin. "He's using the holy water now."

A few minutes later, the priest came out; a second officer and the reporter flanked him on either side. He stood on the steps, his grey hair tousled, and announced to those assembled that it had gone as expected, adding "She's gone back," without any real conviction. The *Independent* reporter lifted his camera to take a few photos of the crowd. Dermot moved behind Keating and kept his head down. Tomorrow it would be in all the papers, he thought. "County yobs gather for a church exorcism." Things like that still played well in Dublin. In front of him, Keating shifted her ample girth, rummaged again in her bag for the mobile, dialed her sister's number in Spiddal. Some of the crowd picked up their briefcases or gathered their kids. A good number stayed put and stared at the church entrance. Father Whelan blocked the doorway, arms at his sides, wearing a look of near-exhaustion. There were murmurs of disappointment from the crowd — that they were not allowed in, that something miraculous had happened and they'd missed it. The reporter moved around and, in his little notebook, jotted down statements, an inventory of what people had seen and heard: the church bell ringing at odd hours, a fine mist surrounding the congregation on a Sunday in mid-March, a sing-song voice coming out from behind the velvet curtain of the confessional. This last report followed by a quickly drawn sign of the cross. Dermot snorted through his nose again.

It was Friday morning. The sky was clouding over, the breeze getting cooler, although earlier there'd been hope the sun would last. Herring gulls and crows careened over the roof of Saint Brighid's and around the church steeple. Father Whelan, confident no one would try for the door, took off his stole and came down the steps to circulate amongst the parishioners. He shook hands with the people he knew, nodded amicably at strangers, patted the head of the girl wearing the bunny ears before she hopped away in search of her brother. Finally, the mood of the crowd lifted. Music was turned up a notch in one of the parked cars — an upbeat pop song, the kind of music people might dance to. The crowd thinned and headed off, content with the knowledge that things were right in the world. There was the dead, and there was the living, and nothing in between.

Keating heaved herself into the driver's seat of the bakery van, and from the window offered Conneely a lift back to Spiddal. The old man accepted and slowly climbed in. Over by the gates a spaniel, his leash looped around a finial, barked twice then fell quiet. Dermot started the walk back to town, waving once at Keating's van as it passed him. It was only eight miles to the cottage, along the bay road. If he still felt out of sorts when he got home, he could keep walking, maybe as far as Inveran. Or he could just head past the cottage, and across the back field to old Saint Éinde's. Go from one church to another, like a sober man doing a tour of the pubs. Either way, he wasn't ready to go home. Abbey would be up by now and he didn't know what to say when he saw her.

In the parking lot of the church the last few cars pulled out and turned onto the road. Standing on the sidewalk near the hedge, Father Whelan, ready for an early lunch, took a quick look over the trampled front lawn and then headed for the rectory. The gulls circled one last time and then flew off towards the bay. Over by the road, the Bord na Móna foreman in the Nissan truck put his arm out the driver-side window and waved once in the direction of Maam Bog. Five cars started their engines in near unison. The stereos went up another notch. Then one after the other they pulled out onto the road, making their way up the coast.

I

Recensions

At the Church of Saint Éinde

DERMOT enters old St. Éinde's through a gaping hole that was once an entrance to the nave. Goat willow grows up the wall to the left of him and as he steps over the threshold, over a pile of loose stones, he reaches out to steady himself, his palm pushing up against the willow branches. Over by the south wall, the noise of a small animal skittering away. Dermot walks towards the transept looking up at the clouds that sit framed by the walls of the nave, touching the tops of the rotting wood pews as he goes. Towards the altar, a plastic bag in a puddle of water, two empty cider bottles, a soggy *Hello* magazine. He stands over the magazine and looks for the date. Some pop star or other on the cover. Dermot sits down in the first pew, a crushed take-away box at his feet. The edge of the roof above him exactly, so that if it starts to rain he'll only have to lean forward to stay dry.

On his way to Éinde's, Dermot passed the cottage, looked in the bedroom window and saw that Abbey was still sleeping. The light coming in and settling on her arm, her face buried in the blankets. He left a note scrawled on a tear-away sheet from his note pad. It said "at the church" and now he imagines that at any minute she'll step out the front door and see it under the stone on the mat, that she'll pull on her boots and cut across the field to find him. And then what will he do? Dermot pushes his back into the bench and the dampness from the wood moves through him. Last night she said she had to go. *Just the week, to Dublin for work.* Then back. "You'll barely notice I'm gone." And he didn't say anything, just listened to the sound of the tap dripping in the next room, stared at her as if it was starting all over again, the coming and going.

When Abbey walks into the church a half-hour later, Dermot's on bended knee undoing the laces of his left boot. He throws the boot at the wall over what was once the altar. Then he yanks his right boot off, throws it too. It cartwheels once and drops ten feet in front of him. He walks up to it and kicks it with his socked foot, picks up both boots and starts again. Aims for what was once a rose window. Puts everything he has into it. The faint thud of the rubber sole pounds into the stone. Finally, the one boot makes it through the opening, hitting the alder tree beyond. A crack of branches and Dermot, and Abbey behind him, both listen to see if the boot finds the ground. His thin black socks are half falling off his feet. After a minute Dermot turns to Abbey, looks at his socks and laughs. Says, "How long have you been here?" A dozen mossy rot-wood pews between them.

This is when Abbey loves him most: furrowed brow, lines around his eyes, a look that says he's been caught at something. Shaking his head he says, "I don't know Ab," as if he ever knew, as if any day he might figure it out, find the equation. Dermot is fifty-five and looks his age entirely. Abbey's twenty-six and she's been with him almost a year. Going over to him, she takes his hand.

Waits for him to look at her.

"Why didn't you wake me?"

Dermot says nothing, lets go of her hand. Sits back down in the first pew, eyeing the clouds above. After a minute he says, "You're already gone," turning to her after he says it.

Back at the cottage Dermot fills the bathroom sink with warm water and starts to wash up. He rounds the corner with a towel in his hand and looks into the bedroom. She's packing her things.

"I didn't say you couldn't go." Dermot hunches over, the bedroom ceiling two inches above his head. He doesn't want her to leave on a sour note. He wants to be in the clear.

"Yes, you did." Abbey avoids his eyes. The entire contents of the dresser drawer shoved into her backpack; the blue knit scarf he'd given her knotted around the strap.

"Abbey, you're just back." Gripping her wrist now, trying to get her to stop packing. She glances down at his hand and he lets go.

They'd been through this last night. He remembers now. He'd said he wouldn't stand for it, her leaving again.

"Whatever I said," Dermot starts in slowly, "what I meant was that I wanted you to stay."

Abbey closes the dresser drawer and watches the two of them in the mirror above.

"Abbey, listen."

She looks at him, not sure if he's asking her for something or if he's getting ready to state something. Dermot poses everything as if it were a question, his Irish lilt an upswing at the end of every thought. Even when he says "I love you," it sounds as if he's asking.

"It's just a week," she reiterates.

Dermot walks to the bedroom door, taps the curling edge of

the old carpet with his toe. "I'm too old for this."

At the door, Flagon starts barking, her tail hitting the side of the couch. She loops round to the bedroom, knocks Dermot's knees, goes out again into the front room, comes back. Dermot walks over to the front door with her, lifts the latch and the Border collie takes off as soon as the door is open, chasing after Mrs. McGilloway in the postal van.

"Are we over?" He asks it from the living room. Abbey pulls the drawstring on her pack, then goes out with it, sets it on the couch. She takes his face in her hands and kisses him again and again, trying to convince him that she's coming back.

An hour later, driving towards Galway, the Mini chugs and sputters, clunks along like it's losing power before surging forward again. Outside the window: low-rolling fields, a maze of stone fences, heavy clouds coming in. The dark hump of Inishmore barely visible across the bay. Abbey watches Dermot for a minute before turning towards the fields. When they get close to Furbo, Dermot points out the church, tells her about the exorcism, the Garda and the reporter, Father Whelan stumbling out of the building like a man who'd come through a wind storm. He tells her about the kids playing football in the parking lot while the parents looked on. He remarks there was a good-sized crowd from Spiddal, adds, "I should have brought you down."

Abbey looks back out the window and tries to imagine an exorcism. The priest holding the cross out in front of him, altar boys carrying holy water, a look of absolute terror on their faces. What then? Biblical verses and incense? How exactly do you stop the dead from haunting the living? How do you pinpoint that presence and say "it resides here"? For the first time in her life it occurs to

Abbey that revenants might exist. Maybe the dead do come back, the way her father has been with her since the funeral. Not quite here, not quite a whirly spirit, but in her head. Knocking around.

"All right?" Dermot drops his left hand onto Abbey's thigh.

"Yeah. Fine."

Changing gears to pass a transport, Dermot's knee hits the underside of the dashboard. The Mini is still giving up its grief. When they get by the truck there's the line of the bay again, a row of new bungalows going up along the coast road, some only blocks of foundation, some nearly finished. Two-storey peach-coloured stucco buildings dot the fields. A group of similar bungalows is going up on the lot next to Dermot's cottage. Only their foundations are done, although Bord Fáilte plans to have them ready for the tourists by the summer.

"It's just a week." Abbey says it once again to reassure him. "I promised I'd cover Aileen's shifts."

When she looks over at Dermot he is squinting at something up in the distance. He turns the windshield wipers on and lets them flap a few times each way even though it isn't raining.

"And then I'll get work closer to Spiddal."

Dermot scratches the bottom of his nose with his thumb.

Being with Dermot has never been easy. But Abbey knows that's part of what draws her to him. She's been waylaid, which is exactly what she'd wanted. It was the Old Bailey that did it — Dermot, two hands around his pint glass, saying, "I can't help but feel I could have done something more with my life." Abbey'd only just met him. Angela, already sorry she'd introduced the two of them, said, "Fuck off, Dermot," as she dropped her purse on the chair, went over to the bar. Later, she told Abbey she'd heard it all too many times before.

"As if I was on the cusp of something," Dermot had continued, ignoring Angela. And Abbey'd tried to nudge her chair closer to Dermot's, the back leg getting caught in the carpet so that in the end she had to stand and pick it up, lift it by the arms, place it next to his.

Eight miles outside of Galway, Dermot drives off the asphalt onto the shoulder of the road, gravel crunching under the tires. An alder tree on the far side of the shallow ditch. Hitting the brakes, Dermot brings the Mini to a full stop. Turns the ignition off. Abbey half expects him to get out and kick the tire, open the boot, root around for a wrench to beat the engine with. But part of her knows nothing's wrong. He's buying time. Dermot gets out of the car and stands in the open door, laying his arms over the roof, tapping his fingers on the metal. Abbey turns towards him and finds herself looking at his shirt buttons, the one above his belt gaping open. It makes her think of the photos she's seen from his days at Trinity, how needle-thin and angular he was, his hair dark and trimmed. Dermot kneels down to face Abbey, neck craned sideways.

"Abbey I want — " and he smoothes his hands over his face as if ten years in a stone cottage without modern conveniences can be erased.

"If I had it to do over — " he starts in again, shoulders lifting a bit as if to brace himself. But he stops, looks at her directly.

"Marry me." A statement this time, not even a question. "Marry me, Abbey."

Abbey opens her door and then closes it. She sits still, staring at her hands. There are a hundred things she could say here but none of them make sense. She opens her mouth but no sound comes out. Forty feet away the bay laps at the stones that skirt the beach. A car goes by. Then another. Dermot straightens, stands there for a second. Then, without a word, he starts walking up the road.

Carrying On

SOME twenty minutes later, Abbey gets out of the Mini and heads towards Barna wondering if at some point she'll see Dermot sitting or stopped on the side of the road, if he's waiting for her to catch up to him. Or maybe he'll be coming toward her. She adjusts her backpack straps and squints down the coast road until it veers east, inland. To her left a series of fields that slope down to the roadside, towards bent barbed-wire fences. Three cars drive by in quick succession. A few stones settle on the side of the road after the last one passes. Then nothing. Abbey bends down to tighten the laces on her boots and then stands up, starts hoofing it to town. He won't be there up the road. He's pissed off. Embarrassed. This is how it works with them. Dermot will carry on without her. He'll walk up the road, double back through a field, get in the Mini and drive home. Enough cars will pass that Abbey will get a lift into Galway, or once she gets to a phone she can call Corrib Taxi. Either way, she'll maneuver towards Dublin and Dermot will go back the way he came. It's their old argument. She goes to Dublin to work and every time she walks out the door he convinces himself he'll never see her again. When she went home for her father's funeral a week and a half ago it was worse. The look on Dermot's face at the airport. Abbey saying it would be a good chance for her to bring back more of her things.

The truth of it is, she wants to stay. Wishes she was in the Mini heading back to the cottage with him, that at six they'd walk down the coast road to get dinner at Hughes', that they'd spend half the evening in the pub, Abbey sitting beside Dermot, watching how he nods his head at everyone who walks in the door. That's what Abbey's drawn to. The sense of belonging. Of not being afraid who'll walk in on you when you're sitting in a room. Even if she's just welcome by association, even if she's riding on Dermot's good graces, it's something she's never known. But Spiddal will carry on without her. People coming into Hughes will nod at Dermot, converse with him just the same. There'll be music playing in the back room. At eight PM the Guinness taps will gurgle and fart on cue, and Niall will go and change the line. Old man Conneely will sit at the bar baiting anyone who dares to take the next stool. The twenty-year-olds will drink Budweiser and talk about Dublin bands or football. Towards ten someone will open the door and wedge a stone between it and the frame to let in some air. Things will seem the same.

Abbey remembers the last day she'd worked at Gabby's Diner in Windsor, Ontario, how the bells rang above her head as she'd opened the door to leave. She'd worked there for over five years. The staff had thrown a party for her that afternoon with cake and balloons, and had presented her with a going-away gift that consisted of an inflatable airplane pillow, a "Gabby's Diner" t-shirt with the Windsor skyline on it, a bunch of envelopes bearing the staff's addresses, a box of Maple Leaf cookies. Turning in the open doorway to wave, Abbey saw the new waitress they'd hired already putting on Abbey's old apron. Mikki and Jenna were chatting her up, talking about the copper highlights in her hair. Abbey called out "bye" but the word didn't carry over the stereo and the customer conversations.

Now, as she tromps along the road to Galway, Abbey imagines what her life would be like if she was still in Windsor. She looks at her watch. It's nine AM in Ontario. The coffee rush is in full swing at Gabby's. The muffins are selling like crazy, the bells over the door are constantly ringing.

Abbey bends over to pull a pebble out of her boot. She's pushing her fingers down between boot and heel when a car passes. Finding the stone, she straightens up and sticks out her thumb — too late for the driver to have noticed. She looks back, hoping for someone to come along and offer her a ride. Another ten minutes at a good clip and she'll pass through Barna. She could call a taxi from there. Or, if she keeps walking past Barna, she'll come to the caravan park: dilapidated trailers and slick Euro caravans set up side by side in an overgrown field. There's always a good bit of traffic heading in and out, tourists and travelers going into Galway. Maybe she can get a lift from there.

Another car comes towards her and even though Abbey's thumb is out, poised mid-air, the blue Civic drives by without even slowing.

After two more cars race by without stopping, it occurs to Abbey that her rucksack probably makes her look too much like a tourist. Five years ago that would've been an asset but the locals are fed-up with tourists now, especially in Galway in the off season. Without her pack Abbey looks Irish enough — her grandparents came over from Donegal back in the forties — but as soon as she opens her mouth her flat intonation gives her away. "Hi" instead of "Hiya," "excuse me" instead of "sorry."

Two summers ago when Abbey was getting ready to leave Windsor, when she'd finally gathered the nerve to go, she'd gone over to break the news to her Aunt Jane. They'd argued for hours, Abbey standing in the kitchen with her back to the fridge. The accusations non-stop: "inconsiderate, childish, as-selfish-as-your-mother." Jane had looked out the window a good seven or eight times, her disgust palpable. She said, "Your father is dying, for Christ's sake," as if Abbey hadn't a clue. And that was part of it. Frank was demanding too much of Abbey, phoning her at all hours, refusing to eat, to get out of bed, to take his medication. Jane listened, pulled a cigarette out of the pack on the kitchen counter, lit it pointedly. "You can't go," she'd said. Then she turned her back on Abbey, stood in the archway between the kitchen and living room watching the TV while Abbey waited by the dishwasher, nervously fingering the cro-cheted tea cozy that lay on the end of the counter. After ten minutes Abbey pulled her coat on. She asked Jane to look in on Frank, make sure the nurses' aids hired by the home-care agency showed up when they were supposed to.

Jane looked over her shoulder, said, "He's your father," and then, "When did you start calling him Frank?" The news droned on over the silence that followed. Abbey's hand on the door knob. "If you were my kid …" Jane said, shaking her head at that, watching Abbey open the door and go.

He Rearranges the Furniture

DERMOT is pacing. Goes from the front room to the kitchen and back again, grazing his knuckles along the arm of the brown couch as he turns. He taps his head with the flat of his hand. Why can't he ever let things be? Back in the kitchen Flagon puts her snout into her yellow plastic bowl, knocks it once then stands there, waiting for him to feed her. He'd done the wrong thing, said it wrong, and there is no way of going back on it. He thinks about why he'd proposed, makes a mental list, linear, rational, like he'd been taught to do, as he'd shown others when he'd taught at Trinity. Count the versions of the manuscript, write down how they differ, make your notations in the following manner, be precise. There is never one version, every story can be told a hundred ways. He considers writing down "why I love her," revising it until he has it right, leaving copies for future scholars. In six hundred years they could try to make sense of it, put the list in order. Why he first loved Abbey Gowan — her youth, attentive nature; and why he later loved her — the sex, smell of her skin in the morning, for singing off-key in the bath;

and why he finally loved her — for never admitting she thought he was full of shit, or for being naive enough not to notice. There would be a progression anyway, all notes copied in the same hand, a number of recensions filed away, the odd scrap of marginalia: she changed me / she didn't change me / she did.

"She's coming back." He practices saying it. Hates himself for doubting it'll only be the week. "Her shirts are drying out on the line." He says this too, as if it's proof enough, as if in seven days Abbey will be at the door, slipping into his rubber boots, trudging outside to unpeg the clothes, bringing them in flat and stiff with wind. Flagon picks her bowl up in her mouth and drops it at Dermot's feet; she barks into it, paws it until it flips over. Grabbing it, Dermot walks over to the sink, bends down, opens the cupboard, scoops some food out of a bucket.

"An bhfuil tú an madra?" he asks her, ruffles the fur on the back of her neck as she leans in and starts eating. He watches as she burrows her nose around in the bottom of the bowl, half of the food spilling out over the side. "Yes, you are a dog." He says it in English, then in Latin, then French. Flagon's head is in the bowl even though most of the food is on the floor. The whole enterprise moving in increments across the kitchen linoleum as she noses it along. "I told you so," he says, kneeling down beside her. She looks up at him for a second then goes back to eating. Dermot adding, "I won't tell you who I am."

Dermot decides he'll be busy, get some work done so things will have changed while Abbey's gone. Cut his hair, call and make an appointment, go clean shaven. Anything. At least get up off the floor. He rings his friend Michael in Galway. "I'm rearranging the furniture. Would you give us a lift to Hughes?" Dermot sits in his chair by the fire, eyes the couch perpendicular to the door, the coal bucket, the stool against the wall opposite, the big oak table and two chairs by the far window, everything in its place, in the place Abbey has put it. Dermot remembers when she first moved in at the start of winter, the mess of the cottage, the drafts coming through the gashed thatch roof. Abbey, keeping her coat on from the cold, had walked through the front room, stopping to tap the glass of the framed manuscript that he'd hung over the bookshelf.

"What's this?"

"Kiliani Vitae," Dermot said, going past with her bag, not even glancing at the illuminated page.

"Is it real?" She'd traced the capital K, the bold red and blue strokes that curled into a fox's head and tail. After the "K" the writing was small and ornate. He'd looked at her from where he was standing in the bedroom doorway; her bag sitting on the end of the bed.

"A reproduction."

"Oh."

He went over to her then, to warm her hands between his. Abbey's eyes welling up.

"It's a copy of the fourth recension of his life."

Abbey kept her head down; she was watching his big pale hands go bump bump over her knuckles, back and forth. Dermot moved his hand to her hairline, pushed a strand of her hair back.

"My thesis." That's when he knew it for sure. He'd have to be gentle with her, he'd have to explain things, he'd have to weigh what he said.

"There's stacks of books on our friend Kilian under the bed. He met a particularly bitter end."

Abbey laughed and looked around, then started crying.

"If you're not sure." Dermot said it slowly. Still, he had it out before he could retract it. He didn't care if she was sure or not, he just didn't want her coming and going all the time, a day here and there and then the bus to Dublin, another day God-knows-when dictated by her work schedule. He was tired of waiting for her to come around. It was all or nothing, he didn't have the means to manage anything else. They'd only been together two months. He remembers thinking that if he strung the days one after the other they would amount to a week and a half. "Stay with me," he'd muttered the week before when she was halfway out the door for Dublin. The closest he'd come to commitment in years. *Stay. Unpack. Eat three meals at my table.* And then here she was, her bag set down on the foot of his bed.

"Are we all right?" he asked.

"Fine." She walked straight into his chest, scratched her chin on his blue wool sweater. "Really, it's fine."

Dermot's hands on the back of her head, her neck, one hand finding her wrist so that he could bring it up to his lips. Abbey stepping back, accidentally bumping the narrow bookshelf, the framed manuscript knocking back against the wall above, the cup of coins on the top shelf jingling around in their mug. She'd almost started to cry again.

"All right?"

"Yep."

"You'd think we were falling apart here."

Abbey wiped her nose on her sleeve. "One of us, anyway."

"Come here," he said, turning the corner, walking into the bathroom. He turned the taps over the tub on, and pulling up his sleeve he set the plug in.

"Have a bath. I'll get the fire up."

"Where's Flagon?"

"I'll call her in."

Steam started to filter up from the taps. Leaving the room, Dermot saw Abbey unbuttoning her overcoat, undoing her jeans.

Dermot turns the picture frame that sits on the side table towards him. It's a black and white photo from one of those booths in Dublin; Abbey too close to the camera, eyes wide, clip of dark hair angling in across her cheek. He looks rough, like he'd been left out in the elements, forgotten. He turns the frame the slightest bit so it sits on an angle, a gesture she probably won't even notice. He wants the cottage to go back to its original state, wants the gash in the thatch roof to widen, the table to be covered in papers, the dishes left out on the counter instead of put away. He thinks back to when the mud floor wasn't covered by rugs, when all he had he could count on the one hand — dishes, a sleeping bag and kettle. Dermot bunches up the wool blanket on the couch, he throws the candles on the mantle into the bin so she'll think he's lit them, that they've burned down to nothing in her absence. He goes back to the photo and puts it face down so he doesn't have to see himself; turns the ringer off on the phone. Then he waits. It'll be half an hour or more before Michael pulls up. Dermot plants himself on the couch, turns the radio on and then, unhappy with the blather on RTE, switches it off. Sits there in the quiet. Waits for the house to go dark around him.

Spar

AFTER his fourth pint at Hughes, Dermot steps out. Walks
through the rain past the bakery, the closed tourist shop,
careful to stay under the awnings. The street is dark save for
the Spar, which is lit up like a ferry port. The bells jingle
above the door of the corner store as Dermot enters, and he
is immediately stunned by the fluorescent light. Walking
over to the counter he eyes the *Times* but leaves it.

"Dermot," says the cashier; the boy leaning forward,
slack-jawed, eager.

"Jimmy," says Dermot.

Dermot feigns an interest in the magazines, then turns his
attention to the front page of the *Independent*. Picks it up,
puts it down. He walks up to the cash and wavers, plants his
hands on the counter top and enunciates "John Players," so as
not to give off a slur. Jimmy turns, grabs a pack off the shelf,
sets it firmly down in front of him.

"Anything else, then?"

"No."

Or had Michael asked for something? He pictures getting

up at the pub to run over, and Michael asking for … Dermot tries to figure out what it could be. A paper, a bar, a piece of fruit? Dermot looks around for a clue. Was it a snack Michael wanted? It almost comes to Dermot, but Jimmy interrupts and it's gone.

"Did ya hear about Mrs. McGilloway?"

"No."

"She passed on this afternoon."

Dermot staggers back a step and then catches himself. Jimmy watches him; his face a mess of pock marks and freckles.

"Eileen McGilloway?" Dermot's voice is garbled, his tongue feels thick.

"The postmistress."

Dermot shakes his head. "I know."

"McGilloway's only just gone fifty-three." Jimmy starts to ring in the Players.

"What of?"

"That's four fifty-five."

Dermot already has the exact change on the counter.

"What of?" Dermot repeats.

"Sorry?"

"Eileen McGilloway."

"I think it was the heart."

Drunk, Dermot chortles for no reason, turns and walks out under the ruckus of the door.

"Eileen McGilloway's died," Dermot says.

"I've heard." Michael gestures with his thumb to the next table, where a group of women are sitting. "Just like that. After her postal run this morning." He finishes off his pint and shifts around in his seat, turning his attention to the women. They've been talking about McGilloway since they came in.

"Can you believe it?" Margaret Keating turns to Dermot. Her eyes liquid.

"Jimmy just told me."

"She was still in the van, it was parked in the drive." Keating has gone over this detail again and again since she heard. "Tom Joyce found her. Slumped over in the seat."

"The neighbour," Dermot says. Michael nods.

Keating takes her coat off, puts it down on the stool between herself and the seamstress from Furbo. The younger girl, elbows on the table, chin in her hand, says, "I imagine Deirdre'll be coming over from Dublin now." Stirring her gin with a plastic straw.

"I'd say so." Keating takes a sip of her pint.

Dermot leans towards Michael. "Deirdre's the daughter."

"I gathered, but thanks all the same." Michael says it loud enough that Keating looks over, surprised by his British accent. Tries to place if she's seen him with Dermot before. She has. The archeologist. From London. After a minute she turns to Dermot, says, "Ní fhaca mé thú le tamall."

"I was there this morning. At the church."

Keating holds still. "Right. You were."

Michael raises his glass in the women's direction, says, "To Eileen —" Suddenly unsure of her last name. The women lift their glasses and then turn away. Over by the door three of the Bord na Móna lads come in, voices raised. The talk is football, the World Cup.

"He was injured or he'd have made the cut," says one.

"No way," says another, "it was Carsley from the start."

"Kennedy should be there."

"Carsley."

"Catch yerself on."

Niall nods their way from the bar. The three of them traipse over to the counter, mud slaked onto the floor as they make their way past. A few hands go up by the far wall in greeting. A "Hiya Tomás" is called out. People move aside to give them a few stools and they settle in. Two from a second car follow a minute later. They've come from Maam. Every Friday they do a tour of the pubs. Michael nods at a man called Angus; he's met him once or twice while doing surveys out at the bog.

"How's it Michael?" Angus' hand on Michael's shoulder as he moves through the crowd.

"Well enough."

"Grand." And the two men in their rubber boots, work pants and coats join the other three at the bar. Pint after pint appearing on the counter before them.

After another round Dermot and Michael fall silent, listening to the banter at the bar. The Bord na Móna lads have moved from football to the exorcism at St. Brighid's and then on to the upcoming election. Fianna Fáil and Fine Gael posters on every second lamp post along the coast road.

"Bertie'll take it."

"A majority?"

"You'd think."

"You'd hardly know one from the other."

"My mother lives next to the Sinn Fein fellow in Tuam."

"I thought she was in Clonbern."

"No, came over a year ago."

Conneely, his back against the door jamb between the two rooms, clears his throat, leans in to Tomás, the foreman. "Did you know Eileen McGilloway?"

Tomás jabs his thumb at the blond fellow two stools down, "Liam did. He dated the daughter."

Over the next hour, the room becomes more crowded. The seisiún in the back hits its stride and then flounders again when the fiddle player makes for the bar. Everyone is talking about McGilloway. Over at the next table, Margaret Keating lifts her doughy elbows into an old tweed coat. She backs into Michael's seat by accident, almost ends up on his lap. There are stunned looks from the other women at her table. Brigid, Keating's niece, had come in an hour ago, and as her aunt rights herself Brigid counts the number of empty glasses in front of her place at the table.

"All right?" Michael says, steadying Keating's arm. Teetering on her heels, Margaret nods at the two men before pulling her purse straps onto her shoulder. She squeezes Dermot on the arm then goes by him.

Dermot pulls out a cigarette and lights it, inhales. "She was my age."

"Eileen McGilloway?"

"The very one."

"Do you know the daughter?" Michael asks.

"I've not seen her since she moved to Dublin." Dermot says "Dublin" and the right side of his face flinches. He rubs his cheek with his hand. Michael has brought up the issue of Abbey again without meaning to. Dermot had avoided the subject early in the evening, had eventually started in about it, then went to the bar before he'd said too much. When he came back, he'd changed the conversation to Michael's conservancy project at the Museum. When Michael had broached the subject of Abbey again later, Dermot suddenly announced he had to head over to the Spar.

"Where's my Marathon?" Michael remembers he'd asked for a chocolate bar.

"Still at the shop." Dermot turning his glass in his hands.

Michael gets up, walks over to Niall, buys a Smithwicks and a bag of crisps. The pub is stifling — there are coal fires at either end of the room, the low ceiling trapping the heat. A trickle of sweat inches past Michael's ear. On his way back to the table, Michael looks into Hughes' second room, wondering if it's cooler. The bigger room is a mix of wood high-backs and fold-out chairs, a large L-shaped couch along the far wall, an old card table set up beside it. Like a banquet room that hasn't quite come together. There are kids sprawled out on the couch and a woman bounces a little girl on her knee over on one of the far chairs. The musicians pick up again after a break. If it weren't for the large wood beams that cross over the ceilings of both rooms, and the cardboard Guinness coasters set out on every table, you'd never put the two rooms together. By the open window, the fiddle player tunes his instrument. The guitar gets underway.

"It's only a week right?" Michael says as he sits back down.

Dermot shakes his head, sets his arm over the back of Michael's chair. "Listen —"

But there's nothing behind it, just Dermot saying "listen," the word slurred out and bullshit Dermot'll make up on the spot to follow.

"What do you know about —" Dermot's eyes move left to right "—time?" Dermot's known Eileen McGilloway for twenty-two years. He'd even taken supper with her after her husband died, helped look after Deirdre on more than one afternoon.

Michael looks at his watch without thinking. Dermot shakes his head.

"And so it was," Dermot says, looking around the room. A woman in track pants and a shiny blue shirt smiles as she walks past him, the last remnants of her lager sloshing around in her glass. Michael turns in his seat and redirects his attention to the coal fire, pulls at the collar of his shirt.

"And so it was," Dermot repeats, faintly, behind him.

The Bay Road

SEAN O'Riordan steps out onto the main road. The rain has let up, but the street's slick, a black sheen over it. The construction work that's started up all over the village is further underway. Yesterday, scaffolding went up in front of Feeny's butcher shop. The window panes on the second floor of the house were stripped and repainted; Feeny clambered down the ladder whenever a customer walked in to the storefront. By the end of the day he'd finished four windows and had settled on a spot for the B&B sign that was coming from Doherty's. Sean had watched him that evening, outside with his wife, moving a cardboard version of the sign back and forth before Mrs. Feeny decided they'd put baskets of flowers on either side of the centre windows, and the sign directly between.

In Spiddal, things are being torn down and built up in equal measure. The Allied Irish Bank building that sat on the corner next to Hughes was demolished in a matter of two days and the AIB installed a bank machine at the Spar directly afterwards. A grocery is going up in place of the bank, far it's just a concrete pit with metal girders sticking out of the walls. Two roads back, Tele Gael is building a sound studio and a set for an Irish language soap opera. The fish and chip shop is remodelling. Only the new church has stayed the same. Sean eyes it from the main junction. The facade lit up by spotlights hidden in the surrounding hedge. A low railing around the garden. Another spotlight shining towards the coast, a life-size statue of the Virgin. Sean shoots her the finger, shoves his hands in his pockets, starts walking.

It takes ten minutes to get to the end of the village if you turn around at the river. Beyond that, there's nothing except the hotel. There are nine houses between the centre of the village and the bridge, there's the reading room, the post office. All the lights are off until the Folan house. The telly going from blue to yellow in the front window. Back to blue again. Sean stands there a minute and watches the light flicker on their ceiling. He sees one of the Folans stand up and leave the room. Too dark to tell if it's a man or a woman. Someone puts their arm over the back of the couch, the empty space beside them. Sean kicks at a few stones on the side of the road. Picks up a rock and wheels it at the tree trunk in the yard. Misses. When the sidewalk ends Sean keeps walking along the roadside. Counts the paces between street lamps. Fourteen. Fifteen. Sixteen. Seventeen. And Eighteen. Under the globe again. He kicks a puddle, watches the water run over his Docs. At the end of the houses, a byroad angles down to the beach. Across from the byroad is the seafood restaurant his parents go to. Spiddal River's a quarter mile beyond, the draining point for some twelve lakes. Sean's father took him fishing for salmon there once. They caught ling and grisle too. On the other side of the river, in amongst the trees, sits the Bridge House Hotel. Four storeys painted yellow, bright green shutters framing the windows.

Standing on the bay road, Sean looks up the coast, notes how it closes in on itself in the darkness. But he knows exactly how it goes: a quarter of a mile up the road there's the river; then, less than a mile on, there's a bend that curves east before going west again; then, more turns in the road and stone beaches that skirt the shore all the way to Clifden. Weekends he rides his brother's bike that way. The sound of the waves hitting the pier. Beach on your left, fields to your right, sewn together like a quilt that reaches down to the head of the Atlantic, the whole coast of Ireland caving in. The air becomes different the farther north you go. Wind like a solid wall. Men fishing from the piers or coming in on the boats. Sean's Uncle Jack in Roundstone took him out one summer to see what it was like. Sean could end up on the boats; that's what his father tells him.

Sean circles back and stops at the main junction, looks in the chip shop window. They rent DVDs and videos out of the back room now. There's an internet station set up in the alcove by the pay phone. Flynn, the owner, is leaning over the counter in his paper cap, reading a magazine; no one else is around. Sean walks across the road and takes up a position on the low concrete wall of the would-be grocers. The music coming out of Hughes just reaches him, the din from inside getting louder whenever someone walks out the door to straggle home.

After ten minutes of not much happening, Sean sees Jenny Welsh and her mother come up the road and head over to Flynn's. Jenny has a big red hand-bag tucked under her arm. Sean watches as she steps into the light cast by the square of the window. The two women are the same height now; their shoes clip-clop on the pavement, water splashing up onto the back of Jenny's tights. Flynn looks up when they enter. Sean is seventeen, the same age as Jenny, but she looks older — her face, her clothes; something he can't quite put his finger on. When they first met she was thirteen, had moved with her family from Donegal. She was the first girl Sean ever got off with. Out by the pier. If her father, a solicitor in Galway, knew, he'd probably have Sean killed. They were supposed to be in school but Jenny had sent him a note in Maths telling him to meet her by the breakwall after lunch. His hand up her shirt two seconds after he put his tongue in her mouth.

This summer half the kids Sean knows will be going off to college or moving to the city. Jenny's going to UCD for economics. Clancy's doing IT training in Dublin. Sean's grades haven't left him much of a chance to go on. His father talks about the boats by way of a threat, but sometimes he asks Sean to think about apprenticing, becoming an electrician.

Jenny and her mother come out of the chip shop and Jenny looks across the street to where Sean is sitting bundled into his black duffel coat. She calls "Hiya Sean," waving. He wishes she hadn't looked over, caught him glomming around, but he lifts his hand and waves. Jenny's mother, noticing it's Sean, waves as well. Then Mrs. Welsh opens up her umbrella, even though the rain has mostly let up, and she and Jenny crowd together to walk under it as they head towards home. The smell of chips and vinegar trailing behind them.

When the rain starts in again Sean gets up, heads for the side street. Seven houses in is the new two-storey his father bought last year. The door was bright red when they moved in, and Sean's father painted the trim and shutters to match. Wood planters are starting to sprout under the sills. It's a big change from the stone house they had on the coast road. There are neighbours on either side of them now, so in the summer, when the windows are left open, Sean hears their radios, their arguments, their children crying.

Even in the winter there's noise from the village junction, the church bells, people tumbling out of the pub after last call, car alarms whooping and honking on the main road.

As Sean heads home, Dermot and Michael make their way up the side street to the Big House. They'll climb the wrought iron gate and go in, walk the property to the river. Take the tunnel that leads out under the road and then start back from the beach. It's the fresh air they're after, the adventure. At the top of the road they eye the gate. Michael pulls at it. The lock and chain rattle back and forth on the crossbar. Dermot puts a hand up towards the top rung, to the finial. He hangs there a second and then drops down.

"There's dogs. Two dogs."

They listen for the dogs but hear nothing. Crickets sound out from the hedge.

"What's to stop us?" Michael asks. The top of the gate two feet above him.

"The dogs," Dermot says again.

When they turn around to go back to the coast road, Dermot stops to light a cigarette. Michael looks left and sees Sean. He's sitting on the top step of his porch, under the overhang, out of the rain.

"Right there?"

"All right."

Michael sits down on the step. Dermot turns around to see where Michael's gone.

"We were just up the road." Michael nods to the top of the street.

Sean smirks. The guy's accent is pure BBC1. "I saw ya's. You can break in through the tunnel. There's a gate at the end. Just take a pen. It's an old lock."

"What's your name?"

"Sean."

"I'm Michael, and this is Dermot. We're just," and he tosses his head in the direction of the pub.

Dermot lifts his hand, then crosses his arms over his chest. Sean nods at both of them.

"What do you do?"

"Sorry?"

"With your time," Michael clarifies, belching once but managing to keep his mouth closed.

The boy looks at him, a drunk English man in baggy trousers and wet loafers.

"What's it to you?"

"Do you need a job?"

Sean shrugs.

Dermot looks at Michael and staggers back a bit. Michael doesn't even know the kid, and he lives in Galway for Christsake. What kind of work could he give him?

"Dermot here needs a fence around his property. Four pound an hour." Michael looks over at Dermot. "Or Euros. Christ. What about six Euros an hour?"

Dermot shakes his head, steps forward. He no more needs a fence then he can afford to build one.

"You've been complaining about the bungalows all night. It's all you've been saying," Michael explains.

Sean recognizes Dermot — the ex-professor from Dublin. His property backs onto the stream near the old church. A couple of times he's seen him out in the back fields and he's seen him come and go from Hughes.

"I'll do it for four-fifty an hour."

Dermot, his grey hair wild about his head, looks at the boy. Then he looks at Michael. Conneely goes by on a rickety bicycle and rings his bell. The kid wipes his nose with his coat sleeve.

Why not? A fence. Everyone should have one. And at that moment Dermot believes it, thinks that his problems might be solved, solvable, if he can contain them, separate them. Mine and yours. The bungalows over there, the cottage over here and Dermot and Abbey in the middle of it, drawn together by a patch of land, wood and wire around them. He looks at Sean again. The kid can't be more than sixteen.

"Should have tried for five." And Dermot can't believe he's saying it.

"Okay, five Euros an hour."

"Too late." Dermot puts out his hand. Looks over at Michael. "You'll get yours."

The kid stepping forward. Takes the hand, shakes it.

Going Out On the Town

ABBEY wakes up twenty miles outside of Dublin. The bus droning along, the other passengers asleep or staring out the windows into the darkness. In the back a man and a woman talk quietly. Abbey has been dreaming about the funeral. That she opened the casket and there was no one there. In the dream she turned to Jane and said, "Where is he?" And Jane took off her shoes, the black pumps she'd had on at the service, and threw them at Abbey.

The Shaws had come to bury Frank. That was a surprise. And Jane made a big show of welcoming them. Abbey was just off the plane; she'd rented a car at Pearson in Toronto and drove two hundred miles through the flat expanse of Southern Ontario to get to the church in Merlin. On the front steps of St. Pat's, Jane stood with Isabelle and Robert Shaw, introducing them to the city workers who'd had shifts with Frank. "These are relatives of Frank's," she'd said to the city employees and Abbey had to give her credit for that. But when the coffin went into the ground, the Shaws stood on one side of the grave and Jane and Abbey stood on the other. Abbey looking at Isabelle the whole time and seeing herself there, the same height and build, the same dark hair. The Shaws were mostly in their fifties, and Frank was the spitting image of one of the younger brothers.

Midway through the service Jane put a hand on Abbey's arm, was watching her watching the Shaws. Then the priest threw a clump of dirt on the grave. Jane stepped forward and did the same. People turned to Abbey. She bent forward and scooped up a handful from the mound of earth near her feet. Let it go over the casket. A small stone skipped over the mahogany. The Shaws did nothing, as if they had no right, despite being Frank's blood relations. Four brothers and a sister. The sum total of all their parts. Even though they were standing next to the grave, even though they'd driven for over four hours to get to his funeral, making the effort to show up in pressed suits and polished shoes, Isabelle fingering her pearl necklace, Frank wouldn't have forgiven them. One last affront — that's how he would have seen it. As if this was their way of saying "you were never one of us." All of his life Frank had talked about how he thought they blamed him for their mother's death. As if he'd done something in the womb. His father giving him away to punish him. And not so much as a word of acknowledgement from the Shaws all those years. Not even a look that said "we know you."

The twelve who'd come to see Frank off went over to the church hall for the reception. The city workers looked longingly over at their cars. Abbey'd stayed to watch the backhoe push the dirt onto the grave, the driver wary of her presence. After he left she walked over to the headstone and traced the letters of her father's name. Felt nothing. Tried to picture him in her mind in better days. But every thought led her to the last time she'd seen him, the night of the fire. Over by the church the crows swooped around the red-brick bell tower, cawed in the nearby trees. The sun was out but the air held onto the cold. It was mid-April but it didn't feel like Spring. In three days' time, she'd be on a plane heading back to Ireland. She'd be back with Dermot, trying again to find work on the west coast. Jane had asked her to go through Frank's apartment, to take anything she might need before it got hauled away. But Abbey didn't want to go back there; she didn't want to be here now.

Over by the church hall, a few people stood outside the main doors, smoking. They went in and came out again a half hour later. One of the men, a cousin of Frank's, had a paper napkin in his hand. He wiped his mouth with it and let it drop onto the gravel. Abbey tried to picture her father again, from when she was young, that period of time when he could easily please her. But every thought was tinged with grief, with his failure. She could hear the start of an engine in the parking lot. Then the gate creaked as two of the city workers went through it. Tentatively, Abbey took a step forward. Put her right foot on the mound of earth over her father's grave. Then her left. She turned around once and stamped her feet. Watched her shoes sink into the dirt, the barrow.

Abbey steps off the bus in Dublin and Angela is there, waiting by the gate. A cup of coffee between her hands, lipstick along the rim.

"Thank fuck you're here. I'm freezing my tits off."

"Sorry, I thought I'd catch the early bus."

"Well, you owe me a pint." Ange kisses Abbey's temple and then walks over to the waste bin, tosses her coffee cup in, starts for the door.

"When'd you get glasses?" Abbey asks. Angela is wearing a pair of thick-rimmed black frames.

"Last week. They're not prescription. What do you think?" She pushes them farther up her nose and juts out her chin.

"Looks good."

"Slattery's?" Ange asks. It isn't too far from her flat. "You look like a tourist with that thing." She nods at Abbey's pack.

"Yeah? Well, fuck 'em if they can't take a tourist."

They go out through the doors and into the city. The streets full of people, traffic along the quays. Crowds spill out from the pubs onto the sidewalks. A man playing a saw with a fiddle bow nods at the girls as they go by. The eerie sound of the saw, the flex and warp, following them. Abbey shifts gears. The pace in Dublin altogether faster. Angela, walking a few strides ahead, turns around. "Going back to the old codger?"

They're heading along the quays and the wind whips up around Abbey's ears. Her backpack is getting heavy. "Yeah."

Ange sticks out her tongue, rolls her eyes. "Christ, Ab, I'll say it again: you can do better."

They walk past Liffey Street in silence. Over on Ha'penny Bridge a group of kids throw their take-away containers into the river. A pop can glints in the light of the street lamp as it drops. Realizing Abbey is too far into it with Dermot, Angela softens, grabs hold of her hand, squeezes. "I should never have introduced you to that useless wanker. Lesson learned."

At Slattery's a doorman stands with his back to the street eying the crowd inside. Looking in through the front window, Abbey can tell the place is full. On the other side of the glass a man carrying three pints wedges his way between two women to a bench that runs along the front of the pub. The bass of the music reverberates off the glass.

"McDaids," Angela suggests, pushing her glasses up. And off they go, Abbey holding onto the straps of her pack and flexing her back muscles to relieve the knot that's set in. Wondering all of a sudden why she felt the need to bring everything, empty the drawer, take both pairs of shoes. Was she trying to scare Dermot? Ange would tell her to leave him, has said so before. And it was tempting, the idea of it. As if all Abbey's problems, all her aimlessness, would end if she walked away. The Gowans famous for finding the exit, the great revolving "out" door; Frank fond of saying, "Don't let it hit ya as ya leave."

Abbey has tried to leave Dermot before — five months ago, after their first argument. She'd left Dublin to stay in Spiddal for a few days until her next week of shifts started at Connor's. The bus had dropped her in the village; she'd had to double back to the cottage in the rain. It was seven when she got in and the house was in a state.

"She deigns to make an appearance." The smell of whiskey on him. Flagon at Abbey's hand, licking her fingers.

Abbey took off her coat and hung it up, walked over to put her bag in the bedroom. Dermot blocked the doorway.

"You could've phoned." His fingers curled around the lip of the door frame.

"How about 'I'm happy to see you?'" The words came out louder than she'd intended. There was something about the look of him, a desperation. Like her father.

"They'll be waiting for me." He brushed by her, put on his coat. "Who?"

He turned at the door and stared at her. "You'll not have it both ways."

Abbey flipped on the light and sat down on the bed. Wiped her forehead, raindrops trickling out of her hair. He came into the room a few minutes later. A grown man, his hands twice the size of hers, he put his head on her lap and sobbed. Abbey's skirt wet from the rain, clinging to her thighs, Dermot pressing his face against them. She'd never seen him like that, didn't know what he wanted from her, what it was she'd done. Finally she put her hands down onto his head, the mess of greying wisps. She started to say his name, but as soon as he felt her hands on him, he stood up. Like he'd been struck. He stared at her for a minute like he was trying to place her. Then he sat down on the bed beside her, looking straight ahead. "Now we'll see how the story goes."

This is what makes Abbey afraid of him; it's also what makes her stay.

After a while, Angela goes over to the bar for a second round of pints. Abbey rings the cottage but there's no answer. She lets it ring eight times. Angela had suggested, "Let him sit on it for a while. Will you marry me? Fer fucksake." She'd had a good laugh at that, her eyes widening, a pint of Guinness in her right hand, halfway to her mouth. Then she set it back down on the table without drinking. "Jesus," she'd said, rethinking it. Abbey said nothing. "Jesus," Angela said again.

It was Angela who'd introduced Abbey and Dermot in the first place. They were meeting Michael for drinks and Dermot, in town for a visit, had tagged along.

"Abbey, this is Dermot Fay," Angela said as she sat down. Abbey was trying to find a place for her umbrella, so she gave him a sideways handshake; she had too many things — coat, hat, purse. Her fingers were wet. "Dermot used to teach with Michael at Trinity," Ange added by way of an explanation. The three of them settled in; Michael was at the Museum in a meeting, had said he'd make it to the pub within half an hour. A woman came over to take their order. It was early and the place was only a quarter full.

Dermot had turned to Abbey. "Are you studying or having a holiday?" He looked over her face, each feature, and it made her blush.

"I'm working. But I'd like to see more of the country."

"Where've you been?"

"Actually, I haven't," clearing her throat, "really left Dublin." It was Dermot's first good laugh of the evening.

"How long have you been over?"

"Four months." She hated the sound of her voice, the flat accent.

"And you haven't left Dublin?" He looked amused. Later he said he'd admired her for that; after four months most people would be in a Guinness t-shirt, feigning a thick brogue, postcards from every county on the fridge back home. The waitress suddenly between them, ready to drop off the first round. She passed a pint over to Angela. A few drops of stout sloshed out of the glass onto Abbey's shirt. Dermot went over to the bar and got a cloth. Wiped the dark spots off Abbey's sleeve.

Michael and Angela had been going on about work — an exhibition of the Clonard hoard that Michael was involved in at the National Museum. Angela had studied under Michael at Trinity and he'd helped her find work at a local gallery.

"Dermot's going to see me back to the flat," Abbey said, tapping Angela on the arm. It was late and Abbey had to work early. They walked through the crowd that had come in. He put his hand on the small of her back. A woman near the door eyed them wearily then went back to her brandy. Outside things were quiet. Dermot told Abbey he'd come to Dublin for an interview that didn't pan out. Said he didn't know how he'd arrived here, at this point in his life. "I've a thirst," he added, then he asked her if she'd like to stop for another round.

They went into The Old Stand and ordered drinks. He admitted he was lonely, told her about all the things he'd come through. Abbey didn't say much of anything. Dermot watched her reactions as he went on talking, told her later that he'd said more than he thought he would. That there was something about her, an honesty that appealed to him.

Later, they stopped between Meath hospital and Angela's flat where Abbey was staying. She leaned up against a brick wall. Dermot came forward and kissed her. His hands found the back of her neck.

After a minute he'd said, "Can I see you again?"

Abbey nodded her head, surprised by his attention, the kiss. All night she'd felt wrong. Even in the loo when she'd looked in the mirror, she had noticed her eyeliner was smudged below her right eye. She'd taken a paper towel, wet it under the sink taps, rubbed away the kohl under her lower lashes, rubbed so hard it looked like she'd been crying. When she went back to the table Dermot asked her what she did in Canada.

"I'm a waitress."

"Did you not go to College?"

"Night classes."

"What in?"

"English Lit, some sociology."

She didn't know what to say to him, felt intimidated by his interest, by the way he had ignored Michael when Angela got up from the table and Michael tried to join their conversation.

At Angela's door, Dermot gauged Abbey's expression to see if she wanted him to kiss her again. He suggested she come to Galway for a visit. Two doors down a porch light flickered then went out. "Would you come?" he asked again. Abbey agreed and even with that, he asked her again. Each time he asked, it flattered her more. She kissed him for his insecurity and tentatively he'd placed his right hand under her jacket, her shirt, against her warm skin. And then later, from behind the square of glass in Angela's front room, Abbey had watched Dermot stand on the curb on the opposite side of the street. His eyes to the sky for what seemed like an hour.

Tapping her beer coaster on the table, Angela suggests that Abbey move to London. There's a Connor's and Giumbini's there, part of the restaurant chain Abbey works for in Dublin. They could transfer her over. "I have friends in Camden …" Angela talking louder now. McDaids packed wall-to-wall with people, conversations piled over top of each other in the din. "It'd be great. Just tell him you need time away. A break. He'll understand." But Abbey knows that won't solve anything. Dermot isn't the problem.

Over by the doorway a group of young punks barges in through the crowd. People move closer together to accommodate them. There's a girl with blue streaks in her hair and a guy in a leather jacket sporting a bullseye tattoo on his forehead. A few other kids who look about sixteen come in behind them. The girl makes for the back of the pub to the stairs that lead up to the loo. The group by the door spreads out again. The barman changes the music. A ballad comes out of the speaker, something from the seventies. Back at the door an older man tries to push past the same throng of people. He comes in and out of view. Abbey watches the commotion to see if the group of kids will get tossed. The older guy wedges past two men in business suits. He has short hair, a receding hairline. Looks a bit like her father, the same straight nose. And he seems out of place, is getting knocked around, trying to tap people's shoulders to pass by.

Abbey gets the chills. There's something about the man that reminds Abbey of how her father looked before he got sick. The way he looked when she was ten or eleven and they would go to the Holiday Inn on Thursday nights for dinner. Kids eat free, the sign had said. She always had grilled cheese. He had roast beef with gravy and drank Labatt's Blue, would polish off three or four bottles and line them up around his plate until the waiter cleared them; the clink of the glass necks hitting each other when they met in the waiter's hand. All around them were families, American tourists coming over the border to shop in Windsor. That was the worst of it: at every table, two parents and two or three kids, siblings who pinched and kicked each other throughout the meal. Abbey would pretend that her mother was coming, that she was running late. Hating that her father always said "for two" when the hostess asked "how many?"

"At the funeral — " Abbey starts, thinking she'll tell Angela that she stood on her father's grave, that the confession might somehow relieve the guilt, "I …" But she doesn't finish her sentence. And Angela, looking back from the direction of the door, stares blankly at Abbey. The man at the bar is gone from sight but the idea of Frank sticks with Abbey. It's as if he's sitting at the table with her, eying the pints. This doesn't make sense, and Abbey knows it. The dead aren't supposed to stand over your shoulder and watch what you drink at the pub, they aren't supposed to know what you say and how you feel about their going. Abbey looks into her glass and senses the weight of him, a sack of guilt strung around her neck, something portable, something she can carry with her.

When Abbey doesn't finish her thought, Angela goes back to the previous conversation.

"Dermot's not right for you." Angela sums it up, stretches her hand across the table. "For one thing, he's twice your age. And he's so bloody pompous. Now, look at him — " Angela points to the bar where a young guy with short spiky hair and sideburns is paying for a round. "He's in a band. His name's Fenton. Brendan knows him." The fact that he's about twenty-five isn't lost on Abbey.

"Anyway, Bren and I are going out Thursday and he promised he'd bring someone along so you wouldn't feel like the odd man out."

Angela lifts her coat up off her lap. "Shall we?" She takes a last mouthful of stout. Abbey grabs her backpack from under the table and swings it onto her back. Grabs her pint glass and empties it, looks through the bottom of the glass before setting it down. Warbly shapes move through the scope of the base, bits of colour, someone passing close. When she moves the pint glass away from her face, the room comes crisply into view. As it should. There's no room for the dead in McDaids. There's barely enough room for the living. As Abbey heads for the door, a Tom Waits song comes through the stereo speakers overhead and the barman announces last call. "Have ye no homes to go to?" he shouts. A common slag, a way to get people moving. And Abbey laughs, thinks: "No, I don't."

In The Yard

THE BOY will come toward him like an apparition, this is the way Dermot imagines it — as light glinting from the bay, luminous. Even though he knows it will be something as pedestrian as sunshine reflected off the glass casing of the boy's wristwatch; a tiny beacon, measured pulses of light. He tries not to think about it, but there are days like this — a wet Monday, him standing in the yard, kicking a tennis ball for Flagon's amusement, the dog fetching in all directions, taking the ball in the wet pocket of her mouth — there are days when he sees the boy as if he were here. And each time it's nothing more than a murder of crows lifting, a thin sliver of sun skirting their glossy wings, although once it was Fitch's sloped back as he walked the perimeter of his fields.

Dermot no longer trusts his own delusions. There had been a time when every thought could be sifted into its proper place — "Real / seems real / entirely fabricated" — and Dermot would lie awake at night studying the shadows that lashed across his ceiling, mumbling, "Real, a branch, the bottom branch from the white beam, sorbus aria." Thinking,

I ought to cut that down, a strong enough gust will send it through the window. And after he met Abbey and she'd come home with him, slipping in between the flannel sheet and the ratty wool blanket, her small hands, left index finger tracing his spine, he said "delusion" to himself, because he knew she would never stay.

And now, a figure crests the rise at the back plot of land, and even though he anticipates the visitor, an idea takes shape in the back of Dermot's mind, and stays there. Still, there is no glinting, no light, only a dark slump-shouldered form of indistinguishable girth coming close from a distance. Maybe it's the boy. His son. Dermot's chest tightens even thinking it: Rory.

Sophie had sent Dermot one letter saying she'd named the baby Rory, after her own father, saying she'd taken a job as an au-pair in London. The postmark read Cork. Her writing hadn't changed, but this time Dermot wasn't taking a red pen to it, marking off the weak points in her arguments. It didn't begin *Adamnan's account of Saint Columba is said to have been found intact at the monastery* ... Rather it read: *You have a son.* She'd even slipped over into the margins — there was one thin sheaf of paper. A report of sorts. That was 1981, the year after he'd been let go for trying to arrange the abortion. He'd been excommunicated from Trinity, from the high-ceilinged Fellows Hall, from the hoard of papers that were piled on his desk. "Frolicking with a student," is what they called it, and perhaps that was apt. He'd never loved her. If a defence were to be mounted, it could be said, perhaps proven, that she had come after him — stayed late after class to ask ridiculous questions, went right for his belt buckle the moment he bent in to kiss her. The affair had only lasted the month.

The year following his dismissal, Dermot stayed on in the city trying to keep a Rathmines flat he couldn't afford, pretending his circumstances hadn't changed, although there were pubs that wouldn't serve him, and a woman who, upon seeing him, made the sign of the cross. He took to the drink because it was expected, then because it was needed. Michael had put him up when the flat was let out from under him; he'd been two months back on rent, and everything he owned, a couch, table and books, was stacked into Michael's living-room corner. Dermot left town the morning he received Sophie's letter. Packed two bags and caught the first bus near Michael's flat. Felt purposeful, but then didn't know where to get off. Rode the 15A for three hours until the conductor ordered him to pick a stop. He sat on the curb near Georges Street, watched people coming and going. Beside him, two boys ate a bag of toffee. The older boy offered him one and he took it. He read the letter again. Truth be told, he hadn't expected it, was angry that Sophie felt he had to be informed. He imagined she must want something from him. He read the letter again and again on the way to the bus station. Got on the first coach headed out of Dublin, formed a response in his head. When he felt ready to take up a pen they were already closing in on Clifden. The gears shifting as the bus groaned up the hill from Roundstone, then stopped at the rise to pick up an old man and his grandson. The boy was about three. The old man pulled him up the steps with his hand held out behind him. They sat in the front seats and the child hung over the railing, looking not at the road, but down at the floor. A woman carrying a cello case boarded at the crossroad beyond. Sophie had included a return address but Dermot never replied. He folded up the letter and the bus clambered on. He was thirty-four.

Flagon lets out a series of clipped barks and Dermot squints trying to make out who it might be at the edge of his field. When the boy steps out of the shade of the ash tree, Dermot sees it is Sean O'Riordan come to start the fence. A young girl trails behind him, maybe four or five years old, with a mess of curly auburn hair and quick, curious eyes. The eyes settle on Dermot. Already he craves a drink; instead, he looks around as if a pile of wood planks, a wire bale, might materialize out of thin air. He and Michael had told the boy Monday, but Dermot meant next week.

"Hiya." Sean puts out his hand.

"Right."

Dermot kicks the old tennis ball towards the house and Flagon takes off to chase it. It settles in the gorse that cropped up a few years back under the ledge of the kitchen window. Dermot's been meaning to clear it. The girl lets go of Sean's hand and walks over to it. Roots around in the grass. The Border collie wagging her tail.

"Mind yerself." Sean starts towards her, but the girl pulls out the old ball, lifts it up for him to see, grinning.

"That's Mary. I'm looking after her," the boy says, glancing around the yard.

"I haven't got the wood posts yet," Dermot says. "I meant for you to come next week." Still, he could have tried for the posts. Yesterday Dermot had asked Fitch if he could take some of the wood from his old byre which was mostly in planks out behind the house. The neighbour was gruff, didn't think the fence was a good idea. It made him suspect that Dermot is selling.

"Is it the work next door?" Fitch had nodded in the direction of the bungalows. "The tourists?"

"No, no, it's not the tourists."

Fitch stepped out onto the porch and Dermot had to move back a pace.

"I'm thinking of getting a horse." It was ridiculous to say it, a flat-out lie. "For Abbey," he added, which also wasn't true.

Fitch eyed him a minute. "It's the tourists driving me." He looked over Dermot's shoulder towards the cottage and scratched his head. The shadow from the bungalows nearing the road. "In the sixties I taught at the College." He studied Dermot's face. "Worked with Canon McAlinney who'd started the Gaeilgeoirí. An aunt of the Folan's worked in his house. You'd know the students. Niall's father, for one. And Niall came too, though I was retired then. We had great times." A minute passed. "Now they're all writing scripts for Tele Gael. Sobalchlár as Gaeilge."

On the porch, Flagon, her tongue slung over the side of her mouth, watched Fitch as he pulled his hands from his pockets, turned to go in. Often he gave the dog handouts.

"Selling?" Fitch asked again, from the other side of the threshold.

"A horse." Dermot didn't know what else to say.

"Well, take the wood." He'd offered it, gave Dermot the go-ahead to clear it away, cut the beams into posts. Dermot could have started on it over the weekend but he'd yet to organize himself, still had to buy the wire. And now, here is the boy, kicking dirt around with his boot, waiting.

In his pocket Dermot finds a two-Euro coin. He extends it to the boy, as thanks for trekking out. Sean bounces it once on his palm, then sits down on a grassy patch of the yard, rests his elbows on his bent knees. Over by the house Flagon is chasing the girl around, eliciting a high-pitched giggle. Still uncertain of what to do, Dermot gives Sean a once-over: big cuffs at the bottom of his jeans, a bomber jacket, short hair, a tough look on his face. Then he turns and takes in the yard to see what the boy's seeing, how it looks to a stranger. There's the cottage, the thatch coming up near the front, the cracked window on the side wall, the light yellow curtain that Abbey'd put up over the kitchen sink. Against the wall there's a rusted bicycle, a number of plastic buckets under the trough, the initials DF scrawled on the side of them in black marker. A plastic bag of compost for the garden. And just behind the house, an almost invisible clothes-line. Two of Abbey's shirts, three pairs of silky underwear suspended in the yard. Sean looks over at them and it occurs to Dermot that he should have taken them down.

Mary throws herself over Flagon's neck, much to the Border collie's dismay. The second time she does it, Flagon backs up, and the girl falls over the dog's head, thunks down onto the dirt, gets up laughing.

"Wednesday, then?"

Sean looks up. "What time?"

"Noon?"

"All right." And with that the kid stands up, wipes the back of his jeans. Takes the coin he'd been given, puts it back in Dermot's hand.

The Sky on Its Axis

HEADING home across the back field, Sean tugs Mary along
behind him. She's breathing through her mouth like she
always does. By the time they get to the bridge he can hear
her panting. Coming up to old St. Éinde's Sean walks around
a hazel thicket, takes Mary into the church over the rubble
of the western transept. The stones he's been piling up by
the side chapel are still there. The stink of the place remains
the same: take-away containers in the corner of the close, two
old sleeping bags in the chapel. Travelers hole up there some
nights in good weather. Under the fourth pew on the left
Sean and his friend Clancy keep a Lilt bottle filled with gin,
a plastic bag tacked under the seat beside it containing
rolling papers, blem, and a few acid tabs. Clancy's brother
gets the weed from a guy in Cleggan, the blotters from a
cousin in Athenry.

 Sean's been coming to the church more often lately. If it's
dark and no one else is around he smokes a joint or drops
some acid and leaves some money in its place. Then he goes
out to the old stone wall that surrounds Éinde's, takes three

or four of the bigger stones from the top. Hauls them over to where Fitch's field butts up against the church property. Climbs the fence, Fitch's cows raising their heads. If he looks around long enough he can usually find a few more stones in the grass. He dumps them into a big pile. Then he starts arranging them. The acid kicks in. The sky tilts on its axis. The cows grow horns, the lights in the distant houses become eyes. The stones turn into constellations, his fingers running a commentary as he sets them down, so that Sean can look at his hands and listen to what each finger has to say: you worthless bastard / I'm with him / what's the square root of seven-hundred and twenty-nine? / will ya look at Mary Conroy's tits / who's there? who's there?

And when he's done there are whole constellations in Fitch's back field, laid out in the leaning grasses. Some nights if Sean looks straight up it's an exact reflection: stone for star, as if light shot down from the sky, hit the field, and was fixed there. A way of stopping the world. Even if just for a few hours.

"Are you cold?" Sean looks around the church, the damp wood, the puddles. Spots a pot without a handle at the foot of a column. He decides to take Mary home. There'll be something on the telly. He can make them lunch. She lifts up her arms asking to be carried but he takes her hand instead. They start off slowly, Mary turning to look at the church as they head across the field. If he wanted to, Sean could tell her the story of how after she was born, a month too early, Sean's mom brought him with her to Saint Éinde's. He was twelve. Mary was in Galway Hospital. His father was … where? At the pub? No, he was at Uncle Jack's getting the highchair.

That evening, standing in the door to his bedroom, Sean's mother told him to get his shoes and come with her, give her a hand. They went out the back door and hiked across the three fields that sit between their house and the church. Sean pulled apart the barbed wire at the Greaney's so his mother could squeeze through; she was against taking the byroad.

Once at the church, his mom walked over to where the north and east walls met. In the shadow Sean could make out shapes, objects jutting out in all directions. He went closer and saw a crutch leaning against the wall just away from the corner. Then two more. He caught a glimpse of an old coat, an arm brace, a pair of glasses with the light from the quarter moon trapped in the lens. A dozen more crutches and canes came into view as his eyes adjusted. There was a whole slew of things hanging up above on the wall, stacked or set on rusted nails that poked out of the stone. Every few inches there were divots from where the granite had come away. A pair of light blue baby pajamas lay on the ground by Sean's right foot, holes in the sleeves and legs, the seams coming apart. Everything was damp, and the stench made him stand back. He stepped sideways onto a dog's collar, lost his balance, almost fell. Beside him, his mother was unfolding a dish towel. Lying on her palm, on top of the white cloth, was something that looked like a short black rope, thin and curling like licorice, but dry. Like those black seed pods that made noise when you shook them. Picking the thing up in her hand, she reached out and set it over a nail. Watched to make sure it hung there, balanced. Then she said a prayer. He knew it was for Mary, so he prayed too. "Our father who art in heaven hallowed be thy name, thy kingdom come —" and he'd looked up to see what the black thing was doing, but it just hung there in front of them, like it was dead.

His mother'd never come back to the church, but Sean had. He knows every corner now. The crutches, the dog collar, baby clothes, the umbilical cord swept away during the first go at restoration. The Office of Public Works had wanted to rebuild the church, were starting to repair the transept before the funding was cut. Then they more or less dropped everything on the spot.

Sean thinks about those petitions often. Tries to remember what went where, how it hung on the wall. Wonders what people had hoped to get out of the act, what it felt like when they realized those things had been taken away. There is nothing now but mouldy pews and rubble, two good walls, a stash under the bench — Éinde's falling apart stone by stone in a field that few people pass through. The grass up to Mary's waist as they near the road, the thicket closing in.

Bonaventure

DERMOT walks towards the hardware store counter, past bins of nails and screws, a stack of boxed drill presses, feeling like the commonplace country man gone wrong. Everything's modern in Galway now. The counter girl has on lipstick and two welts of blue eye shadow as if she's at a bar on the night of a dance. And the customers, milling about in plumbing and electrical supplies aisles, seem Dublin-sophisticated. It's getting hard to tell the locals from the tourists, the group queuing at the counter a barrage of rain jackets and wool sweaters. Somewhere behind Dermot a mobile phone rings, is answered with a man's brisk "hello."

Dermot tugs at his jeans where they sag at the waist. Runs his right hand through his hair, which won't sit properly to begin with. He'd caught a glimpse of himself in the rearview mirror of Mrs. Sullivan's VW. She'd picked him up when the Mini ran out of petrol and gave him a once over when he settled in, a sorry-your-good-days-are-gone-by-ya followed by a look that said *whatever does a wee thing like that Canadian see in you?* Mary Sullivan, Dermot knows, works in the kitchen at the big hotel in Spiddal, the place Abbey's been trying to get work. She knows everyone's doings. Dermot's often wanted to say to her, "I'm not so bad," and, "look at yourself." She's fifty and soft around the edges — thick brows, a double chin.

"Is it you, Mr. Fay?"

"It is."

"Need a lift in?"

He'd hoisted the petrol can.

"I'll take you."

Took one last look at the Mini where it sat on the side of the road. Opened the door and got in.

"Now is it at the Lisheen Bar or the petrol station that I should drop you?"

At another time, even thirty years ago, he and the widow Sullivan might have been tossed together by circumstance, by lack of alternatives. Except now there is Galway, a micro-Dublin, expanding up and down the coast, population growing in leaps and bounds. A city so sophisticated and tourist-friendly it's closing in on that other hub on the far side of the Island. Nothing but options now. Dermot remembers back to when there were three pubs in Galway. Now there are fifty, with piped fiddle music coming out of the stereo speakers that hang over the doorways, playing out into the streets, hoping to lure the tourists in.

In the queue at the hardware store, Dermot leans forward, tries to steal a glance at the watch protruding from the sleeve of the man in front of him. It occurs to him he's missed decades, and now, after Abbey's leaving, after the botched down-on-one-knee proposal, he is compulsive about clocks. It's 2:25 in Galway, and in Dublin Abbey is probably at the end of the lunch rush, leaning against the bar, drinking water from a pint glass as she was the afternoon last autumn when he stopped by Connor's to say hello. It is 2:25 and Dermot is mired in it, in accounting for the minutes, the three days that have passed since he walked up the bay road, the Mini and Abbey parked somewhere behind him. At Trinity he taught whole centuries in the scope of a term, entire lives rounded out nicely in the course of an hour. *Bonaventure was born in 1217, he wrote about the externality of the world, an argument against Aristotle's theology. These are the documents that remain. This is a Victorian interpretation, this is what we can glean from said article now.* And time would wheel by at his will, all he had to do was close his mouth on the thirteenth century and open it up again starting with the word "Today." Bonaventure in his wisdom had argued that everything which begins to be, begins by way of motion or change. And back then Dermot thought there was truth in it because he was in motion, time reeling by him, bullheaded, the future almost, nearly there.

Back at the cottage the ringer on the phone is still turned off. Abbey might have called a hundred times and he'd never know it. Once last night he was tempted to pick it up, see if he'd find her voice there at the other end. But he doesn't want to talk to her, not yet, and he isn't sure why. She's been strange since the funeral; that is to be expected. But Abbey has never said much about her family, as if her parents have nothing to do with her now, as if they are a part of the past. No, something else has come between them. And Dermot can't place what it is.

Ahead of him the man with the watch, broad-shouldered, moves forward a few steps as the queue shuffles along. Dermot tilts his head, the watch in plain view. 2:26. 2:27.

At the counter, Dermot orders ten dozen posts and a measure of wire to surround the field. He doesn't ask the price, can't imagine what he's doing. Parcelling up the land with money he doesn't have. Easy enough to say the bungalows are driving him to it — Holiday Plans that'll house Dubliners in the off-season and tourists in the summer. Bord Fáilte books them on the net, in the tourist offices, the airports. Already he can see it, the nodding and waving from the gravel drive, "what's your dog's name?" asked again and again in varying accents, an endless parade of foreigners loading the family into their rented cars as they tip their caps at the Irishman next door. Maybe a fence will keep them from coming up to the windows, keep kids from straying into the yard. And, once the land is fenced, Dermot could rent it out to a local farmer. A source of income that would pay for the fence in a few months. The field, gone to seed, just stands there at any rate, Fitch's cows wandering over through gaps in the old stone wall, the grass growing in leaps and bounds around them.

There's comfort in this — coming into town, standing in a queue, a reminder that he can function, measure up. A reminder that these are his people and they know him. "Fay," he says, as the girl writes up his order. She cracks her gum and with every stroke of the pen the bangles on her arm jingle.

"Address for delivery?" She looks up. And then he sees it — or maybe not — a smirk, flickering across her face. And what can she mean by that? *Old man,* or *dirty old man, I know about you and she's half your age,* or *my sister goes to Trinity and we all know.* Either way, if it is there, it's fleeting, because already she's holding the pen out in the air, looking to the next person while Dermot signs his name.

Driving north towards home, puttering along between the stone walls that line both sides of the road, Dermot lets the BMWs and Euro sports cars whisk by him; half the drivers on mobiles or blaring music out their windows. If his own stereo was working he might enjoy some music, maybe Dylan, but all he's got is a tangle of wires hanging down under his dashboard. When he comes to a clearing with no stone walls, just a flat field view to the bay, he pulls over to the side of the road. Sits there, looks out at the thousand colours of grey. Tries to measure the distance a particular wave covers before it rests. Five herons cross over, swooping west, the last two flying towards the water. A truck rumbles by on the road. Down the way a tugboat lolls on its tether. Dermot catalogues everything as if the inventory might have value, as if one day he will be asked to account for his time. But time itself seems malleable. Today the beach is clear and unmarked, even though yesterday a family may have been out there, the son skipping stones, throwing sand at his sister, the parents walking with a fixed distance between them. Even though that existed, there is nothing like that now; everything is washed over. It comes to him like a new idea taking shape, although he has always known it, let it sit like an ulcer in his gut: it's who we are in this minute that matters. Now; who we are. An unmarked beach, save for the worm holes, the "s" marks that surround them, from their turning before they go in.

The McGilloway Girl

THE AFTERNOON of the wake Deirdre McGilloway stands on the edge of her mother's stoop, the shadow of her pregnancy falling over all four of the walkway steps. The baby starts to kick again.

Helen Brennan, who taught Deirdre when she was in school, pads down the far side of the street carrying two bags of groceries in cloth sacs. Seeing Deirdre, she looks both ways down the quiet road, steps out tentatively between parked cars, comes over.

"Sorry to hear about your mother," she says from the sidewalk. "She was a good hen." Deirdre smiles at her and nods, but remembers it was Brennan who'd complained to the general post master that her mother was too lackadaisical with the post. It took three days for the post to reach a Dublin doorstep on average, but Helen Brennan claimed that if a letter was mailed on a day Eileen was working, it would take four or five. This from a woman who only taught math passably, who shouldn't have been allowed to work with kids past the fourth grade.

"If there's anything I can do." Helen Brennan smiles again. Deirdre knows Brennan has never liked her much, even when she was a girl. The word, if she remembers correctly, written in tight print on her school report, was "precocious."

"Thanks, Mrs. Brennan." And she smiles at her, at her nearly white hair, at the silk scarf tied around her neck, at the bags hanging down by her ankles, at her freckled hands. Mrs. Brennan's hair is pinned into curls near her temples and it occurs to Deirdre that the woman might actually be setting her hair for this evening's wake, that it's something Brennan would get dressed up for. Her mother's wake an occasion; her mother's death a reason to go out.

Every now and again people walk down the side road, and more often than not Deirdre recognizes their faces but can't place them exactly. A girl with a red balloon stares at Deirdre from the opposite sidewalk as her mother drags her along by the hand. All morning trucks have come and gone, loaded with building materials for the Tele Gael set that will become a soap-opera village. Last month a sound studio went in on the secondary road. There are more power lines now than Deirdre remembers. Last night she'd stuck her head in at Hughes; people she didn't know were there. A dog stood wait outside the door. She's been in Dublin for five years. Even when she'd come back to visit she'd only really come to see her mum. They'd head into Galway, to the shops. Although sometimes, if Liam was around, Deirdre would hit the pubs with him after he got off work at the bog.

The baby is kicking up a storm. Deirdre's blood sugar is low; since the phone call three days ago she hasn't kept much of anything down. The turkey sandwich Keating made her sits on the table, barely touched, but the fresh air, at least, is doing some good. There's nothing to do in the house anyway. People she barely remembers came over to tidy up under Keating's guidance. Chairs were set up in the living room. Cellophaned trays of food miraculously appeared on the buffet and the dining table. Twenty cans of beer are sitting in the sink on ice and the fridge is filled with a dozen bottles of wine. A keg of lager was dropped off by Niall and left in the utility closet. In the back room a load of laundry was started. Things Deirdre hadn't even seen, let alone touched, were put away. Maybe all that she has left of her mother is in there, in the smell of those clothes. She should have washed them herself, not sat down in the middle of the chaos trying to swallow bites of a sandwich she had no desire to eat.

The maternal instinct is to nest, but Deirdre McGilloway has other things on her mind. The body is coming from Galway in the next few hours to be laid out upstairs. The next time she sees her mother, the woman will be dead. Two months ago Eileen McGilloway was standing on this very porch, decidedly living. Deirdre had come home to tell her about the baby, to make sure she'd be okay with it. She was seven months along and still not sure who the father was, although there were two or three likely guesses. Her mother was angry for an hour; the clock on the mantle had never been louder. Then Eileen had picked up her keys to go into Galway and look for a stroller.

"Come on."

"That's it?"

"Why make a fuss? It's done."

What Deirdre wants now is to go home. She wants her mother to walk out of the kitchen; she wants, selfishly, for things to be as they were. It's hard enough being single and pregnant. Even in Dublin the idea still raises eyebrows. Deirdre thought she'd have to give up her flat when she left the travel agency and went on Mother's Allowance, that she'd have to find a room mate. But her mother had offered to make up the difference, said that they'd work it out together. And so far they had.

Standing on the edge of the porch, one arm wrapped around the porch column, feet perched precariously close to the edge, Deirdre starts rocking. Starts swinging out over the steps, her belly a kind of ballast. She gets up a good swing. The back and forth motion is soothing. Under her weight the porch creaks and something about that makes Deirdre feel good. She swings out again and comes sharply back, her fingers slipping in increments on the column. She swings forward to where she started, almost falling. Stops. Catches her breath. Realizes she could have gone over.

There is No Night

THE CITY goes about its business. Statues cast shadows from the boulevard and the tourists look up. People cross against the light. One car honks and then another. On O'Connell Street at a queue for the bus, Abbey reads over the list in her hand: "Things for Foreigners To Do in Dublin." A few months back Dermot made her an agenda. He itemized where to go, and in what order, and made a few notes underneath about what she should look for: the bullet holes on the front of the GPO, the Behan manuscripts in the Irish Writer's Museum, Bryne's, the best fish and chip shop in Ireland. Against his will Abbey'd made him add the Guinness Brewery. Last month when she worked a week at Connor's she went to The National Museum, Phoenix Park, Kilmanhaim Gaol.

Abbey's first day back at work was busy, the lunch rush non-stop. There was a queue from the "please wait to be seated" sign to the door for most of the evening. Dan, the head chef, and a royal prick, was a bastard all night. Sometime around seven, when Abbey was late picking up a meal, he pointed a butcher knife in her direction and called her a cunt. His

Northside accent combined with a general inability to fully open his mouth meant that "Ye cuntche ye" was more or less what came out. Abbey smiled back at him and said in her clear Canadian accent, "Sorry, I'm busy, but maybe some other time?"

Tonight she'll work the dinner rush and then stay on to sling pints on the pub side of the restaurant until one. At least now she has the afternoon off.

When the bus pulls up, Abbey gets on and pays her fare. She's going to the Hugh Lane Gallery. Then she'll head back to Angela's and get changed for work. People head upstairs. Abbey takes a seat behind the stairwell, next to the window. O'Connell Street is bustling. A group of teenagers in track pants and dark jackets sits around a fountain on the divide. Across from them, pigeons flock to a man throwing crusts. A young girl standing outside Beshoff's taps two plastic straws against the stone wall.

The bus pulls out and Abbey closes her eyes for a second, pictures being back in Windsor. She remembers the Famous Players movie theatre on Ouelette Avenue at the end of the mini mall; the bars that line the strip near Riverside to draw in the drinking crowd from Detroit; the smell of yeast for twenty blocks around the brewery; how guys who worked the line at Ford and Chrysler would cruise the main street in their new cars, trying to pick girls up from the driver-side window. And there was the McDonalds on Huron Church Road, her birthday party at Chi Chi's.

Frank had moved Abbey to Windsor from the county when she was eight. Before that they lived in Woodslee on a quiet concession that ran between Highway 98 and the 401. Across the road there was a farm with cows. Abbey'd gone over a few times to help milk them. Most of the nearby crops were corn or hay. Towards Leamington, twenty kilometres away, there'd be tomatoes. Her father liked to look outside at the farmhouses and fields that dotted the road, say things like "no one here but us chickens."

Before they moved to Windsor, Abbey used to ride a school bus from the house her parents rented to St. John's School fifteen kilometres away. In the morning she'd stand at the back window, scarf and gloves on the square bamboo table next to the door, to watch for the bus coming, small as a toy truck, down the back road. It took five minutes for the bus to get to her stop from the time she saw it crossing the old highway. Time enough to kiss her mom good-bye, to pull her lunch out of the fridge, check her bag for all her books, push open the screen door and make the trek down the driveway. From there it was across the street to the other side of the road. She stood next to the mailbox and waited. Some mornings if Abbey was running behind, her mom would watch the back road for her, sitting at the kitchen table, a mug of coffee in her hands, eventually yelling, "Bus! Abbey!" And Abbey'd have to hurry, packing books and a gym shirt into the school bag, her mom shouting "Let's go, let's go, let's go," because Frank had the car and if Abbey missed the bus she'd have to stay home from school. Her mother's hand hitting her on the backside as she gathered her things; the radio on top forty. Abbey would run out of the house with her jean jacket pulled up on one arm, the other sleeve trailing behind. Then she'd hear the clap of the screen door behind her, her feet kicking up gravel as she ran down the length of the drive. She remembers how sometimes she ran slow, hoping the bus would whizz by her.

There were things Abbey should have noticed; this is what she realizes now. The way everything but the bus — number 602 orange and given to backfiring — how everything but that bus and Mrs. Larevee, who drove it, was unpredictable. Sometimes there was breakfast set out, sometimes not. Even though Frank was usually up early to go to work, there were times her mother would snap at her to keep quiet, stop stomping around because Frank was still in bed. There was a whole month like that once, Abbey coming home after school to find her dad passed out on the couch, four PM, shoes kicked off on the floor, one arm thrown over his eyes. Abbey asking "Is Daddy sick?" and her mother answering, "No, he's just sleeping."

Abbey can still picture her mom down to the smallest detail: t-shirts and jeans, bleached hair tied into a pony-tail, her face made up. A brown leather necklace with a yellow feather on the end of it. An arced scar in her left eyebrow. Abbey's mom made TV dinners. Took her on trips to the beach. The three of them would go to BelleRiver on Tuesdays, to the Charcoal Pit for gyros and burgers. She paid for Abbey's first skating lessons. She helped her pick out a kitten at the SPCA. But, for all that, she wasn't really there.

A year later when Max, Abbey's cat, went missing, Abbey wanted to post notices on the board at Zehrs. She'd made an ad herself. Her mom promised to call the paper but never got around to it, was too busy doing other things. There was a constant stream of strangers trekking through the house, and late-night parties where Abbey was sent up to bed to lie there, listening for hours to the music, the sets of feet trampling up to the bathroom across the hall from her room. One night a guy called Dave walking in to Abbey's room before finding the light switch and turning around.

Before they moved, Frank held a family meeting. Paced around the kitchen. Abbey and her mother sat at the table.

"The rent's going up the first. We'll have to find somewhere else."

Abbey's mom lit a cigarette. "How about back to the city?"

"Can't afford it."

"An apartment wouldn't cost much more than this place and you're driving in anyway."

Frank looked over at Abbey and she smiled up at him.

"She's in a good school." He nodded towards the upstairs hallway. "And she's got her own room."

"There's no work out here."

"Work out of the house."

"People won't come here for a hair cut." Abbey watched her mom exhale, cough. "And the sink's too small."

"There's Ned's place up the road, it's five hundred a month."

"It's a fucking shack."

Abbey smiled at her mother's swearing and her mother winked back. Frank ran the back of his hand over his face, rubbed his moustache back and forth. Abbey was looking at him to see what he'd say. He looked at Karen imploring her to help out. She shook her head.

The Gallery is on the far side of Parnell Square, a banner over its doors. Abbey walks towards it thinking about the old house, about moving to the apartment that her mother picked out. About unloading the last boxes and turning to find her gone. Abbey remembers sitting on those boxes the whole night, waiting for her mom to show up, how Frank refused to start unpacking. Sometime around three AM he ordered Chinese food. Eventually he put Abbey to bed in what would be her room, gave her his sweater for a pillow. When Abbey woke up the next morning, even the cutlery had been put away. What happened to him, she wonders now. What makes a person decide to haul themselves up by the bootstraps and carry on?

Four rows of large brick Georgian buildings make up Parnell

Square. Under "Hugh Lane" Dermot had written *Charlemont House / Patrick Scott retrospective / Maid Combing her Hair / There is No Night* — the last underlined three times. A well-dressed couple carrying a guide to Dublin goes past Abbey, through the double doors, holding the right side open for her. She puts her hand on the door and follows them in. They drop some coins in the glass donation box. The first room is filled with stained glass; a woman wearing a walkman stands in front of a large window, her face reflecting red and yellow. In the next room, Patrick Scott's giant orange sun. Abbey turns around a few times to take in all of his paintings. Hears the sound of her shoes on the hardwood as she leaves the room. A sculpture of a horse by Degas stands in the hall outside. Then, in the third gallery, a large canvas. Abbey walks right up to it. Finds a bench in the middle of the room and sits down. This would be the one Dermot wanted to show her: a man in the foreground with wide eyes. Dark rocks to the left and right of him. The ghost of a horse — quick white brushstrokes — standing in the field. The night sky painted a thick blue. A fixed distance between everything in the frame: the man, the horse, the sky. And behind them all, a quiet. And the dark swell of the sea.

II

Excavations

A Drink at the Door

THE MUCK of the bog is still on them, on their boots, in their cuffs, in the lines of their hands. Car after car, the Bord na Móna workers come down the N59 from Oughterard, tires spinning off the last of their mud. Lough Corrib to their left, a row of beech trees wagging in the wind. Behind them, the mountains appear and disappear, depending on the turn of the road. The clouds threaten rain. Two miles out of town the cars pass rock island, old Aughnanure Castle, an empty souvenir stand. Then the fields begin, some with barbed wire, others with stone fences. A herd of sheep, their backs to the road, bare their red and blue tagged hides to the drivers. Starlings cling to the power lines. A horse and rider circle a paddock. After a while, the houses begin. Then the shops. Bait and Tackle. Larkin's Fiddles. Ride Away Bike Repair. A sign for Doris' Day Spa that points down a side road.

It had been a rough afternoon at Maam, the weather constantly changing. Around three, the spoon harrow had bucked up behind the tractor. Tomás felt it, turned the engine off, stepped down from the cab to see what he'd gone over. A brown stump visible under the milled crumb. Peter and Angus shoveled it out in twenty minutes, hauled it over to the side of the field, the oak's roots like antlers. A line of stumps along the trench. The first set of eleven fields giving them a rough go. It was a bad draw to get this kind of ground. The lads in the next unit were already milling their second set. Sometimes the "pay by results" system worked to a unit's advantage, but this year Tomás felt sure the bog was against them. Friday the tractor had broken down and Peter was up at the main office when it happened. Didn't answer his pager. Had most of the tools. Liam came over to give it a look but he wasn't that good a mechanic. Two hours of work were lost, and then the rain came, so they called it a day.

Tomás' crew last year had been one of the best he'd ever had. Angus and Liam were on it, and a mechanic named Robbie. The fields were easy, the work went straight ahead. The Wetland Unit came and did their surveys and turned up nothing. The crew went from milling to ridging to harvesting in three-day cycles. The weekly tour of the pubs was a pleasure and the lads were easy to be with. Everything had moved along as it should.

Outside Galway proper, the traffic lights start. Angus signals out the window with his right hand and the lads turn their indicators on to follow. They hang a right onto the asphalt expanse of the Corrib Hut parking lot, shut their engines off and get out.

"What did ye's want?" Angus pulls out his wallet.

"Bud," says Liam.

"That's grand," Peter agrees.

"Gin," says Tomás.

"Harp," says Egg.

Money changes hands. A car pulls up into the space beside them. Two girls get out and smile at Liam. Angus heads for the door that reads "off license," goes in without turning around.

The lads lean against the side of Tomás' truck and wait for Angus to come out with the drink. Then they'll be off to the wake, to raise a glass for Eileen McGilloway at the house in Spiddal. Deoch an doras, a drink at the door. Liam lights up a smoke. Tries to remember the last time he saw Deirdre. Summer, maybe Salthill — the time they'd gone down to the arcades then back to his flat in Galway. Or maybe it was the walk in Cleggan. There'd been nothing after she'd gone back to Dublin, not even a call to say hello, though he did get a "Cruise the Mediterranean" brochure in the mail last October. The girls come out the pub door. The older one, maybe eighteen, is wearing a short skirt and denim jacket, too much make-up. The other carries two bottles of cider under her arm. The one in the skirt unlocks her car door and turns to Liam.

"Would ya give us a light?" She pulls a pack of cigarettes out of her jacket pocket. When he leans forward with the lighter, she looks up at him, the cigarette in her mouth, brown eyes flecked with yellow. After he lights it she stands back up like she's waiting for something.

"Off ya go, now," Liam says, watching her settle into the driver's seat, start the engine, back out.

Peter walks over to his beat-up Escort and pulls a duffel bag out of the back seat. Takes a clean shirt out and holds it between his knees while he strips off the dirty blue one he'd been wearing. Then he bends over at the waist and runs his hand through his short brown hair. Wipes his face with the dirty shirt in his hand. Puts the clean one on — an Irish football jersey from the Cup in 90. Banging the heel of his right boot against the asphalt, Peter looks over at Liam.

"Are you heading home to change?"

"Na. Thought I'd go in like this." He pulls at the bottom of a dirty beige shirt.

"Fair enough," Peter replies, knocking the heel of his left boot against the pavement, watching the mud drop off.

The Wake

THAT EVENING the McGilloway house is run through. The whole village has come out for the wake. Eileen McGilloway had sometimes held letters up to the light and read them, later giving herself away in conversations, but she was generally admired. And she had seemed as permanent a fixture in Spiddal as the old church, the pier, Hughes. The last thing Eileen said to her daughter had come over the low hum of the phone line: "Now the bread is splitting, I have to go." Deirdre barely got in "good-bye" before the click and silence settled over the receiver. She'd made great bread, Eileen McGilloway, and there were other things too. She could knit, recite the old stories verbatim, she had a famous stew with a secret ingredient she'd yet to hand down.

The living room is full of talk, of men in suits that haven't been worn since Gerry Folan's wake last winter, of women in skirts or dresses. Margaret Keating rearranges the food trays, fills them back up. Conneely is on the couch by the fireplace, his face red from the drink. Over by the mantle, a group of teachers discuss Irish history curriculums.

"I'd not mind seeing that taken off the list."

"What else is there?"

"Sullivan."

"That man couldn't find Beal na Blath on a map to save himself."

"We should all be after O' Ceallaigh. That's the ticket."

"O'Ceallaigh is right."

The last thing anyone had heard of Deirdre McGilloway was that she was working at a travel agency in Dublin. Every few months she'd send brochures for cruises or discount holidays to her old school friends. Eileen often had a photo of Deirdre on hand when she was sorting mail at the post office: Deirdre in Cyprus, Deirdre in France. Thick black hair and a toothy grin, some monument or the other in the background. The girl was becoming well-traveled. Word had gone round about her pregnancy and there was a fair bit of speculation about who the father might be, though it was generally agreed it could be anyone.

Dermot walks in through the open door and surveys the crowd. He spies Fitch leaning against the settee, looking around at the framed photos and odd objects Eileen had used to fill the room. Porcelain statues of dancing women in colourful dresses lined a bookshelf, a collection of glass bells arranged beside them; above them, a wall of photos of Deirdre that spanned the years. Eileen's wedding photo is in the middle, a black and white of her and John McGilloway, who passed away not long after. Fitch looks at these and over at the old Victrola set up by the stairs, his gaze coming back to the living room, the crowd of people who stand holding glasses, eating the sweets the bakery prepared. He sees Dermot and lifts the glass in his hand.

Fitch has cleaned up for this. He wears a pressed shirt, is clean-shaven, a fresh nick on the chin. Egan, his lab, sits beside him, whipping his tail against the settee leg, nostrils working at the salmon dip that's fallen onto the carpet a few feet in front of him.

"Off," Fitch says, low, and the dog backs away.

Dermot knows that Fitch and Eileen were together some thirty-five years ago. That Fitch had gone off to get his teaching certificate in Donegal and came back two years later to find her married to McGilloway. Apparently they'd not said a word to each other since. At least that's how Conneely tells it, and he generally has the story.

"How's it?" Dermot asks.

Fitch nods and looks away.

Through the archway to the kitchen Dermot can see one of the local kids at the sink. Another boy, a red-head, watches his back. His eyes meet Dermot's and a second later he whispers something to his cohort and the two of them stop what they're doing and straighten up. Dermot walks into the kitchen, takes out a cigarette, lighting it as he goes. The counter is littered with bottles and plastic cups.

"Good evening, son." He lays a hand down on the fair-haired boy's shoulder. "Shame about Eileen McGilloway isn't it?"

Dermot can feel the nerves run through the boy's body as if he is electrically charged. The red-headed kid who was standing guard looks at the linoleum then walks out of the kitchen.

"It's a shame," the boy says, without looking up.

In his hands, a plastic bag sits bottom-heavy in the empty sink. The smell of beer pervades the kitchen. The boys have been taking the last swills from the abandoned cups, dumping them into the bag, hoping to make a getaway. Dermot reaches over and pulls the bag up; a thin stream of lager comes out of a small hole in the bottom.

"And what good does that do?"

He sets his cigarette down on the counter, grabs a cup out of the closest cupboard. Pours the stream of beer into it. When the cup is full Dermot says, "*Now* drink it."

The kid takes the cup but doesn't drink.

"What's your age?" Dermot asks, leaning back against the counter, scratching an itch under his beard. The kid looks up at him.

"Twelve."

"So, be a man." Dermot indicates the cup.

In the sink the beer has spilled out and is almost gone. The boy, looking around, drinks, swallows, drains the cup. Then, he waits to see if there is anything else, eyes the floor for a minute before setting the cup down on the counter.

"Off with you, then."

The boy leaves the room, looking confused. The red-head, his mouth hanging open, is waiting by the stairs. Dermot, waving them off, picks up his cigarette. The ash falls onto the linoleum. He kicks it under the cupboard with his shoe.

The telly in the living room's been turned on to a game of snooker. Three or four of the younger lads watching it. Keating gives them a look as she goes past. The last of the evening's light comes in the big window. In part of the room there's an air of indifference, as if this is just another occasion in which to act by rote.

"I'm not for the water myself."

"You wouldn't know you were on the water, a ship like that's so big."

"It's all you can eat now isn't it? In the price of the ticket?"

"Shuffleboard. Movies. Theatre even."

"I'd go daft with the same people day in and out."

"How's your Aunt's health by the way? We had her out before the stroke to Moycullen."

Mrs. Meehan, who worked as a teller at the AIB before it closed, is talking to Deirdre, the girl's belly huge under her black skirt. Deirdre is saying how just that afternoon, tidying up for the wake, she found a shopping bag of baby presents. "On the floor beside the bedroom dresser. Yellow booties and a green shirt in case it's a boy. Flowered dress and a bonnet for a girl." Meehan eyes the girl's belly then purses her coral lips. "How long now?"

"Two weeks." Deirdre pushes her palm into her side; the baby is kicking again.

"I'm fifty-eight," Meehan says. "I've six children. That's what ended my career in theatre. I was once a Dublin girl, too, you know," she added. Her thinning brown hair is wound up in fat curls and pinned about her head. "Eileen had even come down to see me perform at the Abbey Theatre. Rode the train as I remember. It was Synge."

"Mum always liked the theatre." It isn't true; as soon as the words are out of her mouth Deirdre realizes she is lying. Though if Meehan is telling the truth, it stood to reason that Eileen liked it once. She puts her hand on her stomach again. The baby is pushing against the outer wall, low down. Touching her pearl earring between her finger and thumb, Meehan sighs. "Well, who's to say what tomorrow will bring?" And she kisses Deirdre on the cheek, holds on a long time.

Deirdre rests her glass of juice on the mound of her belly, and when Dermot walks up to her, she turns round and the ice cubes jingle.

"Sorry about Eileen. She'll be missed."

Deirdre is looking at Dermot, her head tilted and her eyes scrunched. He wipes his arm over his mouth in case some of the crackers he's just eaten have stuck in the beard, in case there's something at his nose.

"Dermot Fay isn't it?"

He nods, gives the mouth a wipe again.

"My mother said you're over in Canada."

"No."

"Sure?"

"I've not been."

She looks over his shoulder a minute then looks back up at him.

"She was always the gossip, but I was sure. You're the ex-professor?"

"It's my ..." He stops. "It's Abbey who lives with me. She's Canadian. I've not been."

Deirdre's eyes come back to his face and she tilts her head, distracted. Maybe that was it, he was living with a Canadian, the ex-professor who lived in the old cottage. The baby is giving her a hard time of it. "These things happen," she says, as if that explains everything, putting her hand on his hand before looking away, trying to find old friends in the crowd.

The body is laid out upstairs. People trek up and down the narrow steps to the bedroom and the conversations become more hushed around the top of the stairwell. "She looks grand," Marianne Lynch exclaims, passing by Deirdre as she pulls herself up by the wood railing. "Just as in life," someone says. "Francis, have you had the butter tarts? Aren't they lovely?" The voices, the lilt of exclamation and plodding tones of consolation, traipse down into the din of the living room as the wake-room door opens and closes. And then it's just Deirdre and her mother, the others having discreetly left the room. Deirdre looks at Eileen and starts to cry; the body is stiff-looking, the smile too forced. She tries to imagine the smell of bread rising in the oven, the lavender hand lotion that was her mother's favourite. Instead, there's the stale smell of the powder that someone patted over Eileen McGilloway's face; there's the smell of the lilies on her chest, although they look almost fake. Deirdre has it in mind to sing something, tries to think of her mother's favourite song, but nothing comes. So she sits on the edge of the bed and watches the body's almost imperceptible roll, the head moving a quarter of an inch as if trying to face her. Deirdre puts her hand out to touch the eyelids, wants to feel the flutter of her mother's eyelash, tries to think back to butterfly kisses given at the end of the day, Deirdre's head pushed into the down pillow, her mother's chin gently touching hers. Deirdre reaches across the bed to her mother's face and the tips of her fingers touch the cold skin.

Downstairs, Dermot, along with everyone else, looks up to the ceiling when he hears the resounding scream.

The Space Between

THE MOMENT Deirdre McGilloway reaches down and touches her dead mother's face, she feels her first serious contraction. Stunned, she lets out a high-pitched scream. Downstairs, people consider resurrection, the possibility that Eileen McGilloway was only sleeping. But those who had seen the body laid out know better. Dermot is the first one up the stairs, taking two steps at a time and then miscalculating the landing, going down onto one knee before finding his feet again. When he bursts through the door Deirdre is seated on the bed, her black skirt pulled up to her waist, trying to look over her belly to the space between her legs. He walks over to her and kneels down.

"What is it?"

Deirdre looks around. Candlelight flickers in all corners of the room; the table lamp casts a halo onto the floor. Her mother is laid out on the bed beside her, a bouquet of lilies over her chest.

Deirdre turns to Dermot, stares him straight in the eye. "Is there blood?"

And he doesn't know if she means on herself or her mother — the way people sometimes see things; how once, coming home from school, he'd gone into the kitchen and found his own mother over the sink with a dishcloth around her hand. A trail of blood from the cutting board on the counter all the way across to the sink, the yellow dishcloth going purple and his mother standing there, cold water streaming, unsure of what to do. "It's nothing. But run get Nan just the same." Dermot dropped his school bags and ran next door, later realizing he could've jumped the hedge, could've pushed open the door instead of knocking, waiting for what felt like ages for Nan to make her way from the sitting room at the back of the house. Even after Dermot had moved out to live in Grosvenor Square, he would go home for visits and imagine, in that instant before walking in the door, that'd he find his mother in the kitchen, leaning over something, the front of her dress, her apron, streaked with blood.

Sitting on the bed, Deirdre starts to hyperventilate. She reaches out on either side of her for support, finds the wall with one hand, her mother's leg with the other. It's cold and waxen, and she screams again.

"There's no blood," Dermot says, eying her white underwear. He turns and notices the room is full, half of Spiddal crammed in around the dresser, crowding the landing, although no one is stepping forward to take charge. Even the women stand there, daft. Don't they know exactly what to do? All evening Brennan and her ilk had watched Deirdre, carping on about her — the city girl carrying the fatherless child.

"Call Faherty!" Dermot looks at the dozen faces, the blinking eyes, the whole crowd pleased as punch at the production. He singles out Margaret Keating. "Get Faherty. She's in labour."

Deirdre reaches between her legs, then brings her open palm to her face, looks at it and closes her eyes.

"Is there another bedroom?" Dermot looks at the crowd again.

"There's coats on the bed in the spare." It was Conneely.

Deirdre lets out a low moan, rolls forward, hits her belly with her balled fist.

Dermot grabs her hand, holds it. "Lie back."

Deirdre's teeth start to chatter. She looks over at her dead mother then back at the crowd on either side of the oak dresser, then at the statue of the Madonna on the side table. She goes to put her hand between her legs again, goes to stand up, the mattress lifting up as she comes away from it, her mother's body rolling in the opposite direction. The crowd gasps as the dead woman's lilies tumble loose; her hands still cleaved around a few of the stalks. Deirdre sits down again, Dermot's hands on her shoulders. The weight makes her mother loll close once more, her head tilting, the right arm coming off her chest and hitting Deirdre in the thigh. Deirdre emits a high-pitched whine, her voice quivering. Dermot, thinking it's labour pains, lays the girl down on her back, then walks around to the other side of the room. Tries to think of what to do. Deirdre is lying next to her mother, Eileen's slightly swollen face tilted towards her daughter, her hand next to Deirdre's hip. The family resemblance is startling. From the far side of the bed, Dermot lifts Eileen McGilloway by the shoulders; her lead weight a surprise. He tugs and plunks her body down alongside the edge of the mattress as the remaining flowers tumble onto the floor. With space between her and her mother's body, Deirdre starts to breathe again, long choked exhalations.

Deirdre looks at the ceiling with its brown water stains. She sees the hand of God reaching out from the corner, a trumpeting elephant marching away from the round globe of the ceiling light. She exhales and inhales, trying to separate the panic from the contractions.

"Out!" Dermot yells, but the crowd stands there, old man Conneely set back against the wall but leaning forward, looking down at Deirdre, her skirt pulled halfway up her legs. In his head he's already retelling the story. "And there was the time young Deirdre McGilloway delivered her baby next to her dead mother on the poor woman's wake bed." Dermot yells again, "Out!" and begins to push people, Jimmy from the Spar, Conneely, out of the room. In the hallway the new postal worker Finn butts his cigarette out in the last dregs of his glass, sticks his head in to the bedroom, peeks around the door frame before Dermot yells, "I'll not say it again!"

And when the room is cleared of all but Niall Hughes, who offers his help calmly, Dermot turns back to Deirdre, grabs her hand and says, "It'll be alright, I know what I'm doing." Niall leaves them to it and starts down the stairs for hot water and towels but everyone is congregated at the bottom of the steps and he becomes stuck on the third step trying to decide how best to pass through the crowd. Fitch coming back in through the door just then, Egan wagging his tail beside him, both of them looking around.

When the lads from Maam enter the house they are laughing at a joke that was started in the driveway. But as soon as Tomás and Liam step in through the door they go quiet and so does Peter, Angus and Egg behind him. The whole village of Spiddal is crowded into the living room and lined up on the stairs as if they're queuing for a film. Even the dog looks upstairs, waiting for something to happen.

"What is it?" Tomás asks the crowd. To which Conneely, on the couch, replies, "Just a pause in the drinking."

Upstairs, Dermot slides Deirdre's wet underwear down over her knees. One by one he lifts up her feet, looping the underwear off her ankles. He pushes her skirt up to her hips, and placing his hands on her thighs he spreads them slowly until they are as open as wings. He thinks of Sophie. He thinks of Abbey. For a brief second he closes his eyes. When he opens them he notices Deirdre's left leg hovering just above her mother's.

"Right," he says, "breathe."

Deirdre starts counting and in between numbers she looks at the water stains on the ceiling, some the size of bugs, some the size of her hand and she goes over them again — a cap, a tree, Doyle's pony, a wedding cake but upside down, the bride and groom hanging by their feet, an olive, a — and then she feels it rush through her, a welt of a pain, and then it ripples and slows — a dog house, no a ship with great sails and she starts back at the first one, the one farthest away, the hand of God. At least, she thinks, that much hasn't changed.

All Our Wreckage

NO MATTER what happens, Abbey feels she has no place in it, that the world passes her by. And even on those occasions when she is part of things, when she's with Dermot at Hughes, or after work at Connor's when she stays to drink with the others, there's a part of her that's beyond even herself, a part that's watching the door, waiting to see who might walk into the room, take a seat beside her.

All night as she's been working at Connor's Abbey's been thinking about her mother, about Frank — the kind of confused thinking where it's difficult to ascertain what it is you're getting at, what's going on in your head. Things she hadn't thought of in years are coming back to her, like the time Frank took her to Cedar Point when she was ten or eleven, how she lost sight of him after coming off the carousel. Or the time Frank was supposed to pick her up from band practice when she was in grade eight, how Mr. Stanley, the music teacher, had to stand with her in the parking lot waiting, eventually driving her to the apartment, leaving her with Mrs. Pasic down the hall.

Abbey gets up from the staff table and pockets her tips. She puts the Euro bills and coins in one part of her apron and the pound coins in another. Around the corner a table of German businessmen finish off their drinks. It's nearing last call. The kitchen's closed, although Dan and Devin are still in there doing prep for tomorrow. Anne-Marie, the American waitress Abbey's been working with, is standing at the bar chatting up the barmen. Over by the cutlery station Veronica, the hostess, in a skirt that's too tight, is wiping down the menu covers with a cloth. In a half hour the place will be cleared out and Abbey can do the brass and the windows.

"Hey-lo." Anne-Marie waves her hand in front of Abbey's face.

"Hey."

"What happened with table twelve?"

"Veronica comped them and they didn't tip."

"Figures." Anne-Marie is from California, a valley somewhere near San Something — Abbey can't remember exactly. Last year, before she moved to Dublin, she'd been in the State finals for the Miss Teen USA pageant. "Are you okay?"

"Yep." Abbey looks at her, focuses.

"That thing with Dan was pretty weird. I mean, like, if he came at me like that I'd kick him in the balls." Anne-Marie shakes her head, pushes her blonde bangs to either side of her forehead; they stay there on an angle, like half-open curtains.

"It's no big deal." Abbey was used to Dan's antics. If a waitress showed up two minutes late to pick up a meal, if you missed your number lighting up on the call board, he'd give out to you. He reminded her a bit of Frank, always needing to have someone under the thumb, someone he could push around. Tonight, Dan and Abbey had argued and she facetiously asked him what prison release program he'd come from. So he came around the counter and pushed her towards the door. A hand on her shoulder. She told him to fuck off and that was that.

After cleaning the brass railing, Abbey heads to the phone box at the back of the bar and dials the cottage. Anne-Marie and Matt the dishwasher are sitting a few feet away having their free pints, so she closes the door. The phone box smells of stale smoke and something in it reminds her of Dermot. The phone at the cottage rings six or seven times. Abbey checks her watch, notices a bit of "Brassglo" sludge on her wrist by her watchband. She looks around for something to wipe it off. It's just past midnight and Dermot's not home. The phone rings and rings again. Nothing. Abbey pictures Flagon at the foot of the couch lifting up her head, eying the phone. The best time to call will be in the morning. And then what? "I've taken a few more shifts?" "I'm not quite ready to come back?" "I'm sorting a few things out?"

At the end of the night Abbey walks up the stairs on her way out of the restaurant, putting her coat on as she goes. Behind her, Anne-Marie, Matt, Devin and two of the junior barmen are finishing their second round of pints, the table they're sitting at covered in near-empty glasses and full ashtrays. Other than the row of lights over that section of tables, the whole restaurant is a dark wood surface, the chairs put up on the tables, everything in its place.

"See ya, Abbey." Matt lifts up his arm and flails it around.

"Bye." Sing-songy from Anne-Marie.

Outside the streets are wet. It's a twenty minute walk to Ange's and Abbey is up for the fresh air. Over at the end of Wicklow street a few kids stand around the door of the McDonalds. A guy in his early twenties plays a guitar, the case laying open in front of him. Abbey recognizes the song: "The Sisters of Mercy." Cohen is as popular in Ireland as he is at home. Abbey had all of his CDs back in Windsor.

Halfway to Angela's, Abbey's pace falls into a rhythm, her eyes to the ground. The whole idea of moving to Ireland had been to get away, to get out from under her father's thumb. To figure out who she was without him. And it was working. She'd started reading history books and philosophy texts she'd found at a booksale in the Quays. She realized she had an appreciation for art. And then there was Dermot, opening her up to all kinds of new ideas and ways of thinking. The world had gone technicolour and Abbey was happy to be standing in the middle of it, in awe.

For years Frank had been saying he was dying, but the blood tests, the X-rays, all came back negative. When Abbey was twenty and thinking about going away to University — Toronto or Queen's — Frank went on disability. He told her he'd been blacking out, that his blood pressure was through the roof. He figured it was a tumour — fifteen years of jackhammers; roadwork that jarred parts of you loose until it all balled itself up somewhere, took root. He said he'd been coughing up bits of blood. After a while he asked Abbey to move back in, short-term, to help him with the rent. The night she came home with her bags, she found him passed out on the kitchen floor. She was never sure if it was from drinking or if he was really hurt. There was a piss stain on the front of his jeans. That's when it started: Frank would sit her down in the living room, telling her he had something to say, as if she was a recorder, as if she cared about his childhood, about how hard done by he was, had always been. Frank could list it on his fingers: First his mother dying after giving birth to him; then his father giving Frank to the Gowan family down the road. Just for a while, he'd said. But George Shaw never came back for his son. He walked by the house on his way to work at the dairy and never even looked up at the door. The Shaws lived ten houses away in that same small town. All those years Frank grew up in the Gowan house, guessing and guessing, but never knowing. And the Shaws never offered so much as a word, never said, yes, you're one of us, or even "maybe."

At first Abbey listened to Frank because he was sick and she didn't know what else to do. And because it was funny and sad to hear him talk about her mother. He told Abbey how he met Karen at a bar, how she walked in wearing a mini skirt and leg warmers, sat down on the bar stool, peeled them off. Frank one of ten guys all trying to get over to her first. Abbey listened because he needed her to and because she half-hoped that somewhere in the chronology of his life she might find her own answers. "I'm dying, Ab." Frank said it over and over again for four years, practically willing the diagnosis. But, in a way, when Abbey thinks about it now, he'd been flailing his whole life. What was that poem, the one from English 220? The one about waving. No, that was it: "Not Waving, But Drowning." His whole life was one long drowning. Abbey sat on the couch, listening to appease him. Waiting, in her own way, for him to die, so her life could begin.

DERMOT'S hand has gone white from Deirdre's squeezing. Faherty is telling her she's hours away yet, to take it easy. Down the road an ambulance siren wails. Dermot goes to the window, pulls back the curtain, but can't see the street, sees instead an alder tree lifting up its leaves in the moonlight, the sloped roofs of the houses beyond. When he turns back to Deirdre she and her mother are lying side by side on the bed, Deirdre's head propped up with a pillow, her breathing slow. The lilies he picked up off the floor are on the mattress between them. And for a second there is a sweetness to the two of them lying there — a closeness, an intimacy.

A minute later the ambulance pulls up outside, the siren wailing one last time. Faherty goes down to wait at the door with his satchel. Dermot and Deirdre descend the stairs, her arm around his neck. The crowd of villagers who've been sitting in the living room watching the television and polishing off the cheese and crackers turn to look Deirdre's way: her forehead is beaded with sweat and her left hand cups the mound of her pregnancy as if she's trying to hold the baby in. Liam stands up to go over but Tomás grabs his arm. Dermot and Deirdre make for the door and the Spiddal crowd spills out of the house with them, into the crisp night air.

Out on the road, Faherty and Dermot hand Deirdre over to the ambulance attendants who strap her down on the waiting gurney, putting the belts over her chest and her legs. The whale of her belly sectioned off, reminding Dermot of the magic show his parents had taken him to in Dublin, a girl in a box cut in three.

"Right there?" asks the attendant, bright-eyed and smiling.

His partner, a girl from Barna, goes to the far side of the stretcher and together they lift the gurney. Faherty watches them set her down inside before they close the doors.

Deirdre McGilloway arrives at the hospital with all the pomp and flourish Ian the ambulance driver can muster. He's radioed ahead, he's laid on the sirens, he calls back over his shoulder, "Right there Mrs. MickG?" in an easy tone. He even fishtails the ambulance a bit when he hits a puddle before the round drive, the beams from the headlights panning the hedge before finding the red brick hospital wall again. In the back, Grainne, who is on her first week of duty after passing her paramedic exams, watches Deirdre go cock-eyed. "Are we nearly there?" she calls out. Deirdre grunts again, grips the gurney's steel railings, banging the underside of her ring against the metal rail at the start of every contraction — clang, clang — like a tinny metronome.

Grainne is looking around for gloves. Just when she is ready to commit herself fully to her training, thinking *left drawer, no,* and opening the right one instead, the one full of the hypodermic needles and blood pressure cuffs, the ambulance comes to a thudding halt and the back doors are opened. A gust of cold night air comes in.

Ian is beside the gurney right away and as he smiles down at Deirdre, brawny and good-looking, his brown hair dyed blond, she says, "You fucker, you goddamn fucker," and the fact that he is smiling so much, the fact that he is squeezing her hand, that his dimples are endearing irritates Deirdre enough that she says, "I'll get you, you little git, I'll get ya," although she has no idea why.

Grainne lopes alongside the gurney as they wheel Deirdre in, telling the doctor Deirdre's stats, and the doctor, a tall woman with her hair clipped back into a messy bun, interrupts, asks, "Is she crowning?" Lights, and the smell of ammonia, wash over Deirdre and she closes her eyes, sees pins, little pins floating in the blackness with red, yellow, blue tips. Her mother used to make dresses for her and kept the pins in a cushion, a cushion that used to be one of Deirdre's father's socks. Her mother had stuffed it and sewn it closed with red thread. Deirdre opens her eyes, the fluorescent lights humming, flashing overhead as the gurney is rushed along; the doctor, her lab coat flapping out on one side, pushes rogue strands of hair away from her face. The gurney bursts through double grey doors. Everything is piercing and aching. The whole world hums. There's a loud bang as the doors hit the walls on either side of the stretcher. Deirdre in her haze wondering about her mother, where she might be.

The epidural comes as a wave of relief. It's like Deirdre's floating in a tank of warm water, the pain that seared a minute ago somewhere off in the distance, tugging away. A nurse with squinty eyes and penciled brows is alternating her gaze between a monitor and Deirdre's face, her mouth moving under the green of her surgical mask. Deirdre can't make anything out. She feels fuzzy, buoyant, imagines that if she were to look down for her toes they'd be far off, her feet out the door of the delivery room, maybe even down the hall, her legs a great elastic length and at the end of the corridor, her swollen ankles, feet, toes, the toenail polish chipped and pink. The nurse is holding her shoulder with a gloved hand. From behind the mask comes a muffled, "Push, push Mrs. McGilloway." So polite. She adds pressure to the shoulder when Deirdre doesn't do as she's asked. Then, suddenly, as if Deirdre is coming up out of the water, the noise of the room comes back, the screaming, the blip blip of a monitor, the doctor calling, "Again, again, again," and the godawful screaming over it all, a scream that Deirdre suddenly realizes is coming from her. The nurse with the penciled eyebrows raises them up so that they touch the base of her surgical cap. The doctor is right there, not more than a foot away saying, "Again," sounding almost bored with it, pulling Deirdre apart so that she thinks maybe her legs have been severed at the hip, maybe something has gone missing. Deirdre pushes again and again, feels hands prying her open, impossibly open, as if she's been split. Then nothing at all, only a pulsing all the way up her body, caught in her throat like a chicken bone.

"A boy."

"What?"

"A boy," the nurse repeats, and she looks over to the doctor, who is holding a wailing baby between Deirdre's knees, his clenched fists swinging. Deirdre can just see them, arcing up in the air.

"What?" Deirdre says again. She can taste the salt of the sweat coming off her upper lip, trickling into her mouth.

The nurse, pulling her mask down to her chin, says slowly and clearly, "You've ... had ... a ... baby. A boy."

And Deirdre understands at last. Smiles up at the nurse. Says in a thick fuzzy voice, "Oh. Good. A baby. For a minute there I thought I was dying."

Maam Bog

THERE comes a point when the men find the exact rhythm and things take care of themselves. The machines work and the bog co-operates. The Bord na Móna administrators come out to walk the fields and keep going for lack of any complaint. Tuesday and Wednesday morning had been like that. Tomás and Peter were getting on again because the tractor, the spoon harrow, and the ridger were in working order. There were no more stumps or surprises. The weather was taking a turn for the better and the crumb was drying. Tomás milling the eighth field in their second set, while Liam and Peter were ridging the fifth. Yesterday was a peak day and the lads had gone home at the end of it worn down but happy that the work was coming along at last. Everyone doing their part.

Angus stands at the far trench having a smoke. He and Egg have been moving the ridged crumb from field three over to four. The conveyor belt stuttering along. Angus enjoys the fourth field; its main feature is a rabbit warren, the only rise in the flat expanse of the bog, twenty feet long and five feet wide. The Bord had decided to leave it — there have been a slew of feel-good initiatives coming in over the past ten years to appease the conservationists. Angus eyes the warren for any sign of life. There must be a whole city of rabbits inside, though they stayed in when the machines were close. Yesterday Angus had seen a few venture out as far as the grass and sedge that grew along the trench. The crew sometimes tosses carrots around the burrow holes.

Angus' uncle in Roscommon had kept rabbits in a row of wire pens at the back of the farm. Before holidays the old man would walk out with the nephews, pull one of the bigger rabbits from its hutch, and with it wiggling under hand he'd take it to the barn and twist its neck. He moved quickly, holding on while the rabbit twitched. Then he'd set the body down on a wood table. A row of hooks above. Skinning a rabbit, you always start at the head. His uncle going slow. The boys watching. Tufts of downy fur let loose as he cut, wind coming in the cracked window. Angus has always thought that bog scraw was like that, like animal fur. With skill it can be taken away from the body like a cloak. Cotton grass carried away in the breeze, just like animal down. He'd worked at Maam Bog when Bord na Móna first took it over in 1982, helped dig the first trenches. Went back a few years later to take the scraw and heath off it. The sedge and deergrass lifting like a blanket, the brown muscle of peat below.

Sound comes in fits and starts over the bog. Over by the ridger Tomás and Peter are shouting. Angus can't make it out. When the wind off the lough changes direction the slightest bit, the voices are gone. He puts out his cigarette and heads over to the next field. Tomás is resting the balls of his fists on his hips and Peter is backing off. By the time Angus gets over to Tomás, Peter's standing thirty feet away with Liam.

"What's wrong?"

"This." Tomás hands Angus a thin leather strap. There's wet peat still on it.

"Where'd he get it?"

"Just over there. Came up in the ridging. He was heading down for lunch when he saw it."

Peter, in his muddy boots and grubby jeans, starts walking towards Angus. The kid is tall and wiry with a soft complexion. Tomás swears under his breath as if he knows what's about to happen.

"It was over there," Peter says, and points.

Angus turns the strap over in his hand. It's eight inches long, narrow, with rough edges. Could be anything. "Call them," he nods at Tomás. "Did you mark it, Peter?"

"Aye."

Angus knows Tomás would normally ignore protocol. He's seen him do it in the past. But word traveled in the lunch room, and if the Irish Archeological Wetland Unit found out that you'd come across something and didn't report it they'd be out on their biweekly survey to miraculously find "a location of archeological sensitivity" on each of your eleven fields. And there'd be no easy way to work around them.

When the light-rail car circles by the far end of the fifth field, Tomás hops on it. One of the Bord na Móna workers from the next section sits on the opposite bench, a tool box on the floor in front of him. He's holding his cap in his hands, staring down at it, his work boots worn down on the outsides. Tomás holds the leather strap in his hand. They were always supposed to be on the lookout for any-thing out of the ordinary: bogwood, tracks or walkways, stone fences. The closer your fields were to Maam Lough the more likely it was you'd find something. Every tree stump, every sight of wood made Tomás' heart race. The inconvenience of it should they find so much as a plank. The archeologists had been surveying Maam for three years and hadn't found a single object worth noting, save for a few cooking stones that came up last summer in Flynn's field on the other side of the lough.

Angus pulls the IAWU kit out from under the seat of the tractor Tomás was driving. Inside there's a survey map of the bog, a pencil, a few orange flags, a list of contacts. He reads over the instructions they've included; there are no surprises. Walking over to where Peter is standing he wonders, briefly, if he's doing the right thing. They'll be able to get on with work around the archeologists but who knows what kind of attention the strap will draw to the other fields; maybe all the sections will warrant a further survey. The Bord is superficially in favour of working with the Department of Arts and Heritage, superficially in support of the archeologists and the Museum folks who wet their pants every time they pull a quarter pound of butter out of some corner of the bog; but in actual fact the Bord just wants the peat processed and sent off to the power station with as little fuss as possible.

Peter had pushed a wrench into the ground to mark where he'd found the strap. Angus walks up to him and tosses an orange flag in his direction. The wind catches it. Peter tries to grab it, can tell it's going to fall short. It does, sails down onto the moist peat. Both men look down at the orange marker on the ground between them.

"It's out of our hands, anyway," Angus says, picking the flag up and aiming the marker in the general direction of the wrench. Like a dart he lets the flag go. It falls sideways about half a foot from the right spot but Angus shrugs, figures it won't make much of a difference. They'll cordon off the whole area anyway. The light-rail car goes by again on the far side of their section. For a split second there's the sound of the engine as the tractor pulling the passenger car moves along the track, then the wind shifts and there's a second of silence. Angus feels a cool breeze on the back of his neck. Then the wind shifts again, carries the sound of curlew and kestrel calls. Peter pulls the wrench out of the peat and wipes it off with the corner of his shirt. Then the two of them turn, walk up the incline to where Liam and Egg are waiting.

The Traps

THE AFTERNOON Sean appears, Dermot is waiting. He's been standing for close to an hour with his arms crossed, eyes to the field, thinking, *The boy will come today, from a fixed point in the distance, between the back field and the road to the O'Riordan's. It will be Sean O'Riordan come to dig the fence post holes, it will not be any other.* Though Dermot wishes it were. He doesn't want to talk to Abbey, doesn't want to reason it through, he just wants her to come back. Give her the week, he'd said to himself five days ago; and in two days' time she should be home. He pictures her walking in the door of the cottage, then he imagines it another way, that she might call him from Galway for a lift. He sees the drive out to pick her up, sees her stepping out the bus-station doors and getting into the Mini. This morning he turned the phone ringer back on. If it rings now, he'll answer it.

She's been gone five days but it feels like weeks. Time is slowing and Dermot is all too aware of it. There were years between Clifden and the lobster traps, and Abbey's arrival. A decade that swung past him without so much as ruffling his hair. He'd gone off side, tucked away in the cottage, sleeping in his clothes the whole time, as if it'd been one long night, a surreal dream. These last few months have been different. He has a sense of purpose now; a part of him has announced itself after years of travel, of hiding away. He can't stay here now. Perhaps Abbey won't come back, and even if she does he imagines it won't be for long. Even Spiddal, untouched for twenty years, is changing; every second house is a bed and breakfast, a craft shop opened last year and now there are rumours of a second hotel. Tele Gael turning the town into a set for some Irish soap opera Dermot will never watch. In three months carloads of tourists will fill up the driveway next door. A satellite dish will be set up on the roof. German and Italian children will scream from the swing sets that will surely go up in the yard. He can see himself standing in this exact spot, witness to it all. How, he wonders, have I passed the time? And the answer refuses to come to him. So he turns to the back field, waits for the boy, just as he's always done.

The sound of hammers in the next lot takes on a rhythm and just as Dermot is about to put his finger on what song they're playing, they slow and the music becomes something else. Flagon stands at the property line barking at the workmen. The smell of cut wood is in the air. Dermot takes a bucket into the house and fills it with water from the sink, comes back out and waters the garden. Carrots and parsnips are beginning to come up and the leaf lettuce rustles in the breeze. Turning to go in for more water, Dermot sees the shape of a gangly boy crossing the field. The sun high overhead, the sky clear; the fence posts and wire stacked by the back wall of the house. Dermot watches the boy's progress. Decides Sean can start with the border to Fitch's, along the old stone wall, and he'll mark the rest out later. He could help but he doesn't want to interfere. The boy won't want him there either. Better to let him start at his own pace. If Sean wants a late lunch Dermot will have to drive to the Spar for groceries. He's been eating at Hughes the past few days, mostly going for the walk. Niall had nodded at Dermot as he set the roast pie down on the table. "I guess Abbey's still away."

"Mr. Fay." The boy is out of breath.

"It's Dermot."

Sean sticks out his hand and Mary, in a red gingham dress with a torn pocket, comes to stand in front of him. Dermot ruffles her hair and she gives him a sharp glance, takes her headband off. Dark curls fall towards her face.

"Where's —?" The girl looks around the yard.

"The Border collie," Sean says.

"Flagon."

"Flagon." Mary says it quietly, starts walking around Dermot in circles, the fingers of her right hand lightly touching his knees.

"She's around." Dermot gives a whistle but the dog doesn't appear. "Probably in the field."

Dermot shows Sean the fence posts and wire bales and then waits while the boy stares the material down. Next door, a power saw starts up, there's the loud whirr of the blade and then the sound of it hitting wood. Behind Sean the laundry on the clothesline flaps in the breeze, billows in the direction of the back field.

"Start at the northwest corner and follow the line of the old stone fence. We need a post every twelve feet."

He tosses a yellow tape measure Sean's way.

"Here's the digger," he motions to the ground where the hole digger is lying on its side. "It's a lend, so mind it." Dermot thinks over what else to say. "Start with the holes for now and tomorrow I'll have the posts dropped off a truck so you don't have to haul them. Come early and you can help with that."

He remembers he's yet to ask Niall for a lend of the truck. He'll ring him when he goes in. Sean is still standing with the tape measure in hand.

"You'll need to go down two feet." Dermot bends over, picks up the digger, holds the handle out to Sean. The wood is split by the base. Dermot wonders if it'll last. Suddenly he wants to call the whole thing off.

Mary goes to the back of the cottage. On tiptoe she tries to reach Abbey's underwear, the only bright colours in the yard. Dermot has left Abbey's clothes out, has watched them dry, soak up the rain, then dry again. He knows that if he'd brought Abbey's clothes in to the house, he'd happen upon them, that if he'd wanted to put them in her drawer he'd have to open it, would see that it was empty.

Mary spins like a pinwheel, trying to reach a pink pair of underwear, jumping at them, almost making it. Sean watches Dermot go over and pull the clothes down, the underwear first then the two shirts, stiff and puckered from the wind.

"Abbey's," Dermot says, by way of an explanation.

"Your wife?" Sean hasn't heard of a Mrs. Fay.

"No."

Dermot ducks under the door frame, the laundry bundled up in his arms, his face inclined towards the clothes, the door closing behind him.

Sean finds Dermot's wheelbarrow and with Mary in tow he pushes it, filled with the digger, a shovel, and one post so that he has its measure, to the start of the field. He hits a rock at one point and loses the half of it; Mary gets a sliver trying to lift the end of the wood beam. Sean has worked it out with his father, he knows he has to dig straight down, that he has to fit the post in and then fill the hole back up with packed earth. The wire will come later. Sean puts the two tips of the hole digger down on the corner of the field, on the near side of what must have been a decent stone fence. Then he looks over to Fitch's house to see if anyone's watching. Two cars go by along the bay road. A third car honks and Sean looks up too late to see if he knows them. Behind him Mary sits in the grass, her dress fanned out around her, her blue leggings getting darker in the places where the dew's soaked through.

"Stand up, Mary."

Sean jams the blades of the digger into the ground, and they thud into the grass. He pulls the handle apart. Looks over his shoulder at his sister.

"Mary, stand up."

This time she does and walks over to a rock, pretends to write on it with a blade of grass.

Lifting up on the handle Sean grits his teeth, uses his arm muscles, can feel them strain. A chunk of earth lifts up, a core of dirt between the spades of the digger. Thin white roots throughout, a worm turning over just under the surface. Sean closes the handle, flips the clump over onto the ground and starts in again. Tips down, jam in, pull the handle apart, lift out. He turns to see if Mary is watching but she's busy with her rock. Sean starts again, further down the post hole, the earth coming up in one swift move.

One by one, Dermot sets Abbey's clothes over the shower curtain rod. They're still damp to the touch. Putting his face close to them, Dermot can smell Galway Bay in the fibers, and the hand soap

Abbey used to wash them. If they'd been dry the morning she left she would have taken them too, and he'd have nothing but her empty drawer and a fear of filling it.

In the kitchen Dermot opens the cupboard to the right of the sink. On the lower shelf: four plates, four bowls, an assortment of glasses, all of them mismatched, muted patterns. They're clean and stacked, as Abbey had left them. On the middle shelf, teacups and saucers, and on the top shelf the bag of vitamin capsules given him two years back by Faherty. Reaching right of the vitamins Dermot pulls down a sheaf of papers — Abbey's Irish notes. Verbs written out neatly in his hand on the top sheet; she'd copied them on the sheet below. There are also a few phrases, 'She lives in Ireland, Tá sí ina cónaí in Éirinn,' 'I am Irish, Is Éireannach mé.' Even though Abbey had no idea what part of Donegal her grandparents came from.

Dermot finds what he's been looking for: Abbey had jotted Angela's number and the number at Connor's on the first sheaf of paper. Tomorrow he'll call her at work, to make sure she's coming home. Walking from the kitchen to the front room he stares at the telephone number, knocks his leg against the arm of the couch. The place is a kip. Books are stacked on the big table, along with a number of dirty cups; the rug is covered in dog hair and there's a water-stain along the trim. Tomorrow Dermot will get up on the roof, retie the thatch. He'll borrow a ladder from the lads working next door. This place was a barn when he bought it. Two cows, a donkey and some sheep had all herded themselves in from the rain, slept on a straw bed in what is now the front room. Dermot remembers that it was months before the reek of shit and piss was finally out; the heavy must of wet fleece had stayed longer, as if it was worked into the stone. It was Fitch's place at the time. Dermot took it and nine adjoining acres, used the money from his inheritance.

When he thinks about his parents and about the house he grew up in, what he thinks of most often is going to the solicitor's, getting the keys. He'd walked up Leinster Road in Dublin, knowing the sale would go through that afternoon. He'd even sold the furniture, remembers standing in the entry way, leaning against the door jamb, thinking that nothing had changed, that if he lifted the chair in the living room the leg marks would go down two inches into the carpet. His father had spent years in that chair, one ear to the radio, eyes closed, *The Irish Times* on the table beside him. He'd worked twenty-three years as a typesetter in the *Times'* D'Olier Street offices and his son had never seen him crack open the paper at home. Dermot had gone into the kitchen and placed his hand on the handle to the cupboard door, thinking: toaster, butter plate and small plates above, two of the saucers with nicks along the side — one with a thin crack across the middle. And when he'd opened the cupboard, things were exactly the way he'd expected, although the butter plate was clean and empty and there weren't any crumbs around the toaster. In his old bedroom the spread was pulled back, the brown wool one, as if his parents had been expecting company, as if they'd thought "Dermot is coming home and he may want to stay." There was a way his mother'd had of putting him down at night. She would push her lips into the hollow of his cheek, then wipe the kiss away, laughing. In the end she'd outlived Dermot's father by seven months, had spent that time in and out of hospital trying to find a complaint — "Sure, my heart's going," one week and then on the phone to Dermot about her arthritis the next. The doctor said she'd died of want — to be with her husband, to sit in a chair and know he was beside her. "We should all be so lucky," he'd said as he pulled the x-ray down off the back light.

Dermot didn't want Dublin, not back then. He'd been shoring up in a rooming house in Clifden, working the lobster traps, and that was enough for him. Although the landlady's clanging was driving him away; all afternoon she'd be in and out of the various apartments with a metal cleaning bucket, the clank of it hitting the floor. She'd sing under her breath, and the walls were thin as parchment. Missus McGuire was her name. She'd knock on Dermot's door to tell him supper was ready, and stand there until he answered, craning her thin, lined neck up and over his shoulder to see what state the place was in. The sea had saved him. He was out on the boat at all hours checking traps, lifting them out of the water, both arms straining. The smell of the sea all around him, the glistening Mannin Bay waters draining off the catch.

Fridays, Michael would come up from Galway after sitting in on meetings at the University. He had just started lecturing there after leaving Trinity, and though no one at the University in Galway wanted an Englishman on staff, there were only one or two conservancy experts in the country and Michael was one of them. And Michael was both a brilliant scholar and willing to teach. He'd picked up some Irish, sat on a number of boards, signed on with the Wetland Unit to show his commitment. Although there was no end to his complaining on the nights when he drove up to Clifden to see Dermot.

Usually they met for drinks at Mahones. Dermot would come down in the Mini, right off the boat, smelling of diesel and algae. Michael would be in a suit or dress pants and a collared shirt, would roll up his sleeves as the night went on. It was Michael's easy company that buoyed Dermot during those years. He remembers the nights at Mahones, their odd paring and the looks of the locals, as if he and Michael were on show — the Englishman and the ex-professor who spoke Latin to the lobsters he hauled into his boat. Their regular waitress at the time was a woman called Janey, all of twenty, with wide hips and blue eyes. One night she turned and smiled at Michael when the two of them came in. She walked over to the table in long strides. "Those legs," Dermot mumbled, watching her, and Michael shook his head.

"Hey ya," Janey smiled at Michael, picking up the two empty pint glasses left at the edge of the table.

"How're ya?" She looked right at him, waiting for an answer.

"Grand, thanks very much."

"Two Guinness," Dermot said.

"Be right back," she'd replied, winking at Michael before she turned to go.

Dermot started to ask a question but stopped himself. Michael raised his eyebrows and lifted his shoulders. "I have no idea."

"None?" Dermot eyed him warily.

"None. But I'm fine with it all the same."

"Sad day when a Brit can get laid in Ireland."

Except for nights at Mahones, Dermot kept to himself. He wrote away to foreign universities, pounding out his credentials on an old typewriter with a sticky "e," seeking a post in mediaeval studies. He had no recommendations and knew that anyone who called Trinity would be told he wasn't suitable. The rejections came one after the next, Missus McGuire sliding them under his door then inquiring at tea what the business from Zurich might have been, saying, "My, Mr. Fay, but you seem to have lofty ambitions." After a while Dermot would fill out formal applications with an addendum saying that he was qualified but too liberal for Ireland. He would cite Joyce's problems with publication and go on for pages about how repressive states cripple the educated. He signed these with a great flourish and mailed them promptly before he'd time to reconsider.

In the end, after six years in Clifden, Dermot cleaned out Fitch's old barn and turned it into some semblance of a home. He took two wingback chairs from his parents house for which he paid the new property owner twenty pounds. When Dermot was a boy, his parents had sat in those chairs every night over tea while he was shushed to the back of the house for bed. They'd be sitting there again in the morning, and his mother would rise from her seat when Dermot came in. It was as though they'd never even gone to bed. He didn't miss them once they were gone. He'd understood this when he left behind the photographs, the radio, the cake plate that was his grandmother's. There were too many weighted objects in that house; his mother had been unable to have another child, and his parents' hearts were hung with that sadness so that everything about them, every object touched by them, seemed tinged with regret. No, he didn't miss them. What he missed was being a boy: waking up to the smell of toast and eggs, the cutlery spaced out on either side of his plate on the far side of the table; his mother getting up to ruffle his hair and serve him. He missed being sure of things — where to sit, where to go, who to come home to.

Frank

THE ITALIAN restaurant Angela has chosen is packed — typical for Temple Bar on a Thursday night. Abbey slides into the booth next to Fenton. A candelabra on the table, napkins folded like swans. Over by the far wall a man in a tuxedo sings an aria, his a cappella almost eerie. People speak in hushed tones so as not to disturb him. The waitress, a busty woman in a black dress, drops off four menus, introduces herself as Irene. A waiter comes along a second later with a basket of warm bread. Angela excuses herself and heads for the loo.

"Do you like Hornby?" Brendan asks Abbey. They'd just been to the films where they'd seen a movie based on one of Nick Hornby's books.

"I've only read *High Fidelity* ."

"Did you see the film version of it?"

"No. But I remember John Cusack was in it."

"They made it so American." Fenton sounds disappointed. "*Fever Pitch* is the best."

"Do you follow football, Abbey?" Brendan raises his eyebrows in Fenton's direction.

"Not really."

After Angela comes back, Irene brings a round of water and takes the order for drinks. Doesn't write anything down, just spins the silver bracelet on her right wrist with her left finger. She has a small tattoo, two Japanese symbols, on the inside of her arm. "Back in a min!" She turns on her heel and walks away.

Fenton leans in towards Abbey's shoulder and looks at her menu. His aftershave is musky and pleasant. "What are you havin'?"

"The eggplant penne, I think." Abbey looks across the table to Angela.

"Yeah, the penne's good," Angela says, tapping her teeth with her fingernail, glancing at Brendan. "How's the fettucini alfredo? Have you had it?"

"It's grand, yeah."

"I'm for the mackerel." Fenton closes his menu. He leans back against the booth's velvet upholstery, turns to look at Abbey. Abbey doesn't want him to think this is a date but she hasn't brought up the fact that she's living with Dermot. And she knows Angela probably didn't mention it to him either.

The waitress drops off the drinks and takes their order. The boys dig in to the bread. The conversation goes back to football and the Hornby football novel, and then on to Brendan's work at an indie recording company two streets over. He offers Abbey a tour sometime and she agrees. Waits for an opportunity to mention Dermot, but it never arrives.

What surprises Abbey most is how much fun she has. After dinner the four of them go to Blackhouse Records then to The Mean Fiddler to dance. Angela knows the doorman there, a guy called Buzz whose real name is Fergal. He has a microphone headset on and when he sees Angela, he pulls it off to kiss her. Dance music comes down the stairs from the club, fills the street.

"Goin' in?" he asks. There's a queue of about fifty people waiting behind a yellow rope.

"Is it all right?" asks Angela. Buzz usually comps her.

"Ah, it's grand. There's some big CD release job goin' on but it's a good crowd."

He lifts the second rope at the foot of the stairs and lets the four of them in free, says "Four V.I.P's coming up," into the headset in his hand.

Inside the music is deafening and the crowd pressed in tight. The whole room smells of sweat. On stage, two English DJs spin dance music, adding their own mix over an album that sounds like it's straight out of the 1980s. People jump up and down in front of the stage, everyone to a different rhythm. Abbey can feel the bass line thumping against her chest.

"I'll get us drinks." It's Fenton beside her, shouting into her ear. When he comes back he hands her a pint of lager, tips his glass to hers; the foam spilling over the rim. He licks his hand and smiles. He'd told her at dinner that he's twenty-four, which makes him just two years younger than Abbey. "An older woman," he'd said, as if things were well underway between them. Abbey takes a sip from her pint and nearly spits the lager back into the glass. She looks up at Fenton and shouts over the music "What is this?" "Bud!" he mouths, giving her a thumbs-up.

Fenton takes off his leather jacket and Abbey hands him her coat, watches as he walks over to a booth set up along the wall, puts their stuff over the end of it, asking the girls who're sitting there if they'd mind. They watch him saunter back towards Abbey and it occurs to her that he's probably considered a bit of a catch. He has a wiry build, the kind girls seem to go for, cropped black hair, sideburns, and almost girlish, doe eyes. He showed up for the film in dark jeans that were folded up at the hem, and a white t-shirt, like something out of a Calvin Klein ad.

Fenton nods sideways towards the middle of the crowd. "This music's not my thing, but do you wanna dance?" Abbey turns around and looks towards the bar but Angela is nowhere in sight.

"Yeah. Great."

Fenton takes her by the hand, and holding their pints close to their chests they weave through the throng of bodies. Somewhere towards the middle of the room Fenton drains half of his pint and nods at Abbey to do the same. "So you don't spill it," he shouts in her ear. She takes a few sips and then tries to swallow a mouthful. They start to dance. Two hundred kids bob up and down to techno music around them; the coloured lights over the DJs turntable arc across the walls and ceiling. A flash of a yellow light flicks across Abbey's arm. Fenton, eyes closed, accidentally knocks into her, shouts "Sorry!" And Abbey shouts back, "It's okay."

Abbey's dream that night is so real that she wakes up with her heart pounding against her chest. A noise in the kitchen, a dish settling in the sink, something Abbey can't place exactly, wakes her up. She looks around to get her bearings, sees the TV set in the corner, the other couch on the far wall, the door to Ange's bedroom. In the dream, Frank's coffin was empty. Abbey closed it and turned around to find a bear behind her, rearing up on its back legs. The maw came down towards her head and then she felt a sharp pain and then there was darkness. Her mother somewhere inside it, so that even though Abbey knew she was dying, she didn't care, because her mother was in there too. And Frank. Outside Abbey could hear Dermot. He was looking for her, talking the bear down, using a gentle voice, using reason. But maybe somewhere in the body of the bear, beyond all the pain, maybe Abbey and her mother could find each other. A choice had to be made. Then the sound in the kitchen woke her up and Abbey, scared out of her wits, thinks that Frank is there beside her. She can see him for a second, his hair pressed up against his head as if he too has been sleeping. Abbey wants to ask, "Why are you doing this to me?" Knowing that he isn't really there, that she won't get an answer.

Abbey wakes up a second time to the sound of Angela's alarm clock going off in the next room. The dream was so vivid it's like a film she could play over and over again. Part of her wonders if she ever really fell back asleep. She remembers pulling the afgan down from the back of the couch over top of her, she remembers taking off her skirt because after the dream she'd realized she'd fallen asleep in last night's clothes. They'd stayed at the Fiddler until three and then come back to Ange's for a last round of drinks. They'd had Bailey's at the end of it, on top of all that beer. Abbey had finally gone to bed at four, after checking the machine to see if Dermot had called. Now Abbey looks over at the clock on the microwave. It's eleven. She sits up, pushes the heels of her palms against her eyelids. Everything goes black. She drops her hands, looks over to the living room window instead, the cut of light between the curtains.

The year her mother left, Abbey was eight. They'd just taken the apartment on Ridge Street and Frank was looking to go back to work for the city. One minute Karen was there, in jeans and a t-shirt, carrying in boxes, lugging them from the U-haul truck to the elevator, then into the apartment at the far end of the hall. And then she was gone. Nowhere. Frank took Abbey out to the near-empty truck and the two of them drove up and down the street, trying to find her.

A month after they'd unpacked, after Frank had finally found work and put Abbey back in school, Abbey woke up in the middle of the night to find him climbing onto their tenth floor balcony, his right foot on the top rail. For a whole minute she thought she was dreaming and so she stood there, unsure if what she was seeing was actually happening. Then Frank instructed her to get back to bed, go to sleep, and something in his voice told her "this is real." Abbey remembers she had to take his hand to get him to come down. That she was the one who said not to worry, that everything would be okay.

Getting off the couch and going into Angela's bathroom, Abbey wonders if that's how Frank would have remembered those years. Or if he'd only remember how every so often, while walking with him in the city, Abbey thought she saw her mother. Sometimes it was a stranger, or a woman with peroxided hair, or a woman who happened to be wearing a red t-shirt like the one her mom was wearing the day they moved. There was no reason behind the thought — just a trait, a detail that made Abbey want to go up to the woman, force her to turn around. Once, though, Abbey was sure. They were on Ouelette Avenue and it was late. They'd just come out of the movie theatre. Across the street a woman walked out of a bar and headed down towards the river. And even though it was dark, something about her was so familiar. Abbey tore at Frank to let her go, scratched at his hands as he gripped her shoulders. Choking out "mom," as if that might make her turn around.

Into the Muck

MICHAEL makes his way across the bog, looking ahead to
where Angus said he'd find the orange flag. At the end of the
fourth field, with the workmen behind him, he comes to a
trench. It's six feet deep and about four feet across, murky
brown run-off in the bottom. The Bord na Móna men wait
for him to cross over. Propelling himself forward, Michael
feels the weight of his stomach pull him down, his boot slip
on his heel. He lands with a thunk, his legs taking the impact.
Looking behind him, he catches his breath. The trench looks
like nothing; still, he feels like he's just hurdled a river bed.
Michael walks over towards the slope of the fifth field,
where Angus has directed him. The lough starts at the end of
the field like an estuary, the wind rippling the water. In the
middle of the small lake is a well-treed Island, a ruckus of
birds. Then the bog starts again in all directions, mostly
stripped save for the area along the lough, a narrow plain of
gorse and sedge.

Midway across the fifth field Michael finds the orange
flag and bends down, conscious the workmen by the trench

are watching. He shakes his head. The flag is sitting on its side, not even pole down in the peat. A big enough wind, a curious bird might have moved it.

"Here?" He shouts over to the foreman, a paunchy balding man with a sour look on his face. Tomás mock salutes him, which Michael assumes means yes. He picks the flag up and plants it, pulls the survey map out of his bag, studies the notes his team made last time they were here. Nothing. Five years before, the WU did a preliminary dig in field three. This was before Michael's time. He was still helping out in the office then, overseeing the conservancy process when material was brought in. And he liked the office better, was never a digging man. He didn't have the back for it. Last year was meant to be a one-off, a field supervisory position that would mean four trips to the bog over the course of the year and six assistants who did all the real work. "A favour" was how the Superintendent had put it. *A man of your expertise.* Maam had been a big zero on the find scale and no one, including Michael, expected that to change. He'd only renewed his contract with the WU because the money was good considering the work-load and he thought it might help him get a permanent position at the University or at the Museum. He was tired of the contract work, the bits and pieces. He wanted something whole he could sink his energy into. Things in Ireland had changed in the past ten years. He could get the work — the WU, the University, the conservancy stints at the Museum. But they weren't changing fast enough. He still couldn't get a position. Last year he told Dermot that he'd give it one more year, that if things didn't get better he'd go back to London. But he didn't really want to live there. He liked it here on the coast, he liked the people, his students. He even derived a certain amount of pleasure from the fact that he was different. He appreciated the small bureaucracy that was the Irish archeological community. In London you could never get by on knowledge alone, you had to prove things, loudly and in public, you needed a platform. Knowledge — intelligence for that matter — came second to position. Position came from backstabbing your peers with a degree of civility. And that didn't sit well with Michael. Excavation. Ex cavare. Cavare, to make hollow. That's the way things were seen in the UK. But that wasn't how they saw it here. In Ireland it's about making history, wrenching history from the ground.

Kneeling down, Michael sweeps his fingers over the soil, moves them lightly, drags bits of roots and peat crumb around. He pulls four wood stakes and a ball of twine from his bag, looks over his shoulder. The foreman Tomás, and the blond-haired kid Liam, are over by the trench, smoking. They watch Michael as he gets up, pushes a large spike into the ground with his boot, takes a tape measure out of his pocket. He marks out a two metre square, jams the other smaller stakes into the peat, reels out the twine as he goes.

Once the base line, datum point and perimeter are set up, Michael pulls out his camera and notebook. The lads watch him and Michael signals that they can go. They're off work today, the four days between harvests, but apparently they decided to come down anyway, to see how much of a disruption the WU might cause. Michael knows some of them from Maam. Last year he worked with Angus on a different section of the bog. And two weeks ago Michael and his team did a survey of this block of fields though they didn't talk to the workers and didn't find anything interesting. Maam wasn't like Ballybeg in Offaly. The Wetland Units there are working around the clock. Every twenty metres in Ballybeg there's a trackway or some rise in the field surface that indicates an underlying structure. Annie, the supervisor there, spends more time in the peat than anyone Michael knows.

Michael writes the location of the site on a slate board and sets it by the stake that will act as the main data point. Then he loads a roll of film into the camera, looks up at Peter and the one with the shaved head they call Egg, who are standing by the trench with the others. The film loaded, Michael takes photographs of the cordoned-off area from a few different angles and then turns and snaps a photo of the lads for a laugh. They look suddenly uncomfortable. Tomás stubs out his cigarette and stares at the ground; Liam wipes his mouth with his coat sleeve. To make them feel more at ease, Michael extends the camera directly out from his face. He smiles big and the flash goes off.

Michael loops the camera strap around his neck and opens his note pad. Then he sits down on the driest part of the turf, a few feet outside his newly formed square, and he starts with the notes. Maam Bog, 9:20 AM. He photographs one view from the north, then the east; he photographs the bog from every direction and after each click he scrawls the exposure number and the directional information in his book. Dirt from his hands falls down the page.

The whole process takes an hour. By noon Una and Gerry, two of the younger WU members on his team, should be out with the shovels and brushes to start digging. They'll work six hours today and get back to it on Monday. Michael briefly wonders if that'll mean he can go home early and leave it to the youth. Una is especially keen, although arguably too careful at times, too full of trepidation. Gerry is the first one to pick up the shovel and haul out a pile of soil. Michael chose the two of them for this site in the hope that they might temper each other, find a middle ground. Still, Michael decides he will have to stay with them, pull his fair share of the load. A "find," no matter how insignificant, requires a supervisor and a preliminary dig, and this, for better or worse, is one of Michael's sections at Maam.

Michael looks down at the survey map and then east to the edge of the bog, where it meets the open bell of the lake. He checks his compass and guesses the distance. He'll have Una measure it later to make sure the site's location is accurate. Pointing the camera towards the lough Michael snaps another two pictures, thinking that an underlying contour or structure might be more apparent in print.

Tomás and Liam watch for an hour. Debate whether or not Michael will need more than a preliminary dig.

"I'll give ya ten he's here the week," wages Liam.

"Two weeks," Tomás says. "He looks a right prick."

The whole Bord na Móna crew watch him go through a roll of film, and then another.

"So that's archaeology," Liam says, wishing he'd brought some weed so he could, at least, in the light of absolute boredom, get stoned.

"'Fraid so," Tomás yawns. His mouth opens wide enough for Liam to see the gap where a bottom tooth should have been. "Shall we?"

"Why not?" And the two of them head off in the direction of the train. Peter, Angus and Egg fanned out along the trench, waiting for the Englishman to dig.

Going Under

THE PHONE rings. Dermot gets off the couch, puts his book face-down on the slim mantle that juts out over the fireplace and watches it flip over, onto the floor.

"Hello?"

"It's Michael."

"What time is it?" Looking out the window Dermot sees it's gone dark. He turns to Flagon, who's lying on the floor by the couch; she looks up at him, but doesn't lift her head.

"Half-eight. Listen, I'm just back from starting a dig at Maam. Thought we'd go out."

"What's at Maam?"

"A Bord na Móna crew found a strip of leather in the peat."

"Bord *na* Móna," Dermot corrects his annunciation.

"Right." Michael waits for Dermot to say something about drinks. There's only the faint hum of the line.

"Where are you?" Dermot finally asks. He can hear noise in the background.

"The pub in Gortmore." Flagon rolls over onto her back.

Dermot watches her lay there, eyes to the carpet. "Thought you might come up."

"I'm for bed," Dermot says.

"Suit yourself."

"Ta." And Dermot hangs up the phone, watches it set there in its cradle.

Dermot pours himself a glass of whiskey and sets it on the bedside table. The smell of Abbey is gone from the sheets. He pushes his face into her pillow and there is nothing, no hint of her left. If she'd been true to her word she would've been home this evening. But somehow he knew better. He'd called her last night, got Angela's voice mail and hung up.

Pulling the blanket under his chin, Dermot turns to get comfortable, kicks at the knot of sheets around his ankles. Turns back to the bedside table. Picks up his glass. In the other room he hears the click of Flagon's nails on the kitchen linoleum.

Abbey is not the first woman to cause him grief. Sophie was Dermot's undoing. She'd walked into his classroom late, after the bell. The other students were settling into their seats, but Sophie, unsure of where to sit, had turned to her professor and smiled conspiratorially. Dermot had never seen her before but he was struck instantly. Dark red hair curled down her back against a light blue cardigan. She had almond-shaped eyes and alabaster skin, although later he would find faint freckles, a dozen or so, across the bridge of her nose, two over her left eye. Her books were held up against her chest that first day but Dermot was aware of the swell of her breasts behind them, watched as she turned on her heels and walked over to the last desk, far right and front row. Dermot cleared his throat and took off his suit jacket, scratched the back of his neck, flexed it until it cracked. "I'm Professor Fay and you are in The History of Mediaeval Churches: sponsorship and political bias. Today I will introduce you to Justinian and his great church at Ravenna." The notebooks opened and the students' heads went down. It was the first day of the semester, Fall 1979. Her books still closed, Sophie watched him. He noticed her gaze and looked away.

Juno and The Paycock followed. Sophie was in the Trinity production of the O'Casey play, and although Dermot didn't make much time for the theatre he dragged Michael Dunne along to the opening night. Michael had started teaching at Trinity that year and was still trying to find his place in the melee. Dermot took to him because they were both outsiders, Michael coming from London and Dermot an Irish Catholic, an anomaly at the Protestant university. In a way it was he, more than Michael, who stood out, and he knew it. Dermot had found his way back to Ireland through a recommendation by Professor Lasalle at The Paris University. Lasalle was an authority on European mediaeval studies and he thought Dermot was doing ground-breaking work with his dissertation. Whether or not Lasalle pulled favours to get Dermot a teaching position Dermot would never know. But he was grateful. Lasalle was a dismissive man who rarely made time for even the brightest of his students and the fact that he took an interest in Dermot, that he made sure he received scholarships and bursaries, amazed Dermot. Although, in a way, it was hard going back to Dublin. The best work Dermot ever did, the study of the Táin remscéla, he did while living in Paris.

Midway through the play, "Mary" crossed the stage, came closer to her mother. Sophie as Mary was unintentionally comical. She sighed before starting across, the square heels of her shoes clunking on the wood slats.

"I never said to him what I shouldn't say, I'm sure of that!" She exclaimed everything.

Mrs. Boyle, the mother, asked slyly, "How are you sure of it?"

Dermot liked the actress who played the mother — she was understated, familiar, like his own mother.

"Because I love him with all my heart and soul, Mother." Sophie was feigning tears now. Dermot knew the director, picked him out of the middle of the house, could see by the way he leaned forward in his chair that he didn't think it was going well.

"Why, I don't know," Sophie as Mary continued, "I often thought to myself that he wasn't the man poor Jerry was, but I couldn't help loving him, all the same." Her make-up at this range, fifth row, was pasty. Dermot studied the other cast members' make-up during a period of awkward pause. Someone had forgotten a line. The actors shifted or swayed on the spot. There was a giggle from the audience, near the back row.

Sophie had asked Dermot to come see her. She'd even brought two tickets to class. "For your girlfriend?" she'd said before taking her seat, crossing her legs under the desk.

She wasn't very good, but after the performance the crowd smothered her, especially the young men. One of them, a blond fellow, kissed her on the lips before placing his hand on her back and guiding her through the crowd.

"Well Mr. Dunne, what did you think of the actress who played Mary?"

"Lovely, though a bit perplexed at times, like she'd forgotten a line, or rather," Michael said, "that she didn't understand it as it came out of her mouth."

They were on Westland Row and the rain had started. The sidewalks were slick.

"Professor Fay," said a voice. Then, louder, as he was about to step onto the street, "Dermot." He turned and there stood Sophie, flushed from running, even her chest red and patchy above the white scoop of her neckline. Dermot had a desire to place his hand there, it looked so warm.

"Thank-you for coming. I saw you —" and she turned towards Michael, looking embarrassed. Up close Michael could see she was only seventeen, maybe eighteen. On stage she'd seemed older. When Dermot failed to say anything, to introduce her to Michael, Sophie started to back away, saying, "Thank-you, anyway, for coming," before turning distractedly to her cohort, the blond man who'd followed her out.

It can be a matter of weeks, of hours, of a small, almost extractable, part of a life. Dermot can trace it backwards and forwards: what went right, what went wrong, and how after all his messing about, he arrived here, on a thin mattress set up on blocks that acted as a bed frame, in a cottage that leaned and yowled in the wind. Outside the white beam rakes a long branch across the window. Dermot smells Abbey's pillow again but there is nothing so he bunches it under his arm as if it is her body, the slope of her shoulders just under his hand.

How do you earn your fate, Dermot wonders. He'd studied hard with Lasalle, the Gallic bull of a man tutoring him, demanding he know four languages. That attention had made all the difference, that and the presentation he gave at Paris University on the Táin manuscript, the handshake afterwards. All his success can be traced to that moment and the months he'd spent in the National Library before it. Now Dermot can pinpoint every turn he's made, every room he's entered that has changed him.

Two months into Sophie's third year at Trinity, she came to

Dermot's office and invited him out to dinner so they could talk about her paper on The Battle of Ros na Ríg. They went to a cafe on O'Connell. He drank tea and moved his whitefish and peas around on his plate, watched her sip at her soup. When Sophie talked about her childhood, Dermot only half listened; her feet were moving near his under the table. They paid the bill before either had finished their meal. Undressing her that evening in his flat, he undid the thin gold-cross necklace she wore, grabbing the clasp with his thick fingers, trying again and again to unfasten it.

"Are you sure?" he'd asked, his lips under her chin. And she nodded, undid his trousers for him, laughing at his worn grey briefs, running her hands over the light brown hair of his inner thigh. And then there was nothing, as if she'd dropped off the face of the planet, as if it was all to be regretted. For a week she missed class. So he waited. And that, if anything, is the thin sliver of time Dermot would take back, extract like a tumour. That first time, and also the second, when she showed up at his flat in Rathmines, walked into the bedroom, walked right past him without so much as an explanation. Later in the evening she said she might love him. Maybe. Always had. The bed springs so loud they'd thrown pillows on the floor, had started again down there, Sophie scraping her knees bloody on the short pile of the carpet. She'd left right afterwards, said she didn't want the girls in her dorm to talk. She stood for five minutes inside his closed door looking out the window until she was sure no one would see her cross out onto the street. And then they met every few days. The whole affair went on for no more than three weeks, and it was always on her terms. When he thinks about it now it seems as if that was the whole point of the exercise — that she wanted to be in charge of him, call on him when she wanted, demand he touch her in a certain way, create a desire in him that would make him helpless. To know in the way that women need to know, that she could break him. Hardly any of their time was spent talking, though he did help her with her logography paper for another class. He went to the library with her and left a pile of books on a desk for her to peruse: Soothill's syllabaries from the 1880s, Brown's *Historical Scripts.* He tore small bits of paper out of his notebook to mark the relevant pages. The two of them had circled the stacks like children playing a game. That term Dermot was busy trying to finish his own projects; he was feeling pressure from the department to publish. He'd started to spend his evenings with Michael, talking about a catalog of oral histories from Inishbofin. He wanted to compare the written recensions of myths with the ways they were told on the Island today, hoped it would evolve into a decent paper.

There was a fragility about Sophie that Dermot sees now, when he thinks about their time together. It was as intangible as a look or a gesture, as if she was outside of her self watching her life unfold. It was in the way she always seemed to be playing at something.

Dermot knows he didn't love her, he knew it then and he knows it now. When she slipped a note under his office door saying she was pregnant he didn't believe her.

"I am," she said through the crack of her dorm door.

"Let me in." He was furious, afraid of being spotted.

"I can't."

And it occurred to him there might be a man in there, so he pushed the door open with his fist and it hit the wall. Sophie's luggage was open on the bed, her school books were stacked on the table under the window, there were piles of notes in the trash bin.

"You'll get an abortion."

"How?"

She was crying. Dermot looked behind him. A student walked past in the hallway, glanced in. Dermot met her eyes then closed the door and turned to Sophie. A sinking feeling, a going-under, for the both of them.

The Unfenced Country

IT'S BEEN three days and only half of the posts along the north border of the fence are up. The air is damp and heavy and there's a low mist along the east end of the field. The digger, when Sean went to get it at the back of the house, was covered in dew. Now he wishes he'd brought a jacket, though the work will warm him up once he gets into it. Mary has decided to stay at home with their mom, helping her bake a cake for Nuala's birthday. Sean had told them he wouldn't be back for dinner and his mother gave out to him, saying Nuala would notice he was missing, that his sister would only turn eighteen once. When he left, he noticed a bag of balloons and party hats on the table.

Sean starts in after the last upright post. He measures the twelve feet, jams the blades of the digger into the ground. Hits stone. Dermot told him it would be all right to move farther down, that it would take a year to shovel out every field stone he came across, so Sean jams the digger's blades into the ground to the right of the stone and they cut through; the grass coming up in a clump.

The finer points of fence building are still a mystery to Sean. He knows he has to do the posts and that the wire will follow but he isn't sure if he should wire the first length of the fence or wait until all the posts are in. Dermot hasn't offered much instruction and now that things are underway, Sean doesn't want to ask his father. He's always expected Sean to simply *know*, assumes that he should be able to figure out how to build a fence using logic. Assumes he can make friends without trying, that when he leaves the house he does it because he has places to go. Even when Sean was struggling in school, when the midterms came back Cs and Ds, his father believed that Sean could rally himself to get As at the end of the year if he just applied himself. And Sean did apply himself but the grades didn't change.

By noon Sean has put in a dozen more posts. The sun comes out from behind the clouds and Flagon follows not long after. She watches Sean for a bit until Dermot whistles and she goes running. On the other side of the low stone wall, one of Fitch's cows eyes Sean warily and butts her head in his direction. In another hour or two Sean will be far enough along that he'll be able to see Cassiopeia and Cygnus laid out in the grass. He put them there last winter, was out until two in the morning doing it. That night he'd imagined Fitch was wandering out in the field, had told himself over and over again that it was the acid, that if he focused he could figure out exactly what was happening. Dead leaves in the trees flapped like crow's wings. The moon gnashed its teeth. The field suddenly reft — there was a hole in the middle of it and Sean was falling in, thinking that if Fitch really was there, then maybe the old man could save him. But he was alone and the hole was getting wider. Like a night without stars. Like the black of an eye. Sean going in. It was two in the morning before he was seeing straight again. He went home, climbed the tree next to the house, crawled into his room through the second-storey window. His younger brother Kevin woke up when the ladder to the upper bunk hit the metal bed frame. Ten minutes later his mother was at the door, flicking the light on, saying, "Good of you to come home."

Last week, after a visit to Éinde's, Sean had added Lyra. He'd stopped at the church to see if Clancy had dropped anything and ended up in the field at midnight planting six small rocks above the swan's head. One of these days he figures Fitch will be out walking in the field for real, and he'll catch Sean stumbling around, talking to the constellations underfoot. And maybe that's why Sean has chosen this field — Fitch would be like someone out of the old books, boxing him on the ear and scaring the shit out of him, not liking anything about Sean at all, and saying so. Spitting it out in a string of insults, not keeping it to himself like Sean's father.

Holding a post upright with one hand, Sean scoops the earth back into the hole with the other. He lets go for a second to see if it balances and it does. As he packs the dirt firmly in around the post, Sean starts thinking about the fence, not so much about building it, but why. Dermot had said he might rent out the field to a sheep farmer or that he might buy some sheep of his own. Sean figures he's bluffing. There's something about the old man he can't put a finger on. And it doesn't have anything to do with what was said about him at home, the gossip as his mother packed lunch boxes at the counter and his father made tea. "Fay, you remember, the professor who —" His mother had stopped there, smiling over at Sean, waiting for him to leave the room so she could continue. But Sean had already heard it from Clancy, whose parents had lived here long enough to remember Dermot moving in. No, there was a reason Fay had gone in for the fence and it wasn't the big

English guy bullying him. He was getting ready to sell. Sean was sure of it. Maybe he was tired of it all, the talk, the village, the bungalows. Or maybe he was simply moving on.

In the late afternoon Dermot comes out with a canister of tea and sandwiches. He comes across the field in his muddied boots and jeans, wrapped in a heavy coat even though the sun is up and the weather is mild. Flagon darts over the long grass at a distance behind him, her nose to the ground as she chases something across the length of the field.

"I brought sandwiches."

Sean wipes his hands on his pants and takes the white plastic bag held out to him, sits down on the ground with it.

"It's going well," Dermot says.

Sean nods as he unwraps the sandwich from the plastic. He bites down on the thickly sliced white bread, turns the food around in his mouth, tastes cheese, lettuce and mayonnaise. Looking up he finds himself in Dermot's shadow.

Dermot crouches down and sets his own sandwich on the plastic bag in front of him. He opens the canister of tea and pulls a teacup from his coat pocket — white with faded roses around the border. He pulls a saucer from the same pocket. Sean laughs.

"Just like my mother's," Dermot smiles. From his left coat pocket he pulls out another cup with an ivy pattern.

They sit for a minute eating their sandwiches; then Dermot, tired of hunkering, crosses his long legs under him and hits the thermos with his boot. It starts to tip forward but Sean grabs it before it spills entirely.

"Ta."

The boy nods, flicks tea from his fingers onto the grass beside him. Flagon comes up behind Sean, leans in, smells his hand.

"She'll take tea."

Sean puts his hand out and Flagon licks it for a few seconds before turning to stand the other way. She's watching the far field, and beyond that, the road to town, her ears pushed forward.

"Do you know much about the stars, Mr. Fay?"

"The stars, is it?"

Sean takes another bite of his sandwich.

"Points of light in the heavens." Dermot looks from the boy to the sky. "You know the sun is a star?"

The kid sets down his sandwich and wipes the corner of his mouth with his thumb.

"Plato. Do you know Plato?"

The boy nods.

"Plato thought the stars were divine beings. He thought, and this was back in the days of sandals and catapults, before the telescope, NASA and g.p.s —" Dermot raises his brow and Sean smiles, "— anyway, he thought that stars moved in a perfect order, circular orbits. And that the earth was the centre of the universe."

"Until Galileo?"

"Copernicus, I believe. Although Galileo had some thoughts on it later."

Sean refills his teacup from the thermos and sips at it.

"You have your sights on astronomy?"

"Maybe." Sean shrugs, looks over at the post he's been working on.

"The silent heavens mark all stars that swim the sky."

Dermot takes a bite of his sandwich. A sliver of lettuce falls out and onto his jeans. "That's Virgil."

"What did you teach in Dublin?" Normally Sean doesn't like to ask personal questions but this time it seems to fit the conversation.

"Ask me what I learned," Dermot corrects him. And he fixes his eyes on Flagon who, behind Sean, is still staring across the field.

"I'M OFF."

"See ya." Abbey picks up her cereal bowl and walks Ange to the door.

"What time are you due at Connor's?"

"High noon," Abbey says with a western drawl.

Ange opens her purse and rifles through it. She finds her keys, puts them in her pocket and turns to go. "I'll be back around eight."

"I'm doing a double shift so I won't be back 'til midnight."

"All work and no play —"

"Yeah, yeah, yeah."

A few days ago Abbey had agreed to cover two shifts for Anne-Marie so she could go to London for the weekend with her new boyfriend. Abbey and Anne-Marie had gone together to the Best Deals Travel Agency on Dawson Street for tickets. The whole office was covered in Irish flags and a banner hanging over the front desk read "Book Japan and Korea now! Special Cup rates!" Abbey had noticed a list that read "other destinations" on a chalkboard beside the banner. Anne-Marie was at the back desk talking to an agent while Abbey eyed the board: Toronto one-way — three-hundred and ninety-nine Euros.

The white shirt Abbey needs for work today is dirty — brown sauce on the sleeve. She rolls the cuff up twice and it isn't as noticeable. Does the same with the other. The television is tuned to a BBC breakfast show Ange likes and the kitchen table is covered with exhibition photos from the Gallery where Ange works. A *Cosmo*, opened up to the "get your best hair ever" article, lies beside them. Crumbs from Ange's toast line the crack of the page. Abbey goes into the bathroom and stands in front of the mirror. Then she opens the medicine cabinet and, finding the hairbrush, rakes it through her hair. There are times when she can see how much she looks like her father. And like Isabelle Shaw. And also like the one photo she's seen of Frank's real mother, Stella. She has the same narrow eyes, the same slight wave to the dark brown hair. Just before her sixteenth birthday Abbey had dyed her hair blonde, the same shade she remembered her mom using — Pure Platinum. Then she didn't look like anyone, not like Frank, not like the Shaws, not even like her mother, although Jane, at Abbey's birthday dinner, had said otherwise, probably trying for once to be nice.

When Abbey told Frank she was going to Ireland she said she wasn't doing it to hurt him. She was just tired of waiting for her mother to magically appear. Staying in Windsor meant waiting for the day they'd run into her. And Abbey watched for it all the time — imagined her mother in the Kmart, at the Magic Cuts, in the Shop and Save, at a phone box; imagined her mother, after seventeen years, simply boarding a bus.

"What I have and what you have are two different things." This was Frank's response. "You know me, right?" thumping his chest, hitting it with his thumb. "You might not like me but I'm your father."

Abbey was changing his bed sheets and he was standing near the window, where he had a view of the neighbouring apartment building, the plastic flamingos on someone's tenth-floor balcony, the potted plants, a pinwheel tied to the rail. There were strands of his hair on the pillow case — more than usual, as if it was coming out in clumps. Abbey'd wondered briefly if he pulled it out on purpose and then felt guilty for even thinking it. She tossed the dirty sheets into the hamper and went over to Frank. He smelled like piss, like piss-stained clothes.

"Go take a shower, Dad."

"While you pack?" He'd turned back to the window. "Thanks, but I know that trick."

The last time Abbey saw Frank was a week before she left for Ireland. They'd had a row about her going. At the time she was calling it a vacation, though she had a work visa and thought she might stay as long as six months. She wanted to travel around, to find out more about where the Gowans and the Shaws had come from. The plan was to come back, nurse Frank through whatever it was he needed nursing through, maybe go full-time to the University of Windsor. But he wasn't having any of it. He refused to let her go. Abbey'd pointed out that he couldn't stop her, but dead-pan Frank had replied, "Oh yes, I can." So Abbey had walked out on him, had gone over to her friend Lisa's house to watch a video. Later, around one AM, Frank called Abbey on her cell phone, telling her to come home, insisting it was important.

As soon as she opened the apartment door Abbey felt the heat coming off the flames. There was Frank on the balcony with his back to the railing, looking at her, at the blazing sway of the polyester curtains between them. The wind drew them towards him then billowed them back into the apartment in orange licks. The fire had already spread onto the couch, the spider plant in the corner, its wicker pot crackling. Frank stood in his underwear behind it all, a gas can in his hand.

Abbey ran for the phone on the wall in the kitchen and dialed 911, screaming at Frank to get out of there, calling him an asshole. The fire alarm went off, the sprinklers started. Frank stayed there, out on the balcony, watching her on the phone. All he had to do was step into the living room, toss the gas can over the railing, come forward. But Abbey knew he was waiting for her to save him.

Draping a blanket over her head, Abbey reached past the curtains, waved her hand around until she found his wrist and pulled him through the flames. All the while she prayed to god that he'd drop the gas can, that he wasn't trying to take her with him. The harsh clang of the fire-alarm was still going off in the hallway and the fire was climbing the wall above the couch, routing its way around the family photos Frank had asked Abbey to put up.

Abbey pushed Frank out the door of the apartment and made him roll over the cinders that had caught on his jockeys. People in pajamas and overcoats came out of their apartment doors, hurrying for the exits. One of the neighbours, a middle-aged man, looked in Frank's apartment then went in with a fire extinguisher, aiming it at the couch. The corner of the room was a mix of orange and yellow flames and Frank was laughing.

At first Abbey let Frank lean on her as they went down the stairs and across the concrete driveway. But once they got to the front lawn Abbey let him go, and he crumpled into the grass. This was his way of begging her to stay. And if she did, and if it only worked for a while, he'd do it again. They both knew this. Abbey looked at Frank lying in the grass, thinner than she'd ever seen him — yeah, okay, dying — but trying his best to ruin her life as he went. He laughed again and Abbey began to walk away. Frank tried to get up and follow her but a fireman came over to him to see if he was hurt. The fireman's two gloved hands held Frank down.

"Sir, I'll need to examine you ... Sir ..." and Abbey was already at the far edge of the lawn.

"Abigail?" He'd raised his voice. "Abbey, come back —"

When Abbey looked over her shoulder, Frank was using his bony arms to push away the oxygen mask they were putting over his mouth.

"Abbey!"

Abbey started running then, trying to remember what clothes she had at Lisa's, what she could take with her to Ireland. Her bank card, plane ticket, and passport were all in her backpack. She thought about what she'd want from the apartment and then realized she never wanted to see Frank again. She could walk away from all of it. Abbey ran ten blocks as if he was behind her, her heart thrumming up in her ears, the sidewalk tilting towards the road. When she reached Riverside, she stopped and looked around to see where she was. The Detroit skyline was lit up on the far side of the park. Her fingers kneaded the stitch in her side and her breath was visible in the night air. She was on Water Street, which meant Lisa's house on Highland was only four blocks away. She made for the hill. The smell of gas on her clothes from carrying Frank down the stairs. What had he been thinking? What if she hadn't come? The street lamps loomed above her as she came to the top of the rise, and turned onto Elm, moving through a circle of light one second, and heading into darkness the next.

The Bog Man

MICHAEL is a few inches down into the soil, his right arm
sore from constantly brushing away the earth. The peat is
moist here, so he has to apply pressure to get it to lift. Gerry
beside him is using the trowel, removing the peat, the dead
roots, by the shovel-full. Una's on the far side of the dump
site going through the surface layer of peat with a screen. It's
Monday, their second day at Maam, and protocol dictates
that if Michael doesn't find anything by the end of the week,
the boys can go back to working this part of the field, can pat
the three of them on the back as they're leaving.

"Una?" The girl — cropped black hair, almost Asian eyes —
looks over from the far side of the pile of peat. "Give us a hand
here, will ya?" Michael nods his head toward the northeast
corner of the pit. Una stands up, brushes the dirt off her khaki
shorts. White bra straps poke out from under her yellow tank
top. "You can use the small shovel. You and Gerry work from
the corners." Michael draws a line out from the corners with
his fingers.

"From here?"

"Yes. And don't be afraid to dig down. Just pay attention to any resistance." Una picks up the small shovel and Gerry, looking over his shoulder, watches her step into the pit, lean over, pitch the blade into the ground. Michael catches his eye and shakes his head. It's not quite a reprimand, more a look of consolation. *She's out of your league, out of mine.* Una's nineteen, smarter than both of them, a feminist who wears tight t-shirts with slogans like "Porn queen" printed in block capitals across the front. Gerry's more out-going, and maybe, in Michael's opinion, a bit too chummy, but he gets the work done. Despite her cautious nature, Una is the first student of Michael's who has ever excavated a find in the field. She'd just finished her first year classes and was working that summer with the WU at the Bog of Allen when she found a trackway. Dug most of it up before the fall term began.

In all his years as an archeologist, as a student, associate professor and professor, Michael's never unearthed anything of consequence with his own hand. He's worked next to people who've come across pottery shards, a broken bead; there was a girl in Dublin working ten feet away who found a lead bulla. But Michael hasn't spent enough time digging to warrant a find. He has a gift for pulling papers together before presentations, for making it all sound worthwhile and good. He even fakes a certain glamour when attending funding meetings, discusses great finds as if every dung heap in every corner of Dublin could contain them. And the truth is, he believes they could. Michael spends most of his time pouring over other people's papers or arranging for the preservation of objects traveling from Dublin to museums around the world. He teaches Archeological Methodology and Conservation Science as a sessional in Galway. He makes a trip out to Maam once every six weeks to supervise the WU. Occasionally he takes up the brush. But not like this. Not for years. Down on his knees in Maam bog — the thought of it gets him laughing. *An English bog man. This is what the Irish have made me.*

The summer Michael turned twelve, his father, a crane operator in Millwall, took him to the British Museum. They went up the steps, through the doors and into the main foyer. Stopped there. Looked up at the domed ceiling. It was off-white with gold coffers, a simple design. This was the first time Michael saw how set apart they were. Maybe it was a matter of education, or class, but everyone else entering that building kept going, right past it, as if they'd seen a hundred such ceilings before. When he thinks about it now, he remembers how they spent the day wandering around, both of them amazed at the smallest things: Egyptian combs, a bent sunflower pin, cuneiform carved on the side of a stone. But what he thinks of most is that ceiling. Not the Sutton Hoo exhibition, the photographs of the site, the archeologists in their garrison caps and fedoras, a large pit behind them; but the ceiling, and his father next to him, looking up.

Michael leans forward with the brush in his right hand, sweeping it back and forth over the peat. He pulls at a thin white root with his left hand, snaps it. Gerry and Una are due back from their break any minute. Then Michael can take one, walk around the field, get the circulation in his legs going again. His back is aching. Sitting up, lifting his arms overhead, Michael breathes in and then exhales deeply. Listens. A group of frogs are sounding out in a nearby trench. Under that, there's the dull roar of the tractor engines carried over the bog. Every now and again, the clang of machinery; once in a while, someone shouting. Sitting back on his heels, Michael undoes the buttons of his jacket. The clouds have moved past the sun. The wind coming off the lake has died down.

The peat underneath him is warming up. Layers of it have been brushed and shovelled away, are drying outside the pit. With the sun comes the sound of kestrels. Shielding his eyes, Michael looks up. Sees nothing. When he looks back down and across the bog, he notes that the stockpiles in the sets to the west are coming along. They look like the spines of wild animals; black plastic covering the tops of the ridges like manes. Tomás' crew is working their first set today, and looking north Michael can see three machines going. Tomás is milling one field while someone else ridges the field behind him. The harvester is two fields behind them. Tomás' first set is coming along, although they've yet to move all the smaller ridges to the central field. Standing up in the pit, Michael sees the whole grid of the bog reaching out around him. The rich brown of it, a copse of bushes near the lake. He flexes his back muscles and stretches his neck, first to one side, then the other. Drops his chin to his chest, rolls his head back. Above him, a kestrel flying in wide circles. Michael imagines the bird looking down over the field, what it would see. A man standing in a small pit. The ground turned over around him. The bird thinking nothing of it and flying on.

Dialectics

HAVING lied to the administrator about his credentials, Dermot makes his way across Maam, a "guest" badge pinned to his shirt. He hops onto the light-rail car and takes a seat, hoping to find Michael. The two Bord na Móna workers on the far bench haven't a clue about the dig.

"Sure, there's always a dig somewhere."

"Wouldn't say now, where it might be."

"You'll likely be doing the circle for hours."

"Pack a lunch?" The laughter is at his expense, but he finds Michael fairly easily, in the form of an orange WU sign posted at the edge of the fifth field.

"There's your man now," called out as he jumps off.

Michael's been at it three days, with Una and Gerry helping out in the afternoons, the three of them working quietly, concentrating on the task at hand. At ten, when Michael sees Dermot crossing the field, he has two thoughts: How in hell's name did he find me; and thank god for the company. Gerry, when he did talk, didn't seem to have anything much to say, and Una tended to stop working when the conversation got even remotely interesting.

Michael spends the next hour listening to Dermot yammer on about bogs. "The summer of 1919," Dermot starts, "Alcock and Brown flew the first non-stop powered flight over the Atlantic. All was going well until the two men came in over Clifden." He stops, takes a drag off his cigarette. "The wind shot up and the plane went ass over tail with it. Nose-down in Derrygimla Bog." He kicks at the peat. "What's 'bogach' in English, Michael?"

Michael racks his brains for the exact translation from Irish. "Wet or soft ground, or —"

"Soft ground. Good enough."

Listing them off on his fingers, Dermot recounts for Michael some of the more interesting finds in Irish bogs. "A man's hand in 1978; horsehair tassels; seventeen pounds of bog butter in small parcels, brought up here and there over a period of about a hundred years. A wooden wheel in Doogarymore. The Altartate Cauldron in Monaghan. The occasional clump of medieval animal dung. Musical instruments. Whole forests. The Lurgan boat out at Addergoote."

Michael knows most of it, but listens to the drone of Dermot's voice, the odd list. "The plane itself didn't have time to sink. They hauled it out the next day with ropes and cattle. Did I tell you about a hand in '78? And roads and bridges that the bogach took over. A thousand-year-old farmstead. The best pair of shoes as owned by old man Conneely's father who, one night heading home from Screeb, walked a bit off the path, dropping down to his knees in the muck."

Michael looks up at Dermot and shakes his head. Goes back to the bottom of the pit. Sticking out of the peat beside his right hand, he notices a thick piece of material, a kind of thread. He shuts his eyes and refocuses. Brushes the dirt away and with his fingers moves the clumps that surround it aside. Above him, Dermot is still yammering on. The part of the thread that was buried underground comes up out of the divot Michael clears with his finger. He brings it towards his face. Up close he can see it's only a root, uniform enough along the top to be spun thread, the part he's just unearthed uneven, the white roots more fibrous looking than the length Michael had first seen. He tosses it up towards Dermot, who doesn't notice it hit the back of his leg.

After an hour of pacing outside the pit, Dermot steps in to help Michael dig. They're three-quarters of a metre down into the soil and there's a layer of calluna roots underfoot, like a thin mat they have to trowel through. Dermot watches Michael to see how much force he's using in the digging. Watches him jab the trowel into the ground, heave the peat by the shovel full over the side of the pit and onto the dump site above.

"You're grand company now," Michael says, after a long silence. The two men have taken opposite sides of the excavation site and they back into each other every now and again. Michael makes quick work of his end; Dermot takes his time.

"What's that?" Dermot says.

"What?"

"You're whistling."

"Didn't notice."

"You were." And Dermot whistles the tune back at Michael, trying to place it.

"Brandenburg. Bach."

Dermot stands up and stretches, looks out towards the machines in the next set of fields. Before the work started here, there would have been clusters of gorse and fern all over the bog —

cottongrass, heather, asphodel. This time of the year there'd have been mounds of pink and yellow flowers, curlews near the lough. He knows the arguments for conservation, even goes that way himself when push comes to shove, thinks there are better ways to power the country. But the sight of the Lurgan boat, the idea of it being pulled out of the peat — fifteen metres long, an internal keel, some four thousand five-hundred years old — that's another story. The ground giving history back. Something returned to you, long after it had been forgotten.

When the wind starts to come west across the bog, Dermot hunkers into the pit, leaning his back against the cut-away edge. Michael had wondered about Abbey, and Dermot snorted through his nose, said he'd heard she'd called to the pub, left a message for him, that she'd taken a few more shifts.

"But I thought she was due back four days ago?"

"She was." Dermot left it at that.

"What about the fence?"

"It's half finished."

"Going well?"

"It'll stand."

Sitting in the pit, his jeans damp, Dermot reaches over his shoulder and grabs at the top layer of the bog, pulls a clump of peat from the ridge overhead, brings it down and breaks it apart in his fist. "I might go to Dublin." He says it slowly.

"After Abbey?"

Dermot looks over at Michael, who is digging out the peat in front of him with a trowel and then dumping it unceremoniously over the side of the pit.

"To live."

Michael stops, turns to look at him. Sits back on his heels. "Dublin?"

"Maybe so."

Michael shakes his head.

"I'm as lost here as I would be there," explains Dermot.

"What about money?"

"I'd get by. I could find something."

"Dublin's changed."

Dermot pulls a cigarette out of his pocket, puts it in his mouth, roots around for his lighter. Taps his left pocket. Finds it. Shielding the cigarette from the wind, he tries twice to light it.

"It's very cosmopolitan, very EU now. You won't recognize it." Michael is still shaking his head.

"That's what I was hoping."

That evening, mud is tracked into the house, but Dermot doesn't say anything. It would have never crossed his mind before, but Abbey had started to straighten the cottage up, put things away. She'd even kept at Dermot to take his boots off by the door when he came in. Today he leaves them on and as he heads to the refrigerator, clumps of mud drop off, scatter over the kitchen floor. Michael's boots are just as bad and when he sits down at the kitchen table, falling into the chair, a layer of dirt drifts down off him.

"It'll be the death of me, that bog."

Dermot winks at him. "You'll conquer it yet." He opens the fridge, leans in and moves a few jars around on the metal racks. "Any preference for dinner?" Flagon comes into the kitchen, stands behind him. "I've cheese for a sandwich." He backs out holding a plastic Spar bag.

"That'll be grand."

"Dublin?" Michael says again.

"It has to be something."

"But Dublin?"

"Spiddal. Galway. Dublin. An leabhar céanna."

Dermot waits for Michael to beg for a translation. When the sandwich is ready, Dermot places it on the table in front of Michael, who ignores him, bites into the sandwich, swallows without chewing.

"That means it's the same book, that it's all the same," says Dermot. He walks over to the kitchen window and moves the curtain aside, leans over the sink and looks out. The framers have started on the interior of the nearest bungalow and they're pouring the foundation of the bungalow just down the road.

"Do you want another sandwich?"

"Might do."

"I'll have to go for bread."

Michael puts the last bit of crust into his mouth and wipes the crumbs off the table and onto the floor. "Don't bother, I'm grand." He stands and puts his hand on Dermot's shoulder, looks out the window at the bungalows. "She'll be back. Give her a few more days."

"Will she?"

"Yes."

"What makes you so sure?'

Dermot goes into the front room, turns on a lamp and sits at the big table. A series of books he'd pulled off the shelf are spread out around him. Michael picks up *The Life of Anselm of Canterbury*. Opens it and flips through it. A number of pages are dogeared, and he discovers a handwritten receipt for eight pounds, dated 1972, at the start of Chapter Four, Hanna's Books on Nassau Street. Another piece of paper, crisp, falls out a few pages on. There's a passage underlined in black pen: "He does not exist in place or time, but all things exist in him."

Dermot looks up. "Anselm is it?"

"It is."

"Useless wanker."

Michael smiles, puts his hand on Dermot's back. "I'm off."

"Suit yourself."

Closing Time

ABBEY throws a chip across the sidewalk and into the grass. A duck waddles up from the edge of the pond. He's nearly there when a seagull darts at it, hops a few feet away with the chip in its beak. Stands in the shade of the park bench guarding it. Abbey checks her watch. She's due back at Connor's at six for the evening shift, has been taking work left, right and centre, doesn't care how many hours. And Veronica has agreed to spread it out on her cheques so it doesn't reflect the fact that yesterday, for example, she worked fourteen hours. Suspicious, she'd asked Abbey at the end of the night if she was trying to save enough money to fly home.

Abbey misses Dermot. She hadn't thought it would be like this, had expected more of a choice. Maybe it's Dermot's silence, the act of letting her go, the fact that he'd let her have the last word, even if it was a lie. She was supposed to have returned five days ago. He hasn't called, and Abbey's given up on phoning the cottage, has started to leave messages for him at Hughes.

Closing her take-away container Abbey looks around for

a trash bin. Her cod has gone cold. On the next bench two girls wearing green and white Dunnes uniforms eat sushi and complain about their manager. Their hair up in clips, as if they work in a kitchen or bakery. Abbey stands up and heads for the gate, drops her container in the bin. Eyes the statue of O'Donovan Rossa. Once out on the sidewalk she waits with a dozen other people for the light to turn. A couple on the other side of the street carry grocery bags, the backs of their hands touching. The last time Dermot came to Dublin he and Abbey had a picnic in Stephen's Green. He bought a bottle of wine, grapes and cheese at Dunnes, and they sat over by the northeast corner of the park, away from the benches. The weather was miserable — cold for November, and damp. It started to rain. Eventually they went over to Kildare Street and got into the Mini. His hands on her in the car, the two of them laughing. What is different now? How have things changed between them? Part of her is afraid of him. At least that's what he says — that she's afraid this is it, that if she stays with him she'll be circling his moods, his needs, the rest of her life. That she's afraid he might need her the way her father did. Abbey recalls the look on him, on Dermot's face, when he said it. Standing in the kitchen after a fight, a broken tea pot on the floor between them, and the realization that it might be true, that he would insist she be subservient, that he didn't know how to be with someone any other way. But she's not afraid of him, not in the way he thinks she is. What she's really afraid of is that she'll give herself to him fully and it won't be enough.

At nine, the pace in the restaurant slows. Abbey goes over to the work station to polish cutlery. Every minute or so she checks the call-board lights in the dining room to see if either of her tables' meals have come up in the kitchen. Holding two butter knives in her left hand she runs a clean rag over their smooth faces, then over the fat handles. The cutlery reminds her of her mother's silverware, a place setting for eight that was given to her mother by her grandmother as a wedding present. Abbey remembers how heavy it was when she was a kid, how the handles, mediaeval looking oblong bulbs, got bigger until the bases seemed to fill her palm. For a joke her mother would tap her on the head with them when they set the table at holidays. Abbey would pretend to fall over, unconscious, onto the floor. The good set of silver was the only ornate thing Abbey could remember her parents having. After her mother left they never used it, even though none of their everyday cutlery matched.

The number six comes up flashing on the overhead call board. Abbey drops the knives into the tray and they make a loud clunking sound. She walks into the kitchen and Dan and Devin, both in their chefs hats, are pushing steaming plates across the metal shelves in her direction.

"Roast Pie, Lamb, Halibut and Risotto!" Dan shouts. He glares at Abbey.

"I'm right here, asshole." Abbey makes as big a smile as she can muster.

Dan shows Abbey his teeth, runs the back of his hand over his forehead. "Go fuck yerself, Princess."

"It's not a roasted potato, it's supposed to be baked." Abbey puts the Halibut back down on the shelf in front of Dan. He checks the order and then turns the plate around. Looks at the offending spud.

"This is supposed to be baked!" He turns to Devin, shouting, even though Devin is beside him. Abbey can tell the kid is almost shitting himself. Devin's maybe eighteen, nineteen, and Dan is at least forty. Devin picks the roasted potato off the plate with his hand and sets it on the cutting board. Abbey gathers up the three plates that are ready and starts to go out.

"Wait!"

"I'll come back for it."

"You'll fuckin' wait!"

Abbey stops and stands there a second, the heat from the kitchen on the backs of her legs. Devin calls, "Almost!"

The plate on Abbey's arm is steaming, hints of basil and pepper, the musty smell of the grains, fill the air. Abbey hears the whirr of the microwave and starts heading out; it'll be two minutes for the potato and the plates are hot, her back is aching. Dan says "wait" again but Abbey is already nudging the double doors with her hip, heading out into the restaurant. When she comes back less then a minute later the halibut is up and the potato is open, a curl of butter, sprig of parsley inside.

"Thanks." She grabs the plate and turns to go and suddenly Dan is behind her, his hand around her throat, forcing her chin up. The plate in Abbey's hand tilts and the food, then the plate, hits the floor. Abbey's hands go up to her neck but Dan's palm is against her throat, pressing into her larynx. She can't breathe. Things become confused. Her father is holding her back; her mother is across the street and Abbey wants to run over; and her father's hands are on her. But not like this. Devin is in front of her now, yelling, "For fuck's sake, let her go!" Heading out the doors to get help. And then it's just the two of them, Abbey in shock, trying to get a breath, digging her nails into his hand. Dan loosens his grip, just enough to let her breathe, his chest pressed against her back, mouth to her ear. "Now let's see ya try that again."

Veronica drives Abbey home from the hospital, tells her she did the right thing, pressing charges. Dan has never done anything like that before, but maybe, in retrospect, someone should have seen it coming. Corrects herself, "*I* should have seen it." She puts her hand out to Abbey's, tapping it maternally. The brake lights of the cars in front of them go on and off; traffic crawls down Harcourt Street, people queue outside the nightclubs. And all Abbey wants to do is get out of the car and run to Angela's flat.

Later, Abbey sits in Ange's kitchen drinking tea. Every light in the flat on. Angela is out with Brendan, her mobile phone going straight to messages. After a while Abbey goes into the living room and turns the television on, curls up on the couch. An episode of Coronation Street coming on TV3. She puts a warm cloth over her throat. The doctor had said her neck will be fairly bruised in the morning.

What bothers Abbey most are those two or three seconds when she closed her eyes in the middle of it and thought Frank was behind her — that it seemed possible he could do that to her. That even when she opened her eyes and saw Devin standing there, panicked, telling Dan to leave her alone, it still seemed conceivable that Frank was behind it all. Willing it to happen.

When Abbey was ten, Frank took her to Nipissing Park saying they were going on a vacation. But after a quick swim in the lake, he locked Abbey in the truck for six hours while he went door to door, cottage to cottage, asking whoever answered if they remembered Karen Delaney and did she ever come around here anymore? Abbey was left in the parking-lot for what felt like days, the sun coming in through the windshield, a large wood cutout of a bear by the gate, the sign above warning hikers that there'd been two sightings in May. Frank promising Abbey ice cream before he left and then forgetting to bring some back for her. Admitting it all when she was twenty-two or twenty-three, in the phase of "just listen," in the non-stop dirge of "these are my sins." "I hit her you know. Once," he said while drunk, as if he was proud of it. "Two weeks before she left." Made a fist with his right hand as he said it. Eying Abbey to see if she'd do anything about it, to see if she'd move the couch cushion off her lap, stand up and walk out.

From the moment Abbey stood on her father's grave, he's been with her. Memories coming back to her, images of him she'd forgotten: sleeping on the couch in Woodslee, the stubble coming up on his chin, and six-year-old Abbey touching it lightly with her fingers but not wanting to wake him. The smell of diesel on his hands after a day of work, the tar sometimes staining his clothes; Frank telling Abbey he made holes for a living, trying once to get her to put her hands around his arm muscle the way Karen would, saying, "Look at that, sweetie, your daddy's a damn strong man." The buggy ride in the Zehrs parking lot — Abbey, maybe twelve, straddling the grocery bags while he wheeled her around in the cart. And the year before she moved back in with him, when he was just starting to get sick, Frank begging her to take him for lunch, telling her he hadn't been out of the apartment in days. Abbey said, "But Dad, it's three o'clock," and Frank looked up at her sheepishly, got out of bed just the same, opened his closet. "But I have a class," Abbey had explained, lying. Adding "Wordsworth," as if that made it real. Frank crawled back under the blankets, shrugging, "You bet, kiddo. Maybe another time."

Abbey gets up and turns off the TV. Goes to the kitchen and runs the dishtowel under warm water, heads back to the couch, pulls the afghan over her, and drapes the cloth back over her throat.

The warmth feels good. Once, when Abbey had a fever, Frank, not knowing what else to do, took her nightie off and put her into an ice bath. Stood there watching her turn blue. Panicking, he called the neighbour, Mrs. Pasic, after twenty minutes. The old lady pulled Abbey out, warmed her up with a fleece towel, even brought over an electric blanket from her apartment. Told Frank that he should have taken Abbey to the hospital. She stayed there all night until Abbey's fever went down.

It wasn't so much that Frank had failed her or that he'd lied. Abbey had done enough of that herself. Even at ten years old, she knew they were in Nipissing Park to track down her mother, had gone along with the vacation idea anyway — sitting in the cab of the truck with the window cracked open, running her Barbies back and forth across the dashboard for six hours because she wanted, in her own way, to please her father. It wasn't the lies, how Frank insisted Jane was her real aunt even though Abbey knew better, that he told her Karen would come back and that everything would be all right. In the end, it was his lack of trust in her — trust that Abbey could handle knowing the truth; trust that he could have let go of her hand that night on Ouelette Avenue, watched her run over to her mother and try to hug her; trust that even if Karen, seeing Abbey, chose to walk away, Abbey could've dealt with it. Because that, at least, would have been something real.

When the phone rings, Abbey is in the shower. By the time she hears it, turns off the taps and grabs a towel, the machine has picked up. Wiping the condensation from the mirror with her right hand, Abbey tries to get a good look at her neck, but the mirror fogs up again. She puts on Angela's terrycloth robe, goes into the living room, hits the play button under the answering machine's blinking red light. She's expecting Angela to call, say she got Abbey's messages. There are a few seconds of silence, then: "Abbey. It's Dermot." Followed by a long pause. The sound of him breathing. "Listen. I want you to come home."

III

Finally Away

The Director from Annagassan

SIGNS INDICATE a detour. Traffic on the bay road is diverted inland and the drivers eye the actors' trailers, the arc lights, the dolly, as they wheel past. A hundred people are milling about; the lawn at the new church is trampled. A make-up tent, set up by the statue of the Virgin, bucks in the wind. A woman in track pants runs across the road with a wedding dress in her arms, the crinoline lifting. All the trees in Connaght point east.

At the far end of the church parking lot, the film crew queues for cappuccinos. The catering truck is lit up like a carnival, fairy lights hanging from the awning. The filming stopped after the twenty-third take. In an hour they'll do the scene at the chip shop again: The actress will come out the door and meet her neighbour, they'll talk for a minute about the weather and then he'll absentmindedly let slip that he saw Maeve O'Brien at the O'Malley wedding yesterday. The camera will move in close, the boom over the actors' heads will pick up a sharp intake of breath. A look of understanding will cross the actress' face. Then she'll rush off down the road.

A few of the locals have gathered on the corner to watch the action. Niall and Conneely have come out of the pub, Jimmy's at the Spar window a few doors down. Helen Brennan and Marianne Lynch stand by the gate to Éinde's, craning their necks to see over the film crews' heads. Dermot, coming up the bay road, stops to talk to the director. He's wearing a padded jacket, has the weathered face of a coastal man, is holding the script in his hand.

"Are you from around here?" Dermot asks.

"Annagassan."

"Near the peninsula is it?"

"That's right."

"And the Cooley mountains."

"You've been over?"

"I know it."

"Fierce weather," the director nods towards the bay.

"What's it called?" Dermot asks. "The show."

"Ros na Run." He pauses for a second, moves closer, "It's huge in Dublin, the Gaeilge."

"Well, good luck." Dermot offers the director his hand. Turns towards Hughes. Looks back once as he crosses the road. The wind against them both.

The smell of fried food wafts across the set; twenty orders of take-away curry have arrived at last. A girl in a baseball cap calls out the meals. The arc lights by the chip shop are turned on and that whole area, and Feeny's beside it, is suddenly brighter than day. Over by the prop tent, the grip, a Galway boy, looks up, then goes back to crushing pop cans with his boot. The trash cans are overflowing and a plastic cup tumbles across the road. In the centre of the crowd, a Dublin man in a stiff Arran sweater holds a bullhorn. People study him warily as if waiting for him to use it. Dermot meets up with

Niall and Conneely. "So the circus is in town."

O'Nia, an Irish teacher from the local College, sits in a chair outside Feeny's with a sullen-looking brunette, his white hair standing up in the wind. There's a script in his hand, the pages flipping up at the corners. The woman, both arrogant and plain, looks down her nose at him. A few feet away, Roxy, Hughes' dog, lifts his leg on a light stand. Dermot sees him do it and laughs.

"Again," O'Nia says. He reads the actress' lines in Irish. "Beidh mé romhat ag an stáisiún."

"Beidh mé romhat ag an stáisiún," she repeats, tossing her hair over her shoulder.

"Again."

"Beidh mé romhat ag an stáisiún."

O'Nia looks at her, and with two knuckles taps the script. "Correct me if I'm wrong, Ms. Lowell, but your character's not from Portmagee."

The election posters that lined the road in Spiddal have been taken down from the poles and "Ros na Run" signs and arrows for parking have been put up in their place. A large Tele Gael sign has been staked into the corner, pointing to the studio they're finishing up the road. The series is in its second year, and they were shooting in Galway until the cost of permits went up. The producer, in her wisdom, killed off the main character to create a subplot in Spiddal. A whole new village storyline is coming along. Conneely watches it every week to laugh at the Dublin actors' Irish.

"Anyone for a drink?" Dermot asks.

Niall checks his watch, sees it's just past two. "I'll go in with ya."

"I'll be a minute yet," Conneely says, watching the actors make their way to the chip shop door. "That one is about to leave town and your man just gave away last week's secret."

"Which is?" Dermot asks.

"The wedding guest." Conneely lifts his chin.

The director from Annagassan takes his seat, and the assistant to the producer holds up the clapper. Dermot and Niall turn to go in but Conneely grabs Dermot's arm. "Watch this," he whispers, "it'll all be out in a minute."

"What's that?"

"They're about to bring Maeve O'Brien back from the dead."

The Breakwall

"ANOTHER, Michael?" Dermot tilts his head towards the bar.

"I'm grand."

In the corner by the fire a woman with dull eyes and high cheekbones launches into song. Her voice is rough and the noise of conversation hushes for a minute. Soon the rabble starts up again. Michael studies the callouses that have come up on his hands.

"What's playing in Galway?" asks Dermot.

"At the films?"

"Anything."

"A Friel at the Druid. Music. The usual."

Dermot eyes the last crescent of stout in his glass. Sits back in his chair. "I'm not up for it."

Over by the bar the cooking show on television goes to commercial — an ad for the Ab-Buster machine. A woman rows herself over the carpet of a bright living room.

Dermot turns back to Michael. "Do you suppose there's anything down at the water?" The local kids sometimes have bonfires on the beach. Dermot would know a few from town and Michael would recognize some from the University. There'd be drink and a measure of company.

"How would I know?"

"We could walk over."

They take the short cut through Costelloe's field, Michael catching his coat sleeve on the barbed-wire fence as he climbs over, Dermot turning his ankle in a rut. The two of them silent as they cross, the sound of the wind in the hawthorn. When they get down to the beach, the light from the bonfire becomes visible, an orange globe over by the pier. The black ink of the bay a skirt that obscures even the Islands.

All that week, fish heads had been washing up on the beach. Dermot steps over one, then another. Pocked eyes, bone showing under the gill. Michael ambles along at a distance, watches Dermot bend down, study the fish at his feet.

When they get to the bonfire the kids make room for them. Dermot knows two or three by name — a McGilloway nephew from Furbo, Jimmy Greenon, a girl called Barbara that he sees some nights at Hughes. He looks over at her, nods, and she looks away. Michael has found one of his students, stands with him over by a bucket full of beer cans. The sound of a guitar coming from the breakwall.

A log is thrown on the fire and the flames lift. Over by the road a few kids break branches off the low shrubs that line the field. A car parked near the low wall to the beach has steamed windows. The moon is half full.

Michael walks back over to Dermot, pulls a can of Kilkenny out of his coat pocket, and gives it over. Produces another from under his arm. Opening his can and raising it in Dermot's direction, he intones, "To the composting of elements. Or fish guts, at any rate."

Dermot flips the tab on his can and sips at the foam, lifts the whole enterprise in the air. Thinks for a second then adds, "Between wood's rim and the horses of the sea." He takes a long drink from the can.

Michael lets himself be baited. "Wood's rim?"

"In three days' time he stood up with a moan?" Dermot narrows his eyes. "And went down to the long sands alone / For four days warred he with the bitter tide / And the waves flowed above him and he died. It's Yeats."

"My apologies."

"Who the Christ let you into Ireland anyway?"

Michael drinks from his can of lager, swallows. "I believe it was your Prime Minister."

Michael does as expected. He finds a group of students he knows and stands with them by the fire, talking about their programs, their professors, the new Gallery the University is building near the canal. It isn't lost on Dermot that these students could have been his. Not these exactly, but this generation. He'd have been at it for twenty-five years by now. If he'd stayed on course, if he'd hung on at Trinity, fought for his position; if he hadn't met Sophie.

Dermot sets off along the beach. Once he'd brought Abbey down here so she could meet kids closer to her own age. As soon as he saw her in conversation with one of the boys from Salthill he'd discreetly walked away. They were on about Toronto, the boy having gone there one summer to stay with his aunt. That was last November. It had been cold away from the fire so Dermot made for the shadowy outline of the breakwall, climbing the hill that joined it to the upper road. Then he'd dropped down to the far side of the concrete barrier, the last lick of the sun straddling the water.

The noise from the party had receded, and only now and again could he make out music from the stereo as it was carried over the wall by the wind. When he first came to Spiddal there were musicians who'd come to the beach with instruments to play. Now it was all hip-hop and portable stereos, music he didn't recognize. That night, Dermot had watched the sun bleeding down until it was underwater, the bay going from blue to black. He must've been there an hour. *All I want,* he was thinking, *all I want,* and his mind had looped around that idea like it was a song lyric he'd once known. *All I want,* and it had occurred to him he wanted Abbey to go home with that boy from Salthill, to fall in love with someone who didn't need her. It had occurred to him that he wanted to bow out, to stay on the other side of the breakwall while the world churned on without him. He had lit a cigarette and the smoke burned the back of his throat. The cold became more apparent. He'd lifted his back away from the concrete. He wanted out, out of everything. If there was a vote going, if it was his lot in life, his fate, that was up for consideration, he'd abstain. And he felt heavy, wondered if he'd even be able to lift his foot, move it forward over the sand, lift the next foot, pull himself up the stubbly grass hill that led to the parking lot above. He'd moved his hand towards his mouth and picked a strand of tobacco off his bottom lip. He'd listened for the music, concentrated hard, but there was none. Perhaps everyone else had gone home. He'd leaned back against the cold wall and tried to sort through the different shades of darkness. He was waiting for Abbey to find him and the realization made him sick.

Now Dermot walks towards the breakwall, and, squinting, makes out a group of kids sitting on the near side of the pier. Finn, the new postal worker is among them. And the girl from Hughes, and a guy wearing army pants and a bright sweater, strumming a guitar. Much to Dermot's surprise, he sees Flagon with them, lying beside a black girl he's never seen before, the girl scratching his dog's chin. As soon as Dermot is close enough, Flagon picks up his scent. He whistles low and she trots over. Circles him a few times, nuzzling his legs.

"Ya big hussy."

She sits down and looks up at him, tilts her head.

"All right, all right."

Seeing Dermot, Finn raises a hand in greeting. The girl, Barbara, looks away again.

"How's it?" Finn calls.

Dermot nods, raises his hand.

"What happened after the wake?" Finn had been there, saw Dermot take Deirdre out of the house. All the kids now, all four of them, looking over.

"A boy," Dermot calls back, then louder, "she had a boy."

Dermot walks towards the bay and Flagon trots ahead, turning around every few feet, waiting for a command. When they get to the water the dog stands there with two paws in the soup. Barks once into the darkness. Dermot watches the tide lap up around his shoes, recede, lap up again. Waits for the water to soak through.

Finn Eason had taken over Eileen's job at the post office. One morning he was simply there, in the van, dropping off a bill for the fence material, a credit card application, and the next moment he was backing out of the driveway without as much as a word. Dermot had run into him again on the road a few days back. Finn had pulled over and rolled down the window, his walkman on. Fumbled through the mail on the seat beside him. Handed a letter over — an ESB bill. Dermot recognized the logo for the electricity company in the top left-hand corner. Finn put the van in gear and spun away. Dermot had hoped for something from Abbey. Or even a social word from the postal boy. He'd enjoyed Eileen McGilloway's chatter. She'd pull up and say, "You'll have to try my lemon squares, Mr. Fay. It's a new recipe, quite tangy." And the next day, wrapped up in aluminum on his doorstep, Dermot would find two lemon squares. And McGilloway would always apologize if there was no mail, and comment on any that there was. "Ah, but where'd we be without electricity?" Standing at the edge of the bay, the line between the sky and the water all but gone, Dermot can hear McGilloway as if she was right beside him.

"Where'd we be, Mr. Fay?"

"In the dark, Mrs. McGilloway, in the dark."

Climbing Bray Head

WHEN Dermot gets home he lights a fire, sits on the couch, and Flagon comes to stand in front of him. "Stop staring." He tries to usher her off, but she won't go. "I mean it. Away with ya." He walks into the kitchen, pours a drink, and she stands behind him, watching. He drinks the whiskey, staring back at her, and then turns to top up the glass. The light in the front room on and the rest of the house gone dark.

Dermot gets a blanket from the bedroom and lays down on the couch. Closes his eyes. Listens to the spark and hiss of the fire. Flagon panting over by the door. There's something familiar about those sounds together and he tries to think of what it is. Can picture licks of long grass, bracken that crackles underfoot as he steps on it, making his way up a hill. Then nothing. He goes back to it again, the walking uphill. Tries to see the size of his shoe. What age is he in this memory? There's the grass, the bracken. He goes down on his hands for a minute to scamper along. And then he sees her. His mother. Standing on the rise towards the headland in Bray.

His mother had taken him to Bray when he was seven and for the first time that he could remember, the trip was about him, not the world of adults where you're bribed into going to an aunt's with promises of fruitcake and tea. Like the times Dermot's mother had brought him along to visit her older sister Kate, who was suffering from rheumatism. She would tell Dermot they were going on an outing, that it would be fun. That if he behaved himself, and his cousin Joe was home, maybe he could ride their pony. And he did, once. The cousin, all of fourteen, his torn brown jumper held together at the shoulder with a stitch of red wool, walking Dermot, legs slung over the pony, around the paddock while his mother watched from a window in the upstairs of the house. Dermot going in circles, still more waiting than riding. The pony dead-eyed. Dermot's bare legs feeling the pull of skin over her rib cage. The cousin saying, "Atta boy." The flies buzzed around all three of them as they wore down a wheel of grass. Dermot had watched the ground the whole time — the weeds near the byre that came into view again and again just to the left of the pony's bobbing head. It was mid-summer and the thick stalks arched out of the ground. Then his mother came out. He remembers her hands under his arm pits, Dermot pulled awkwardly down from the pony so that his shoe, already untied, slipped off. Then the cousin bent down to pick it up, farting once, a loud pop — looking up to see if anyone had noticed, and everyone had. So he'd slapped the pony's rump, as if to blame her. "Right, see yas." Going in to the house to check on his mother.

But it's Bray that Dermot wants to think about — climbing up Bray Head, stumbling over the grass and scree, and then, for a while, walking the clear path straight on, until it arched up again and the two of them had to lean forward, use their hands. "Good boy, son," she had said, and he'd looked back to see if she was coming, holding up sometimes to make sure she didn't fall too far behind. She was wearing trousers, beige ones; they were grass-stained by the end of the day, mud up along the one hem from the right foot slipping. Near the finish she'd raced up ahead of him, on her own then, not even looking back. And that's how he remembers her now, at the top, looking out, not even seeing him crest the ridge.

He'd expected more from the top — more than the view of the sea, the gray stretch of it. He'd expected something monumental. The two of them clambering up after each other, racing towards a grass and mud peak. "Ever since I was a girl I've wanted to climb it." His mother reaching for his hand and starting down.

He doesn't hear the first knock.

"Dermot, let me in." Abbey's knuckles against the wood of the door, raw and red from the cold. The road, the beach, everything had gone dark since she started walking. "Dermot!"

Her head is throbbing at the temples, her neck's still sore every time she swallows; the cold goes right through her. It's close to midnight. Other than the ride to Barna, she's been on foot.

"Dermot!"

Abbey's voice comes to Dermot the way sound travels through a tunnel, distilled and faraway, until the pitch of his dream subsides and he can hear her clearly. In two strides he's at the door, opening it, her pinched face in front of him, arms crossed over her chest, backpack at her feet. He wants to touch her, to cup her face in his hands but instead he stands back, lets her go past him, has a sense that he should be angry although he isn't sure why. His hand still on the latch, holding the door open. Abbey heads through the front room without a word. Goes into the bedroom. And for a second it's as if time has rolled backwards, transporting them into some old, unresolved argument. Where had they left off? Dermot tries to nail it down, figure out what part of it they'll go forward from now. The proposal? The tug-of-war before she left for Canada? The day she first moved in? As if the past two weeks never happened. Behind him, Abbey turns on the light in the bedroom, pulls the second blanket off the bed, wraps herself in it.

Dermot rubs his face, his eyes, with his hands. He can hear Abbey in the bedroom moving around. When he looks up, she's standing in the doorway watching him. Then she goes over to the dresser, opens her drawer. *Empty,* he thinks. She took everything with her. She throws the blanket back onto the bed and walks around the corner into the bathroom. After a minute Dermot moves away from the door. Thinks, *this is all going wrong.* Unsure of what to do about it. He wants to say something to Abbey about her being home, but he doesn't. Instead he stands there bewildered, watching her from behind as she turns on the immersion switch, starts taking off her clothes. It occurs to him then that maybe she's come back to pack her last few things, that tomorrow she'll leave him. So he walks out of the room and sits on the couch. Gets up again and opens the far cupboard to find a bottle. The sound of the water running through the pipes.

Between the Cottage and the Bay

DERMOT stands beside the bed watching Abbey sleep, the covers pulled up to her chin and balled around the one fist. He's
been watching her a while, the way she opens and closes her
mouth, turns and nestles the pillow. He'd gone for a walk,
made it as far as St. Éinde's. Sat on a pew holding a bottle of
whiskey in both hands, willing himself not to drink it. When
he'd come back to the cottage, into the bedroom, he thought
she'd wake up, but she didn't. So he stands by the bed wondering if he should get in.

Abbey opens her eyes in the dark room and waits for
them to adjust. She isn't sure how long she's been sleeping or
if she's even slept at all. Slowly the room comes into focus,
and looking up, Abbey sees Dermot standing there in the
dim light, still in his sweater and jeans, the smell of smoke
clinging to his clothes. He's watching her, his body swaying
a bit. "Is it you?" he asks.

Abbey slips her hand out from under the blanket, touches
his palm, pulls at his arm until he sits on the mattress beside
her. Moving over to the far side of the bed, Abbey makes room

and Dermot lies down, puts his back to her, his boots clapping together on top of the blanket.

"I'm glad you're back," he says. The peach scent of her shampoo on his pillow. The spin of the room starting to slow. Abbey puts her arm over his chest, her forehead against the back of his neck. "Would you believe it," he declares, turning his head in her direction, "we're finally away."

In the morning Abbey wakes up to the sound of Dermot dragging one of his clothes boxes out from the closet. Then there's a *thwap* from the other side of the room as he airs out an old pair of pants.

Abbey sits up, her back stiff from carrying her rucksack from Barna. She stretches and the blanket slips down off her shoulders. Dermot smiles at seeing her bare breasts. "I know you," he says. He's at the window, the shadow of the white beam bobbing up and down his face. "I thought you three were for Canada," he nods at her chest.

"No such luck."

Dermot starts putting on his jeans, looks up at her. That's when he sees it, the brown welt around her neck.

"Jesus, Abbey. What happened?" His hand lifting her chin. Two fingers lightly touching the bruise.

"A psychopath at work."

"A customer?" He's angry. Looks around the room.

"A cook. It's okay, I pressed charges, they picked him up, he isn't allowed near me or the restaurant."

Dermot lifts her chin again, touches her neck. She flinches even though he can tell she's trying not to. "You should have phoned." Angry about it, that it could happen, that he wasn't there.

Later, when Dermot is kissing her chin, he realizes he has

remembered exactly the slope from her lips to her neck. He kisses her ear lobe, the spot behind her left ear, goes along her hairline to her forehead. He stands up and from the edge of the bed he pulls her pajama bottoms down, kisses her thighs.

Abbey has chills all over from his touch, from the cold in the room. She pulls up his sweater, Dermot bunching his shoulders close. "Christ we need a heater!" Laughing, they get themselves under the covers and Abbey can feel Dermot undoing his belt, pushing down his jeans, hooking his finger over the top of her knickers. When he leans down on top of her, Abbey kisses his shoulder, then down the slope of his arm. She says his name over and over in her head, *Dermot Fay, Dermot Fay, Dermot Fay* and she touches him, his grey hair, his shoulder blades, the soft cant of his back.

Lying in bed Abbey starts to explain what happened, why she'd stayed away. Dermot, putting his clothes on in the doorway, says, "you're here now," longing for that to be the end of it. But Abbey's afraid it'll start all over again. That if she keeps what's been bothering her to herself, Frank will come between them.

"Either I'm going crazy or he's really here."

"Here?" Dermot sits on the edge of the bed, trying to sort out what she means. He looks at Abbey and around the room; the corner crammed with the boxes he's hauled out from the closet, books lining a shelf above the window.

"In my head, at McDaids, at Ange's. I don't know. Getting Dan to come after me." Abbey pushes her face into her palms, not sure if it's the saying of it or how stupid it sounds that makes her want to cry.

Dermot looks at the top of her head. "There's no one here but us."

"I know. I know." And then, "I'm losing it, Dermot, really I am. I just keep thinking about him. And about my mother —" Abbey looks up at Dermot, her face pinched and red. "And the other night, with Dan, for a half second, in the middle of it, I thought it was my father," the words punched out, "trying to get back at me for leaving him."

"Abbey."

She's shaking her head, doesn't want to listen.

"Abbey, it's all right." Dermot tries to pull her to his chest. "The man just died. It's a way of grieving."

"No, it's not." Her nose congested and her eyes welling up so that Dermot puts his hands out, takes her face in his palms, smooths his thumbs over the skin under her eyes.

"Is that what all this has been about?"

Abbey nods.

"Since you're back from Canada. All this time?"

Abbey nods again, tries to burrow back into his chest, all the smells that comfort her mingling there in his sweater, a burl of wool tickling her nose.

"Come here."

Suddenly it's clear to Dermot — the reason for her uneasiness, the restlessness since the funeral. They'd been so settled in the weeks before, and she'd said more than once that she didn't want Dublin, that a job in Galway would do.

Dermot cradles her head in the crook of his arm and he rocks her, looks at the ceiling then down at her hair, saying, "You're crazy, you know." His one hand tucking her hair behind her ear as he's seen her do a thousand times. "And you're with me, which proves it."

When Abbey comes out of the shower Dermot is in the yard talking to someone — short sentences, as if answering or asking questions. Abbey takes an old pair of Dermot's jeans off the pile he's pulled out of the box, puts on her jumper then takes it off, grabs a t-shirt from his drawer to wear under it. She slips her arms through the wide sleeves and throws her boots on. Out the front door the sky is clear. The sun is out and as soon as she's outside, Abbey is warmed by it. Overhead crows caraw, passing in between the cottage and the bay. Abbey steps round the corner of the house and Dermot stops talking, has just said "fortify —" the word hanging there, a boy with dark hair facing him, a mess of shovels laid out on the ground.

"Hello." Her voice is loud and awkward, and Abbey is aware of how Canadian she sounds.

"Hiya." The boy's voice quiet, like Dermot's.

"I'm Abbey," she says and she feels like a parody, a visitor from another planet, her hair messed up and the front of her neck a blue-brown, Dermot just standing there as if he's never seen her before, all dressed up in his oversized clothes.

"I'm Sean." The boy folds and unfolds his arms. They stand there like that for a minute, Sean with his chin to his chest, glancing up at Abbey with curious eyes.

"Sean's building us a fence." Dermot says this to Sean as much as to Abbey.

"Great." She looks from one to the other. A young girl comes around the back of the house then, in corduroy pants and a red plastic jacket. She's making aeroplane sounds, looping around the rusty pole of the laundry line, and then she stops, says "beep beep" and jumps once, lets go the pole and goes back to the aeroplane sounds, walking with her arms out, fingers and thumbs arrow-straight.

"Mary!" Sean calls her and she turns around, her arms still out but tilting from side to side, a plane making an awkward landing. She "rreeuuunnns" up to Abbey, the sound coming from the back of her throat. When she reaches Abbey, the girl jumps up and down, says "beep beep" again. Abbey bends down to greet the girl at eye level, notices Dermot is finally looking at her as though everything were normal.

"Hi. I'm Abbey," she says to the girl.

"Are you Dermot's friend?"

"I am."

"Beep Beep."

"Beep Beep." Abbey says it back and the girl goes off, her blue eyes open wide and her arms out.

"C'mon, Mary," Sean gestures to the field and the girl heads that way, teetering left as she goes. The boy places the shovels into the wheel barrow, picks up the handles, sets off with all the dirt-caked tools.

"See ya for lunch," Dermot says and the kid nods, looking back at Abbey after he reaches the beginning of the field.

Found

THE CAMERA'S shutter clicks. Pivoting, Michael aims the lens
to the left of the area he's just photographed. He mentally
notes that shots 17, 18, 19 are from right to left, documenting
the south wall of the pit. Nothing has come up. God knows
why he has to be so thorough. He's lost a week out here on his
hands and knees; maybe taken years off his life because he
stayed out in the weather. The last two days have sent a flood
of rain under the tarp, the run-off coming like a stream down
the side of the pit, turning the bottom to muck. On Monday the
Bord na Móna lads will be back at it and Michael will be on
the sofa at home. He's already looking forward to the weekend, can feel a chest cold coming on, the beginning of a cough.
Una and Gerry were good sports to the end — Una was especially patient, although Gerry's off-beat humour was its own
kind of reprieve. Yesterday Dermot and Abbey came out for
an hour before heading over to Oughterard for lunch. Dermot
arguably happier than Michael's ever seen him, and Abbey
only back two days.

Turning to the east wall, Michael rubs his eyelid with his thumb, looks through the camera viewfinder and focuses on the black, chiseled mess of roots and peat. Another twenty minutes of photographs and notes and he'll be done.

The first spit of rain starts just as Michael is leaning over the back-panel of the Canon, loading a new roll of film. He hunches his shoulders to keep the rain from getting in. The new roll snaps into place and Michael pulls at the spool of film, lining the end of it up into the slit of the opposite spool. It catches and he closes the back of the camera, looking down as he advances the film to " 1." Then he puts the roll he's just finished into his right pocket, thinking he'll label it when he gets to the car. He doesn't even look up. If he had, he would have missed it — but instead he sees it, just there, jutting out of the east wall of the pit. He keeps his chin down but refocuses, looks again at the spot on the far wall. Dark as wet wood — but he knows it isn't wood. Michael drops the camera and on his knees rushes over to the peat wall, keeping his eyes on it so he doesn't lose it. He finds it a meter down from the top of the bog, and with less than a square inch exposed. All this time they'd been digging alongside it.

It takes two, maybe three strokes of the brush to see it clearly, Michael moving the white calluna roots around with his fingers, his shoulders aching, the knees of his jeans wet right through. It's human skin. Dark brown and leathery. He can feel it, immovable, the brush skirting its smooth surface, the resistance against the bristles. Carefully he leans against the wall of the pit and with his thumb and finger he digs at the peat on either side of it. He pulls the tendrils of roots away, tugging at them until they break. Leaning forward to be at eye level, he recognizes the line of a hand, palm down in the peat.

Later, he'll have no recollection of climbing the ladder out of the pit, of jumping the trench, of rifling through his bag for the car keys, of driving down the road to the phone at the local hotel. He'll remember shouting for a drink midway into the conversation with the Chief Archeologist at the IAWU; he'll remember calling Jack Hopkins at the Museum right after. Telling Hopkins this was it. Jack reminding him that they'd have to call the Garda first, that the Garda would meet him down there, that it would take a few days to get all the proper permissions in order before they could do a full-blown dig. Michael saying, "Okay and okay and no, it isn't animal hide," saying it again and then pounding the paneled wall behind the phone box when it beeps for more change.

"I'll wait at the site," is the last thing Michael gets in before the phone goes dead on him, before he stands there a minute listening to the dial tone, staring not so much at the receiver, but at the hand holding it.

Michael drains a pint of Guinness, the locals lining the barstools looking at him with amusement. He is every inch the bog man with his muddy pants, dirty hands, his brown hair plastered down on his head. Michael puts five Euros down on the bar. The barman at the taps gestures with his head that he'll be right over. Michael shifts from foot to foot, says, "Keep it," pushes open the oak door to the street, whistling on his way to the car.

When the Garda arrive they come down the road that runs beside the light-rail track, their white cars muddy and teetering as the wheels dip in and out of the potholes. While he waited for them, Michael worked off an inch of peat from the middle of the east wall, covered the hand with damp turf and marked its location with an orange flag. Farther along the wall he came upon what he guessed was a knee, its round cap delineated, its skin the colour of a chestnut. He covered that up too, marked it. Michael knows they can't start excavating until the Garda's determined whether or not the remains are recent. Then the Bord has to apply to Dúchas for a license, assemble the right group of people for the work.

Michael stands back and mentally works out the parameters of the dig. From the look of it, most of the body runs parallel to the pit they've already excavated — everything but the shins and feet, which Michael figures end just past the the southeast corner of the pit. They'll have to dig farther out into the turf. Then they can cut a wedge into the wall under the body, cut another wedge vertically from above. They'll pull the body out onto a gurney, peat blanket and all.

Sergeant Joyce is in the first car and two inspectors are in the car behind him. There's the sound of car doors closing. Michael climbs up to the sixth rung of the ladder and watches the sergeant, a well-built man, jump the trench between the fourth and fifth field, his right hand holding onto his baton to keep it from swinging. A minute later he's standing in front of Michael, looming over the pit. The two inspectors stand on the far side of the trench.

"Now, what do we have here?" The sergeant takes off his cap and sets it under his arm. He has a mop of white hair, thick brows, a prominent forehead.

"A body," Michael says, still standing on the ladder.

The sergeant looks around. "Where exactly is this body, Dunne?"

"Here." Michael points at the flat, muddy peat bank beside him. "I've a hand here," he points to the first orange flag, "and what I think is a knee over here."

"I thought we had a body?" The sergeant puts his cap back on, then tips it up off his head, pulls his hair back before setting his cap down again.

"We can't uncover it until we can secure it for preservation."

The sergeant lifts his walkie-talkie off his belt and says something into it that Michael can't hear. He turns and gestures for one of the men to come over. The taller of the two inspectors steps over the trench, bridging it. He stands beside the sergeant and they converse for a second before the sergeant goes back to the walkie-talkie. Michael finds himself looking down at the turf wall, measuring the slant of it, as if waiting for it to move.

"There was a girl missing —"

Michael looks up sharply. The sergeant is talking to him. "1982, around about these parts, body never found."

Michael shakes his head. There was no evidence of a recent burial and the hand looks like tanned hide — that takes at least a hundred years.

"When can we bring it up?"

Michael does the math. Jack needs enough time to get out here from Dublin, and first he'll have to secure a temperature-controlled fridge if the one at the National Museum is on loan. Dúchas and the Bord will need to sign off permission. "It might be three or four days."

"What's the name of your Museum man again?"

"Jack Hopkins," Michael says.

The sergeant brings the walkie-talkie to his mouth. "Get Jack Hopkins on the phone will ya?" He listens for a second, then drops the walkie-talkie back onto his belt in one swift move. Steps up to the edge of the string perimeter. Looms there a second, looking at the wall of peat, the orange plastic flags.

"We'll keep a guard posted in a car overnight and I'll be back in the morning. Will you be here for a bit until I can send someone back?"

Michael nods.

"It'll likely be Charley who comes." The sergeant jabs his thumb towards the young inspector beside him. "It'll just take us an hour to get organized."

Then, as if it's just sinking in, the sergeant says, "It's an odd thing, that." He's looking down at Michael, and at the flags, at the ground between them. And for a second or two there's no sound but the distilled voice of the Garda on the mobile phone by the trench, the croak of a nearby frog, the flags rustling in the wind.

The True Love Show

THE HOUSE is in a state. Deirdre hasn't slept soundly in the ten days since she's been home from the hospital. The baby is colicky, up at all hours, probably wondering, *where am I?* Deirdre feels the same. Her mother's house is not hers. There's a familiarity to it but also a formality — things are in their place; a whole life packed neatly in boxes, tucked away in the drawers. Standing over the baby it occurs to Deirdre that she could have this life if she wanted it. Her mother's life. Raise the baby alone in Spiddal. But then Deirdre's son might have *her* life, and she wants more for him than that.

Ben, Eric, Nolan, Tadg … the baby without a name starts to roar. Deirdre drops her *2000 Best Baby Names* book and walks to over to where he's laying on a large square couch cushion in the middle of the living room floor. She rubs his belly with her hand, sings "Blackbird" up and down, going over the chorus again and again until his face relaxes and he slips back into sleep.

In the early afternoon Deirdre turns on the television.

Flips channels. Finds "The True Love Show" on RTE. Three women in closed booths are made to answer a male contestant's questions about their likes and dislikes. Deirdre used to watch the show before she went to work full-time at the travel agency, and then again when she was working half days in the last stages of the pregnancy. The man can't see anything of the women but their legs. Today, one of the girls is wearing trousers. Deirdre assumes he won't choose her on that basis alone. He gets twenty-one questions and then has to pick his most likely true love. "Question four," he says. Deirdre makes out a Limerick accent. "Where's the best place to go to get out of the rain? Number one?"

She's quiet for a second and then shouts out "Spain!" The audience erupts in laughter.

"Number three?" He skips right over the trousered girl.

"The bedroom." The audience yells "woo." Deirdre stands up and turns the TV off, looks over at the baby. He's clenching his fists in his sleep.

She hasn't seen the will yet, but Deirdre knows this house is hers and everything in it. She walks over to the old oak sideboard, looking at the baby to see if he stirs. The sides of the top drawer stick until she yanks it open. Inside are writing papers and pens, old postcards Deirdre sent from Cyprus, France and New York, bundled up in an elastic. The TV listings from two weeks ago with four shows circled in pen. Sellotape, coupons cut from the paper. A long crow feather in the back corner. An address book with two dozen names.

The baby lets out a gurgle but Deirdre, walking over, sees he's still sleeping, pink feet kicking up once before falling back down. "A fighter, aren't ya?" Names. She's been thinking about names. His skin is fair, and the almost invisible arcs of his brows are cherry blond. There's the tuft of a curl, one wisp, on the back of his head. Liam Conroy — the father.

The stairs creak, one after another, as Dermot mounts them. Once on the porch, he knocks, looks back at the steps to see if they're about to go, notices rotted wood on the bottom one. Deirdre answers the door, and seeing Dermot, opens it wide. "Jesus, I've been meaning to ring ya. Come in."

He goes past her, tries not to look at the breast-milk stains on her shirt.

"I'm a state. The house is a state." She speaks quietly, leads Dermot past the living room and into the bright yellow kitchen. "But that one's sleeping, thank Christ."

Dermot puts a paper bag on the table, looks at the dirty plates stacked by the sink. "I brought some scones from Keating's. Didn't know if you'd been out."

"No, I'm not really out on the town yet," Deirdre replies, indicating her shirt, track pants. "But we did get a drop-off from my friend Marianne. And Margaret Keating came by."

Dermot puts his hand on the back of the kitchen chair. Now that the scones are delivered he's not sure if he should stay. "I'm just by to look in on you. Maybe I should go."

"Listen, I've really been a wreck but I should have come by to thank-you —" Deirdre uncrosses her arms and Dermot looks over to the living room. Sees the baby wrapped up in a blanket on a cushion in the middle of the floor. "You saved my life, I swear. I thought I was going to lose it."

"Can I see him?"

"Aye, the tyrant."

Deirdre leads Dermot into the living room and they lean over top of the baby. His face is a darker shade of red than the upholstery under him, and his sausage-like arms are stretched out to either side.

"He's big isn't he?" Dermot guesses.

"Just over seven pounds." Deirdre wants to reach down and pick him up but knows better. She puts a finger over his hand instead.

"Has he a name?"

"Not yet."

Dermot straightens and looks towards the door. "I think you've a rotting step. I can come by this week and replace it."

The baby turns his head and it lolls sideways, a burble of spit between his lips. He kicks his feet once and then settles. Deirdre watches him, bends down, pulls the blanket back up over his blue pajamas.

"I'm due back in Dublin in a week, but thanks, if you've a chance. My da built the porch for my mother. I'd say the whole lot is going." Deirdre looks up from the baby and meet's Dermot's eyes. "I hear from Keating that your Canadian is back."

"Aye, Abbey."

"And she's half your age."

"She is."

"Keating's quite the gossip, God love her." Deirdre shrugs. "Well, are you happy?"

"I am."

"That's the stuff." She puts her hand on his arm. And Dermot is surprised at the intimacy of the gesture. Nothing at the wake — not her skirt up, not his hands on her — carried this kind of empathy.

"Will you sell?" He nods to the living room.

"It'll pay for a flat in Dublin and I've been renting."

"He's a good baby?"

"I'm not sure there is such a thing."

Bellowing in Greatness

CUTTING across Deirdre's yard, Dermot heads for the bay road. Thinks he might meet Abbey on her way to the Spar. She was flipping through the papers at the cottage this morning when he left, said she was going to type up a CV then head into town for groceries.

The film crew has come and gone again. Yesterday there were trucks all along the road and the church yard was turned into a cemetery. Mottled styrofoam gravestones and fake grass lining the bluff behind the rectory. Feeny's door painted yellow, a sign that said "Prim's Flowers" mounted overhead. Buckets of roses, irises, and snapdragons were set up around the butcher shop door and inside a backdrop was hung over the counter. All to film the Dublin actress with the Kerry accent as she stopped, reached out her hand, touched the lilies.

The construction workers at the corner grocery are back at it — the concrete two storeys high and covered on one side in scaffolding. The tinny sound of a radio, muffled conversation, comes from inside the walls. The scrape of a cement trowel on the near side of the building. A Punjabi fellow Dermot's met in Hughes eats his lunch on a pile of cement blocks. Dermot raises a hand in greeting and the man nods back.

Two doors down, Dermot passes the tourist office, closed until June. The blinds are partly drawn, the chairs and tables gone. Brochures are stacked on a desk at the back of the room. A defaced Fine Gael poster stapled to the pole outside catches Dermot's attention. An ad offering gardening services in fine handwriting is pasted beside it, alongside another ad propounding discount airfare to Japan. *Call Declan in Screeb. Go Ireland!* Dermot steps off the curb and looks down the road for Abbey. A Lada and a Volkswagen drive by, swerve into the other lane to avoid him. A warm wind coming in off the bay. The clouds over Inishmore opening up, sunlight sifting through them.

The first day Dermot walked onto the Trinity campus as a professor, the air was crisp and the leaves hung on the branches of the trees like banners. Dermot Fay. Professor Fay. He'd turned the words over in his mind, and self-consciously pulled his briefcase close to his chest, a battering ram against his nerves. The sheaf of papers inside was meticulous, poured over. *Today we start with the history of illuminated manuscripts in Ireland. Turn to page one.* And he'd unroll the class map above the blackboard, hit Ireland with the back of his hand.

When Dermot thinks of his time in Paris he's embarrassed by how crude his doctorate work must have seemed. Bumbling over his French the whole time, explaining the Táin in broken sentences, giving the academics a good laugh with Irish myths of battle and pissing contests. But when he'd explained the geography of the Cattle Raid as not just a setting but a map, as a memorized history of place, they'd sat up, listened. He'd said, "We travel as a way of physically remembering the past. We tell stories so we can locate ourselves." And he'd analyzed the Táin verse by verse, described the place names in the Cooley mountains as a guide for safe travel, showed how commoners could traverse unfamiliar ground by following the footsteps of the heroes and armies that had gone before. He'd mapped out the land from the text and demonstrated that one could navigate that part of the country through story alone. "History doesn't stand still," he'd said, "but the land does." A map in the guise of a story, one that took ten centuries to be written down.

Five years later, when they called him into the Dean's office at Trinity, when he strode in, misguided, over-confident, almost swaggering, he was stopped in his tracks by Sophie, pale and hovering in the far corner of the room. The Dean held out a letter to Dermot, and on it he saw Sophie's name as he'd written it, underlined. Dutifully he opened the envelope to be sure it was all there. The note folded three times over, creased across the doctor's name, the address in London. The Dean and Associate Dean waited and the silence was palpable; Dermot would've choked on it if he'd opened his mouth. Sophie stood in the alcove, starting to show under the navy one-piece dress, a hurt look on her face as if somehow Dermot had demanded she come forward, as if it was his fault matters couldn't be kept between them. Dermot watched as the Dean looked out the window at the end-of-term students walking in haste from Berkeley library, cutting across the square. Bicycles zigzagged to avoid the slow-moving groups. Someone somewhere had lost a few sheaves of paper and they drifted across the stones. Class had ended and in a few minutes both Dermot and the Dean knew the square would be empty. And Dermot would be sent packing.

"I can't say, Mr. Fay, what this means to us at Trinity." The Associate Dean stepped closer to Dermot while the Dean turned from the window. "And Ms. Keegan," he paused, puffing out his cheeks, "is arguably ruined." Sophie was looking into her hands, clasping and unclasping them. Her hair was tied back in a ribbon, a pearl sheen that ran from her ponytail down the side of her cheek, settling on the top of her shoulder. Dermot wanted to set it back, or to pull it out of her hair, to show the two men in their suits, with their grim faces, what the girl was capable of. The Associate Dean pushed his wire rims in at the nose. He surveyed Dermot, who stood there still as a man facing certain execution. They'd always wanted him out.

"These are your dismissal papers." Another envelope was pushed into his hands, even as the letter to Sophie was taken away, the Dean leaning so close to him that Dermot could see the stubble along his chin. "You're to have no contact with Ms. Keegan and you'll have no recourse to appeal the dismissal." He looked Dermot up and down as if taking his measure. "You'll be lucky if we can keep it from the Press." The hiss of the word "press" said between clenched teeth. Sophie backing still further into the alcove, pressing up against the book that was set in it. To Dermot it looked like the open book was coming out on either side of Sophie's head, as if it was about to close, cup her ears. Her eyes were wide. A line from the Táin remscéla was suddenly in his head: "… and a cow's eye apple." Dermot tried to think back to how the verse started: "This was the Brown Bull of Cooley — dark brown dire haughty with young health"; and then later, the ode to the other bull, "he romps in rut, born to bear victory, bellowing in greatness, idol of the ox herd."

The Associate Dean was watching him. Dermot cleared his head. What did it matter now?

When Sophie stood forward, the light from the window crossed her face and Dermot could see that she'd been crying. It made him want to hit her. It made him want to rain his fists down over everything and everyone in that room. And he knew they took pleasure in it — Protestant administrators hanging him with the sins of his own religion. Pointing out in no uncertain terms that he had brought this upon himself. Outside the square was empty. The leaves in the courtyard turned silver-green in the wind. Dermot moved towards the door, opened it, went out. And the three people left in the room made no motion to stop him.

Loony Toons

WHEN ABBEY walks out of the Spar, Sean sees her. She's carrying two plastic bags, is heading in the direction of the cottage. He runs up behind her. Taps her on the shoulder.

"Hey." Abbey's happy to see him. Lifts her bags. "I'm just picking up supplies."

"You've no car?" He looks around for the Mini.

"No. I can't drive stick."

Sean takes one of the bags, looks down at it. "Fuck. What's in here?"

"Cantaloupes." She laughs.

"Here." He tries to grab the other bag but she starts walking with it. He lopes up beside her, hits himself in the shin with the cantaloupe. A light breeze coming in off the bay.

"It's the other side of the road in Canada, right?"

"What?"

"Why you don't drive."

"Yeah, that too."

Abbey smiles at him. She's wearing an orange-and-brown flowered skirt, a short-sleeved turtleneck and army boots. Her hair's in braids that stick out on either side of her head. Everything about her indicates she's from somewhere else.

"Shouldn't you be working on the fence?"

"Yeah. My mum had to run out so I was looking after Mary."

Abbey turns and walks backwards a few steps. Turns around again. The beach on their right. A family by the rocks having a picnic. A terrier standing at the edge of their blanket waiting for scraps.

"Come here. Let me take this." Sean tries to grab the second bag.

"I've got it. But the chivalry is impressive."

Abbey starts heading down to the beach, along the grassy berm. When she gets to the sand her boots sink an inch, leave imprints. The sun is high overhead and gulls swing left and right over the bay. "It's beautiful, isn't it?"

Sean sneaks up behind Abbey and grabs the plastic Spar bag out of her hand. She turns around and watches him run down the beach, a lanky kid in a black t-shirt and dark jeans. When he's fifty feet away he turns around and holds both bags up in the air. Abbey walks over to him, tries to grab the bag. "Give it back."

"No."

"Sean, I can carry my own bags." She imagines this must be what it's like to have a younger brother.

"Take it." He holds the bag out, stands still. Down the beach the terrier trots away from the picnic blanket and a young boy follows it. Abbey studies the outline of the apples in the bag to the left of Sean's head. The cantaloupe to the right. Sean getting impatient. "Come on." A stupid grin on his face.

Abbey considers kicking him, but takes a tentative swipe at his right hand instead. Misses. Behind Sean, the terrier runs up and down the sandbar, chases pebbles the boy throws into the swash. Sean starts walking backwards down the beach, in the direction of the cottage. Abbey follows and he winks at her, enjoying himself. When he stops five minutes later to look out at the water Abbey runs up behind him and throws herself onto his back, reaching her right hand around to grab one of the bags. He falls over and Abbey goes with him, landing on the canned goods and apples.

"Fuck." Sean laughs.

"Asshole." Abbey pulls the bag out from under her back, sand sticking to her legs. From where he's laying Sean stretches out his hand, grabs the other bag, sits up. Holds it high in his right hand. There's sand in his hair, on the left side of his face. Abbey's trapped underneath his right leg. She tries to push him off her. But Sean wrestles her down. Straddles her, a hand on each of her wrists. There's something of Dan in it, something of her father, the time he pulled her across the living room by the arm, a bruise developing below the elbow. How he saw it the next morning at breakfast and didn't say anything. Waited for it to go away.

When Abbey doesn't fight back, Sean gets up. Moves off her. Wet sand everywhere, along her arm, on the backs of her bare legs, up her skirt.

"Twit." She doesn't know what else to say.

Sean laughs, tosses a handful of sand at her legs. Her skirt stretched across the top of her thighs. A scar on the side of her calf. A white angry seam. Abbey sees him looking at it.

"Monkey bars."

"What?"

"The jungle gym. Grade four. Marty Syred pushed me off the top." Abbey leans sideways and looks at it. She'd hit an exposed bolt on one of the rails coming down. Her father had tried to band-aid the cut but it kept bleeding and bleeding. Finally, after an hour on the couch watching Loony Toons and pressing kleenex against her leg, he drove her to emergency for stitches.

"You're beautiful."

Abbey looks at Sean, realizes he's leaning towards her. Everything is fuzzy for a second, Abbey still on the couch with Fog Horn Leg Horn prattling on and a blood-stained pile of kleenex on her lap, her dad making Kraft Dinner in the kitchen.

"Don't say that." She says it like she's pissed off. Then gets up, shakes the sand out of her skirt.

"Why not?" He's baiting her.

"How old are you?"

"Why?"

"Fifteen? Sixteen?" She picks up the bag beside her, grabs the other one out of his hand.

"Seventeen."

"You'll grow out of it."

He doesn't know what she means.

"Listen," she snaps. But then she doesn't know what to say. Stands there for a second trying to line up what just happened.

Sean puts his hands in his pockets. "I didn't mean anything."

And that's all that Abbey needs. She feels a wave of relief. A seventeen-year-old kid stands in front of her looking totally relaxed, staring at her like she's gone crazy and he can't figure out what went wrong.

"You have sand in your hair." Abbey brushes past Sean, climbs the berm. The bag handles stretched, the cantaloupe and the apples swinging down around her ankles.

"So do you," he volunteers, hurrying to catch up.

Another's

WHEN ABBEY gets home she finds Dermot in the garden
pulling weeds. Sean nods at him, picks up the digger and the
wheelbarrow, starts out towards the southeast end of the field.

"Where were ya?" Dermot brushes the dirt off his hands
onto his pants, leans in and kisses Abbey. Kicks the bind
weed he's pulled farther away from the plants.

"Walking back with Sean."

Dermot peeks inside the Spar bag, frowns. "What have
you done with the food?"

"It's called vitamin C." She sticks out her tongue, heads
into the cottage.

"I went to The Bridge House this morning." Abbey sits down
on the couch beside Dermot, hands him a slice of cantaloupe.

"And?"

"They said to come back Tuesday. See Aidan. Do you
know him?"

"Aye. He bought the Big House off the German woman
last year."

"It's just part-time. Cleaning rooms. I think they're worried about keeping me away from the tourists, though. In case I ruin the 'Irish' feel of the place."

"Just don't open your mouth." A bead of juice from the cantaloupe in his beard.

"How was your friend?" Abbey takes the rind out of Dermot's hand and goes into the kitchen. Dumps it in the compost under the sink. Outside, Flagon starts barking.

"All right." He goes to the door, pulls the latch, watches the dog trot in. "I dropped 'round NUI after, looking for Michael, but he was at Maam."

"You went to the University? Dermot Fay stepped into an institution of higher learning?"

"He did." Dermot goes into the kitchen, cuts another slice of cantaloupe.

"Well, how was it?"

Dermot thinks about the middle-aged secretary in the archeology department office, her frosted hair tied in a tight bun. "Mr. Fay?" She'd said it with a question mark, but not in the usual way — "Where've I heard that? Fay, Fay," cataloging, the eyes going up and left until they remember: ex-Trinity professor, gone to Spiddal to go mad. No, this was flat, uninterested. She wrote a note for Michael on a square of pink paper and promptly ignored him.

"I think," he says, gently touching Flagon's head with the tips of his fingers, "that maybe they don't know me anymore."

Around ten, Dermot and Abbey go down to Hughes. Abbey picks up their pints at the bar, happy that people are nodding at her, that old man Conneely asks after where she's been.

"Thought you'd had it with Fay," he says, hands wrapped

around a short glass of whiskey. And when she doesn't respond, he raises his glass. "Gives us all hope to have ya back," knocking the knuckles of his right hand on the top of the bar. Niall appearing in front of them as if summoned. Conneely saying, "for luck" and demonstrating the knock again, "that we should all have young women to keep us."

Tomás Sullivan and Liam Conroy come in the door first, part of the body of workmen that stumbles into Hughes every Friday night. Angus, Peter and Egg follow. The men sidle collectively up to the bar, the five of them causing a great shift in the room. Even Conneely gets off his stool to make way for them. Black pints appear in convention on the bar. Euros and coins are dropped in the wet half-moons that are left after the glasses are raised. Angus telling Niall that they've found a body in Maam Bog. Word spreading. Soon everyone is talking about it, crowding around the lads asking if they'd seen it, what it looked like, if they had any idea whose body it was.

"Did ya hear?" Jimmy asks Dermot, his wide mouth gaping open. He's turned away from a group that has been squeezing him out. Dermot recognizes the girl from the beach on the chair next to Jimmy's, touching her hair, turning around to Finn and the fellow beside him.

"Ever seen a dead body, Abbey?" Jimmy is leaning in to her, his knobby nose and pit-like eyes right in front of her face. He's had too much to drink.

"No."

"Never?"

"Afraid not."

Looking at Abbey, thinking about the fact that she hadn't seen her father's body, Dermot wonders if maybe that's what did her in, the not knowing. Remembers how he saw both his parents laid out on their deathbeds, how he knew in that instant they were beyond his reach. It's the body that matters — and to some degree, the objects that come with it. Maybe that's why he didn't keep the house, the furniture, the black coat his father hung in the front closet. It would have been too much to carry around. He'd seen them; they were dead. And he decided everything that was theirs should pass with them. Otherwise you look to the dead all your life, in everyday objects that solicit your grief.

Coming back from the jacks around eleven, Dermot circles the room, trying to remember where he and Abbey had been sitting. All night the talk has been the body in Maam Bog. Is it the girl gone missing, the one whose name no one could remember? Is it a sacrifice like the one in Meenybradden? Or the body of whatever spirit they'd sent out of St. Brighid's two weeks back? Conneely suggests that it's the soap opera actress who'd been killed off in last season's final episode.

"You don't really watch that shite?" Niall asks Conneely, pouring another whiskey.

"I do." Putting his hand out to take the drink. "Fine, fine stories."

"Maybe they'll have you on?"

"Oh, the Mrs. would never permit it."

Dermot walks past the bar just then, looking around the room for Abbey. He puts his hand on Conneely's shoulder. "Joe, she's dead twenty years."

Conneely raising his glass. "But she's in charge just the same."

It's the living who haunt Dermot. Seeing Abbey over on the far side of the bar, talking to Liam Conroy — Liam Conroy who works at Maam, and who, according to Deirdre McGilloway, is her baby's father — it occurs to Dermot that he's assumed certain things about his own son, about Rory. Assumed he'd been a healthy baby, assumed he'd survived his childhood to become a man, skirting all those accidents and illnesses that whisk children away. When Dermot has imagined Rory, he's always seen him walking across the bridge at the end of the field, coming across the long grass to the back of the cottage. He's seen him as if he were whole and healthy. Now he begins to wonder, but stops himself. No, Rory would be the man Dermot had almost been, could have been. And, Dermot thinks, enough like his old man that he would never seek his father out. Or enough like Dermot that if he did, if he ever came to the door and Dermot opened it, Rory would not be there to forgive him.

"Will we head?" Dermot touches Abbey's arm, nods at Conroy.

"Sure." She watches Dermot study Liam's face. "Do you know each other?"

Liam puts out his hand. "I've seen ya around. Liam." He looks from Abbey to Dermot and realizes that they're together.

"Dermot Fay."

Liam narrows his eyes. "Were you out at Maam last week?"

"I was."

They stand there a minute, the talk of the pub around them. Niall's youngest daughter comes out of the back room with a parfait glass in her hand. The last of her ice cream in the bottom of it.

"Do you know Deirde McGilloway?" Dermot asks.

Liam nods, reaches past Abbey to his pint on the bar.

"Have you seen the baby?"

"Not yet."

"You should." Dermot moves to walk past him. "I'd say he has your eyes."

On the walk back to the cottage, Abbey is lightheaded and warm from drinking. Flagon had followed them in to town, had lain outside Hughes' door when they went in. On the way home she's full of energy, runs out along the sand to the water, barks at the crash of waves, running toward the surf as it recedes. They're alone on the road. Only two cars have passed since the edge of the village.

"Do you believe in ghosts?" Abbey asks. She's wanted to ask this question for days. She doesn't look at Dermot, watches Flagon by the water.

Dermot smiles to himself in the dark, thinking she should know better. "Not the kind you're after."

"Not even a bit?"

He kicks a pebble with his foot; it rolls twice over gravel before skittering onto the road. "Well, if I did, I'd probably believe in my own before another's."

Later that night Dermot wakes up to the sound of Abbey saying something in her sleep. He leans over her in the dark, tries to make it out, but all he can hear is a sob welling in her chest. He puts his hand on her cheek to wake her, just a bit. Turn the dream around.

"Hey," he whispers, wondering if it's the old business with the father. Wondering if he's there, in her head.

"Abbey?" he whispers again, gently pushing her hair off her forehead. She turns towards him, eyes still closed. In the moonlight he can see her pupils moving back and forth under her lids. He strokes the fine hair over her left temple with his thumb. She feels cold.

The world, Dermot thinks, is a changed place. Abbey's come home and he's still at sea. It might as well be him with the restless dreams. Somehow he thought her return would right things. But it's like he's slipped through the cracks anyway, as if the boat he was sitting in had turned over. The secretary in Galway did not know him. Michael is over at Maam doing work that Dermot could be involved in. And Rory is still in his head, a fiction he's constantly spinning. *So here we are.* Dermot runs his finger over the arch of Abbey's brow. *The two of us going under together. And I don't even have the wrongs I've done to hold onto.*

Isle of the Dogs

AT THE south end of the Isle of the Dogs, there's a green space called Millwall Park. When he was a boy, Michael and his parents lived five minutes away. The spit the Park occupied narrowed towards the Thames and ended in another park called Island Gardens. The gardens led to the Greenwich Foot Tunnel which led to Greenwich Pier. These were the boundaries of Michael's childhood. Never allowed on the docks unaccompanied, never allowed to cross Manchester Road. When he saw Crossharbour, he was meant to turn around. By the mid-sixties all that changed. Michael was old enough to ride the train into London alone. The area modernized, and development brought the police in. The only dangers left were the construction zones. Then his father lost his job and there was no reason to stay by the docks. By 1968 the family had moved to Wapping.

Now, standing in the pit at Maam, it occurs to Michael that he's always done exactly as he's been told, that he never goes beyond the perimeters set for him. Never went to the Quays to mix with the dock hands, never stopped to talk to the old drunk who raised a chess piece in Michael's direction when, as a boy, he marched past him on his way to school. He wonders if he should regret this. If it's diminished him in some way. Lifting the tarp that covers the east bank of the pit, Michael looks at the orange flags, touches the peat beside them with the flat of his hand. The outer layer is dry even though they've kept it covered, even though Michael has brought jugs of water to keep it moist. It'll be five days before they're ready to dig. But every pore of Michael's being is ready to start in now. To break the rules. Just once.

There was a point in time on the weekend when Michael thought the paperwork would never end, that he'd be dead and buried himself before the Maam body was ever cleared for excavation, but now, at least, the forms are done. Hopkins has taken them to the Minister, to Dúchas, himself. First, there were the methodology statements, then the arrangements for the body fridge from St. James', then assembling the team, tracking down the paleobotanist from Clare. Then getting Bord na Móna and the Museum to agree on the size and scope of the excavation. All Michael's patience is exhausted. At least the Garda had assessed the hand and the site, agreed it wasn't a crime scene, allowed the work to go forward.

Michael sits on the west bank of the pit and looks around the bog. Tomás and his crew are off for three days, having harvested both sets. The sound of another team's tractor comes across the field from the north. Everything else is quiet. No birds, no frogs sounding out in the nearby trench. The strata of the pit goes from dark to light brown, depending on the level of moisture. The tarp beside Michael catching the glint of the sun, like a glass held up to the light. It occurs to him to call Janey. He could ask her down from Clifden; invite her out to watch the excavation. But maybe she'd bring Simon. Michael weighs it out — why would he want her to come? Would it matter to him if Simon came with her? He was over it now. He was. Would only ask her along because she might find it interesting, because, in those years they were together, she could never wrap her head around what he did, that archeology involved the lab, involved writing papers, as much as it involved digging in the ground.

Michael was with Janey for two years. He'd commuted between Clifden and Dublin the first year, a ridiculous and impractical move, but one that seemed completely natural at the time. In the summer he'd stay in her house on the coast but in the autumn he was driving back and forth again. Finally he just threw his hands up in the air and moved in with her. Took a sabbatical for research, worked a few sites freelance on the islands. The fact that she wouldn't give up her job at Mahones, her uncle's pub, never really bothered him, though he saw the humour in it. His twelve years of education, his career, having to accommodate her desire to stay in a small coastal village at a pub that paid her five pounds an hour, in a house that was near falling down. But he loved her. Really did. And they were happy. And after a while her family got used to having Michael around. The father was a Nationalist, the uncle more or less the same. And maybe that was part of it. Janey asserting her independence, taking up with an Englishman. And Michael asserting his place in Ireland, saying *Okay, maybe I'm not one of you, but don't assume that makes me one of them.*

Simon had come into Mahones just as Michael had done. Sat down for a drink. He was even Michael's age, and no better looking. Probably gave her a decent tip. Went off down the coast on business but came back again. Michael was on Inishbofin for the weekend, getting a hard time of it from the locals. Simon worked in exports:

"Kiss Me, I'm Irish" buttons, Connemara-stone key chains, Sláinte t-shirts, pint glasses bearing the tricolour, tiny ceramic houses that came with impossibly small bricks of Irish peat. He sold mostly to the US. Everything made in China and shipped from Belfast. Janey mentioned him the day Michael came back. "Had a drink with Simon. Was a good laugh." Making fun of his line of business.

Two weeks after Michael moved out of Janey's house in Clifden, Simon moved in. Michael found a flat in Galway and sat on a chair with his back to the window, reeling from the blow. And just when it seemed like he was ready to start over, weighing the idea of returning to London, she started to call him again. At night mostly, from Mahones, or in the early evening when the pub wasn't too busy. "Just to see," she'd said, "how you're doing."

"Fine."

"That's it? Fine." Her voice uneasy.

"What did you expect? That I've become engaged to be married?"

"No." Followed by silence. Followed by, "Michael? Don't hate me."

If there was anything he could take back, it would be the fact that he never gave her that — never allowed for the possibility that he didn't hate her. He liked her unhappiness then, the guilt he knew she was feeling. Janey became the conduit for everything that had welled up in him all those years in Ireland — the times he'd had to suffer the looks; the talk, the flat-out racism heaped on an Englishman living in this country. Fair enough, he'd think when it happened. But he was convinced even then, that things could be different if the Irish got to know him. So he thought: let the guilt get to her. He'd done everything by the book. She was the one who'd left him. She'd brought it on herself in the end.

Settling

SEAN WALKS over the rise in the back field and heads towards the cottage. If Dermot's in he'll ask him something about the fence, about payment, maybe ask him for a first installment. But what he really wants is to see Abbey. The past three days, since the fight on the beach, he's been thinking about her. And this morning, up at the house to collect the wheelbarrow and the wire, she was out in the garden watering the plants. Saw him and said hello.

When Sean enters the back yard he sees that Dermot's clothes are up on the line now — three pairs of men's pants, a white shirt, some underwear, a sweater. The line sags with the weight.

Knocking on the door, Sean goes over what he'll say. Shoves his hands into his front pockets. After a minute Abbey answers. She's wearing a tight red shirt and jeans. There's a bruise on her neck he hadn't noticed. An old bruise turned yellow.

"Hiya." Sean looks down at the floor.

"Hi." Abbey hesitates, unsure why he's there.

"Is Mr. Fay here?"

"No, Dermot's in town."

"I wanted to ask him about the fence."

"He's due back in an hour or so."

The two of them stand there a second and then Abbey asks, "Do you want tea?" Turns to go to the kitchen.

"Thanks." He steps into the cottage, closes the door behind him. Something savory is cooking on the stove.

"I've got black tea and …" Abbey reaches for a tin in the cupboard above the sink, her shirt lifting at the back. Sean watches the swathe of her bare skin shift above the top of her jeans, "… lemon."

"Yeah, grand. Lemon. Can I use the loo?"

"Sure. Over there." Abbey points around the corner. Sean takes his jacket off and drops it on the floor by the door, heads through the front room, rounds the corner and closes the door behind him.

"Fuck off." Sean looks at himself in the bathroom mirror and says "fuck off" three times to his reflection. He runs the taps and puts cold water on his face. A sunburn under his eyes, over his forehead. The nose peeling.

When Sean comes out of the bathroom Abbey is standing at the sink looking out the window. The kettle is whistling. Stepping behind her, Sean reaches out and turns off the burner. When the tea's poured Abbey sits down at the table and Sean takes the seat across from her.

"How's the fence coming?"

"All right." He slouches down in the seat. Drums his fingers on the edge of the table.

"So what kinds of things do you like to do when you're not building fences?"

Sean lifts his right shoulder up, an exaggerated I-don't-give-a-shit gesture.

"Do you like music?"

"Yeah. Ska mostly."

Abbey takes a sip of her tea, burns the roof of her mouth. "Do you speak Irish?"

"Yeah. Fuckin' hate it."

"That's too bad," she smiles. Sean's sitting across the table with a tough look on his face.

"Do you speak French?" he thrusts his chin at her.

"Un petit peu."

For the next half hour, it works this way between them. Abbey asks Sean a question, studies his face, and then after he answers her, with one word or two, she asks him something else, something more personal, until he starts telling her things he doesn't talk about with anyone. And Abbey's interested, wonders how his mind works, what it's like to grow up on the coast in Ireland with six brothers and sisters and two parents. What it's like to know almost everyone in the village. She tells him about Ontario when he asks, about a whole childhood spent in front of the TV. Confesses that she couldn't name a bird or a tree to save her life but she knows the plot of every episode of "Charlie's Angels" that aired in the 1980s. Sean telling her how his father's always riding him to get his shit together, his mother pawning Mary off on him when she's too busy with the baby. Every now and again Sean kicks the heels of his Docs down on the rug under the table, and then aware that he's doing it, both legs nervously bouncing up and down, he looks up at Abbey and stops. When he asks her what happened to her neck, she tells him. Then she gets up and takes the tea cups away, starts wiping the table.

After Sean goes back to the fence, Abbey walks around the cottage waiting for Dermot to come home. She picks Dermot's sweater up off the couch, puts it on a shelf in the bedroom closet. She does the dishes from tea, washes the plastic cutting board. Throws out last week's *Irish Times* which was still occupying the far corner of the big table. Then she runs her hand along the front of the bookshelf in the bedroom, trying to find something to read. Back in the living room Abbey touches the frayed wool blanket on the couch, the petals of the iris Dermot brought in two days ago. She picks up the photo on the side table then sets it down, happy to be settling in again. And when Dermot comes home, he puts his arms around Abbey and heads into the kitchen, tests the chili and tells her, with tomato sauce on his chin, how wonderful it is. He pulls two bowls and two glasses down from the cupboard, opens a bottle of wine. Turns the radio on to music. Proclaims lunch. And for a minute or two, for an hour, everything is perfect between them.

All that afternoon, Dermot stays in and watches Abbey move from room to room as if she is a product of his imagination, a quirky manifestation out of his control. Just when she is standing in a square of sunlight, her hand to the window, just when Dermot is struck by the simple beauty of the image, Abbey will turn and laugh, say that Flagon is out in the yard chasing a gull, that it's close and she almost has it. It amazes him that she is so much a woman and then sometimes a girl; the way her face opens in amazement at things she's never seen. After lunch they had gone for a walk to the beach and talked about her father, and talking about him made Abbey feel better. Dermot had made a joke about ghosts, had opened the door after coming home, had stepped across the threshold before her, saying he was checking to be sure the cottage was clear. And if he is here, Dermot reasons now, if by chance Frank is watching, if he's not just some byproduct of Abbey's grief, let him look at this woman, let him see her as Dermot does. Let him see her the way the dead should see the living, as something apart from themselves. Dermot has his own superstitions, has seen his fetch come across the field to call him father. Everyone haunted by something.

Around three, Dermot pulls Abbey into the bedroom to make love. She rolls her eyes, says "not this again" and he isn't sure if she's joking or not. But time is ticking and Dermot can hear it. He remembers Bonaventure. The Franciscan insisting that every instant of time is a beginning of the future even as it is a terminus of the past. The act, Dermot thinks, of being stuck in the moment before the hand of the clock moves. And Siger of Brabant, a favourite of Lasalle's: "Potentiality precedes act in duration." Dermot mulling it over as he lifts Abbey's shirt over her head.

Later, when he's kissing her — one breast then the other, then the yellow bruise along her neck, the two of them laughing — he feels an elation, feels outside of himself in a way that is oddly tactile. As if he's standing there watching his body with hers, anticipating the feeling that's to come, thinking *this is what happiness is.* His happiness, hers, theirs together. As if she's pulled him out of himself, the way she kneels at the foot of the bed, teases him with her mouth. But in the middle of it, just as enters her, he feels her body tense up. Pushes himself up on his hands, wondering if he's hurt her.

"Are you all right?"

"It's nothing."

"Tell me. Did I hurt you?" His left arm quivering so that he has to roll off her.

"It's Billy McKay." Abbey puts the palm of her hand over her eyes.

"What?"

"My father walked in on me and Billy in grade eleven, and pulled him off me."

"Abbey, what are you talking about?"

She sits up. Puts her hand on Dermot's chest. "I just spaced out. For a second I thought we'd been caught. That Frank had walked in on us."

"You and me, or you and Billy?" He swings his legs over the side of the bed.

"You and me."

"I'm for a drink." He looks over at her but she shakes her head no. Then, naked, he walks across the room, heads into the kitchen.

Later that afternoon when a water glass falls to the floor and no one is in the kitchen, when the radio loses its station for no reason, Dermot will look up at the ceiling and shake his head. Abbey picking up the glass shards in the blue plastic dust pan, tuning the radio back to RTE.

"C'mere." Dermot pulls Abbey into his arms and she kisses his neck. He takes her right hand in his and they start dancing to the bluesy music that's playing. Dermot waltzing Abbey around and into the kitchen, trying to get her to follow his lead, laughing when she trips over his feet, hits her elbow on the fridge. They start again and move from room to room, stepping over Flagon's bowls on the kitchen floor, over the furled edge of the living-room rug. *Watch this,* Dermot thinks, turning Abbey in circles. *Watch this, Frank Gowan. The woman your little girl has become.*

The Bridge House

TUESDAY morning Abbey wakes up to the dull thud of hammers hitting wood at the bungalow next door. The framers are putting in the interior walls. She rolls over and grabs her travel alarm off the window sill, looks at the time. Just after ten. Dermot's in the kitchen and the house smells like sausage. Abbey has to be at the hotel in two hours to see Aidan. They'll talk about the kind of work he might want her to do, about her experience. The only cleaning she's ever done has been after-hours at Gabby's, end-of-shift stuff at Connor's. And taking care of her father. Although how emptying a bedpan qualifies her for room cleaning might be beyond Aidan's comprehension.

"You're up, then?" Dermot is standing in the doorway. He's trimmed his beard and combed his hair. He's even wearing a shirt with a collar.

"What time did you get out of bed?" Abbey walks over, goes up on her toes, kisses him.

"A while ago. Breakfast is almost ready."

After they eat, Abbey gets dressed. She chooses a short green skirt she bought two weeks ago in Dublin and the white blouse she usually wears to work at Connor's. She slips on her black shoes and puts on some lipstick, checks herself in the bathroom mirror and then goes outside. Dermot is tossing the ball to Flagon, eying the bungalows. He said he'd drive Abbey in, wait by the bridge until she was done. Then he wanted to go into Galway and drop by the bank. Maybe stop at the Brasserie for a pint.

"Ready?" Dermot kicks the ball one last time towards the start of the field.

"Yep."

"Do you have your work visa?"

"In my passport." Abbey taps her shoulder bag.

Then the two of them get in the car, dressed up for the first time since last November, when Dermot met up with Abbey in Dublin and they went to the Gate to see a Stoppard play.

Aidan is nice enough. Very Dublin, very congenial. A man in his early forties with two prominent lines across his forehead. Lines, Abbey thinks, you could sink a ship in. He says "I see," in response to everything she puts forward. Folds his hands. Index fingers tapping each other in contemplation. They sit out in the back garden, and every now and again when she's in the middle of saying why she wants to work at the Bridge House, Abbey can see his attention drift. His gaze goes from her face to the potted flowers beside her chair and then off to the stone wall at the back of the garden. He tries to deter her with "it's just part-time" and "the wages won't be what you're used to in Dublin, and the tips are minimal if you get anything at all." But Abbey insists she wants the work. At the end, he looks back over at her and asks, "How long will you stay in Ireland?" And maybe it's the fact that he seems so sad, that there's a weight hanging off him, but Abbey tells him the truth. "I can't really say." Just then, a woman in gardening gloves comes out the glass patio doors. A tired-looking laborer with a big gut, carrying two large sacks of fertilizer, follows her. He looks once at Abbey then drops his eyes back to the ground. The woman's gardening clogs slapping up and down against her heels.

"Aidan, will you mind the desk?" A bee zigzags past her. She fans the air, raises her eyebrows at Abbey.

"This is Abbey Gowan." He drops a hand in her direction.

Abbey steps forward and the woman smiles thinly at her, pulls at the fingertips of her gloves.

"Aidan — the desk." The woman turning to examine the geraniums.

The west-facing bedroom on the second floor is filled with Queen Anne lace and gold tassels. It's not the kind of room Abbey would have put together but it's delicate and clean — the type of suite old women love to sleep in. Aidan takes the keys and heads down to the desk, tells Abbey to take a minute and look around. When she comes down they'll go over the cleaning responsibilities she'll have. Abbey goes into the bathroom, flicks the light switch on. Small heart-shaped soaps by the sink. Mini shampoo and conditioners. A shower cap. Ice bucket. Four glasses in paper wrap. A bag for sanitary napkins. Ten towels of varying sizes on the rack by the wall. It occurs to Abbey that she'll hate this job, that slinging food around for tourists is bad enough, but this will be less pay, harder work, maybe even a little lonely. Looking at the toilet she realizes that she'll be the one responsible for cleaning it, the way she had to clean up after Frank before Doctor Kaplan changed his meds and things righted themselves again. A month of diarrhea and Frank saying "see," as if that was proof positive that he was dying. He'd taken some pleasure in it, in the look on Abbey's face as she carried the bedpan from the table where he left it into the bathroom. She'd wash her hands for ten minutes afterwards, telling herself there was nothing she could do. But wanting, the whole time, some kind of a declaration. "There's been some internal bleeding, but it's stopped and we can't say what caused it. The CAT and PET scans don't show anything out of the ordinary. The lethargy is a concern, but until the tests show something abnormal ..." Dr. Kaplan, in his office at the hospital, had been almost sorry, looked at Abbey as if he knew what she was going through, patting her hand as he dropped the folder containing Frank's medical history into a file cabinet. Abbey walked back to admitting to find Frank on the bed in a hospital gown, grinning. The green curtain had made him look more sallow than usual. Abbey went over to him, watched him swing his legs over the side of the bed, stand up, take his IV with him. Frank saying, "Let's get lunch at the cafeteria." The back of his gown open as he started down the hall.

Dermot is at the bridge. Flagon down in the river pawing stones in the shallows.

"How was it?"

"Okay. I start next week."

"Is that what you want?"

Abbey looks at the trees, skylarks rustling in the upper branches. A dragonfly dipping up and down over the stream. "How long do you think this'll go on?" she asks.

"How long will what go on?"

"I hate him. I really do."

"Hate is a strong word, Abbey."

"But that's it, isn't it? I hate my father but there isn't anything I can say that he did to deserve it. He never really hit me, not really, he didn't dump me by the side of a —"

"Ssshhh." Dermot reaches out and puts his hand on her shoulder. After a minute he says, "Do you remember when we first met?"

Abbey nods.

"We were at the Bailey and Angela had introduced us and I was talking about the past and you were hanging on every word that I said."

"Well, not every word."

"You were."

Abbey laughs.

"And then you dropped your hand on my knee."

"I did," she agrees.

"A small thing, Abbey. But here we are. Never underestimate how even the simple gestures can change us."

Later that afternoon when Dermot comes out of the bank, he sees Abbey waiting for him by the car. Happy to see him, lifting her hand. This pixie girl, this woman who is making a life with him. Abbey, who has grown as strange to him as he has to himself. Her sudden compliance. Her wanting to settle down. The Bridge House job, the afternoons spent lazing around in the cottage with no desire to do anything, go anywhere. Yesterday, she whiled away three hours reading the church-sanctioned version of Kilian's life and then asked Dermot to tell her the Saint's verifiable biography. She is still interested in mining Dermot's head for all the things he knows. Although now, Dermot's starting to wonder if she'll grow tired of it. If he tells her everything, what will happen then? When his knowledge has run its course? If she stays, he thinks suddenly, nearing the car, I'll be the ruin of her. His lethargy catching. The drink, his aimlessness, wearing them both out. Unless he makes something more of himself, then it might work. Still, either way, he might hurt her. But then, there is a comfort in that too. As if causing another's sorrow is one way to define being a man.

The Heritage Service

MICHAEL and Dermot stand at the edge of the pit, contemplating the tarp. After a while Michael walks over to the far side of the excavation, moves back two feet from the edge, says, "We'll take about fifty centimetres off the top here, then cut a wedge down behind the body and at the same time go in underneath. Pull out the whole shelf."

"When's the license due in?"

"This afternoon. If it's in by four, we'll dig tomorrow."

"Has Hopkins come over from Dublin?"

"He and the paleobotanist are coming in the morning. Jack's bringing the license. She's driving up from Clare."

"Who is it?"

"Moira someone. Recommended by O'Flynn."

Two hours pass. Michael sits at the edge of the pit with his legs hanging over the side and Dermot walks over to the rabbit warren, watches Tomás mill the field adjacent. Abbey'd wanted to stay home today and Dermot was restless. He knows the excavation will be starting soon. Yesterday, in Galway, there was even talk of it at the Brasserie. The barman had recognized Dermot and asked if he was from Spiddal, and did he know they'd found a body up the way at Maam. It's a different kind of gossip now, as if finally, after twelve years in the cottage, Dermot belongs. There was a time even four or five years ago when he'd walk to Hughes and not one person driving down the road would raise a hand in greeting. But now he was one of them. Their story was his story. Not like before — he was no longer "Dermot Fay from Dublin." Now the barman at the Brasserie, seeing him, had asked, "Aren't you a Spiddal man?" And Dermot, thinking about it, said, "Yes, I am."

When Dermot gets back to the pit, Michael is down below exactly where he left him. His notebooks in his canvas bag beside him, the camera on his lap.

Squinting up at Dermot, Michael asks, "Will you bring Abbey along?"

"I will."

"I was thinking of asking Janey."

Dermot looks up at the sky, then down at the top of Michael's head. "All that business is the past."

"You're right," Michael agrees. Picking up a handful of dry turf, sifting it through his fingers.

There had been a time, about ten years ago, when Dermot had managed to live in the present, to let go of the business that had come before. He was seeing Nora Leary then. Forty-two and shy, well-heeled for a seamstress. They'd met at the Festival parade on High Street. It was the second weekend in September and he was just back from Clarinbridge. She'd backed into him, turned, and said sorry. There was music on the bandstand. They spoke about the weather. The next week he took her to the films.

In the end, Nora Leary made a number of demands. That Dermot arrive in good time and in good order, that he give up the drink. And he did, but not to please her. It was a study, a course in the observation of the self. *Here I am with Nora in her living room; here I am not drinking. Is this what it feels like to be sober? Is this what it looks like when a man takes a woman's hand?*

There was talk that if all went well for them, he might be welcome in her home after the marriage. He could sell his property in Spiddal and live in the city. He could find work, maybe at the University — he was just forty-five and he had his degree. Nora completely oblivious to the obstacles he was facing. She made a list of things she expected him to do, her life a ranked system of duty and obligation: *If you can stay sober, we can get married. If you can find work, we can get a bigger house. If we get a bigger house, it won't be too late to consider children. I have to save you so you can save me.*

They would stay in most nights, which is what she wanted. Sit in front of her television and eat a warm meal. After six months of it, Dermot grew restless. No drink in the house. Canned laughter echoing in all corners of the room and Nora placing her hand on his as if to say, *laugh along.* He'd yet to touch her.

One night after dinner he'd reached for her. They'd been kissing on the couch and he'd placed his hand ever so gently over her breast, could feel the pert nipple under her shirt. Suddenly she was standing. Wide-eyed, backing away towards the kitchen. "Nora, Nora," Dermot tried to calm her but she kept backing away, patting her hair, turning to the sink to run water. And in that instant, those months of study that said *this is who you are now* or *this,* those months of watching himself, were over. He was completely inside himself then, and for a long time after. Tired of ignoring his wants, of denying who he was, what had come before. It was better, in the end, to be inside yourself. The dark room that he knew was in him.

"Dermot?"

Dermot looks down at Michael, who's holding up the tarp with his right hand. Two flags visible below it.

"I put your name on the list," says Michael.

"What list?"

"The license application for The Heritage Service. I put you down as a medieval specialist. You're cleared to be at the excavation."

"Can't anyone come?"

"No, I mean you're cleared to be here." He points into the pit. "But listen, I don't want to go into the whole thing with Hopkins. Though I think he might know not to ask."

Dermot shakes his head, looks down at Michael. "You didn't have to do that."

"Tá sé sin ar eolas agam." Michael smirks.

"I see you've been working at it." Dermot puts a hand down to Michael when he nears the top of the ladder. Hauls him out of the pit. The day suddenly brighter. The clouds moving off the sun.

Michael wipes the sweat off his brow. Straightens up. "Actually, there are some things I've known all along."

Odds

OUTSIDE the cottage, the yard has settled into a pocket of good weather and other than the odd gust of wind swirling the grass in half-circles, everything holds its place. Abbey wanders from window to window looking outside as if she were in a bathysphere. The radio is on and Flagon follows along behind her as she walks around the cottage, goes into the bedroom to make the bed. Through the window at the back of the house she can see that Fitch's cows, used to the new line of the fence, stay away from it, only come up against the wire to scratch their chins. The lettuce in the back garden rustles its leaves. The wild irises called "flagon" bend and sway at the start of the field. Abbey has no idea how long she stands there. Maybe five minutes, maybe ten. But then her father is with her: *I spy with my little eye something that is red.* And Abbey looks to the clothes on the line, to the field, but sees nothing. Frank's voice in her head, from those long drives across Ontario, the two of them in the truck and Frank playing "I Spy" to keep her distracted.

"Where are we going?"

"To visit a friend."

Abbey stayed buckled into the passenger seat the whole time while Frank hopped out of the truck, knocked on doors, asked a few questions, climbed back in. They drove down one county road after another, past farms and silos, co-ops and shopping centres. The two of them looking for Abbey's mother, though Frank would never admit it.

An hour later, when Sean sees Abbey coming across the field, he goes back to the wire, intent on ignoring her. He holds the "come along" at arm's length and walks backwards toward the corner post, his heel hitting a rut in the field so that he trips, has to balance himself. Cuts above his elbow and along his shins from the barbs in the wire. Sean is wanting to get the fence done, has come out the last two nights after dinner, working by flashlight so that Dermot would see how things were progressing. He'd stopped at Éinde's last night on the way home and pulled the stash out from under the pew. Nothing there but a note from Clancy that said "You owe me twenty Euros, you gom." Sean thinking it was probably more like thirty.

"Hey."

"Hi." Sean glances at Abbey then goes back to hammering the nail into the post.

"Do you want a hand?"

"No." He hits the U-shaped nail three times until the wire is snug underneath it. Then he pulls the wire taut with his right hand and hammers in the nail the rest of the way.

"I brought you a sandwich."

"Thanks." He stands up and starts walking down the east length of the field until he gets to the next post. Abbey walks behind him. Sean sees her and brusquely adds, "Watch it. You'll get cut."

"Are you pissed off at me?" Abbey tries to remember if they'd ended on a sour note after he'd come for tea.

"I'm just busy." He tugs the wire taut and pulls a nail out of his pocket.

"Should I go?"

He turns and looks at her. She's wearing Dermot's Arran sweater. He can see the white of a t-shirt underneath, between the knots of wool. "No."

Abbey hands him the sandwich and he takes it. Opens the wax paper and lifts up the crust.

"I got a job at the Bridge House." Abbey swings her arms back and forth, clapping them in front of her then behind her.

"Doing what?"

"Cleaning."

"My sister Nuala worked there last summer. Thought it was crap."

"Yeah? Well, it might be." Abbey watches him take a quarter of the sandwich, shove it in his mouth. "What are you going to do after this? Go into fence building?"

"I dunno." His face softens for the first time since Abbey's known him. "Maybe work for my Da." Sean looks over Abbey's shoulder towards Fitch's field. "He's an electrician."

Abbey turns around, curious to see what Sean's seeing. But there's nothing there. Just one of Fitch's cows standing over by the back stream. The alder tree's shadow thrown across the field. The wind rustling the leaves.

That evening when Dermot gets home, he and Abbey go for a walk in the back field. The sky has gone black like a great glove above them. They go as far as the bridge but Dermot doesn't want to cross it so they turn around. Flagon nosing the bank by the stream. Dermot talks about the bog and tomorrow's excavation. About Lindow man, how he saw the body when he was in London. The red hair of his beard visible. One side of his face pushed down like in sleep. Skin puckered between the ribs so that it seemed he had no mass left in him. Like a soft outline of the person he'd once been.

At the southeast corner of the field Dermot walks to the last post that Sean had run wire to. He puts his hand on the top wire and tugs at it but it doesn't bend. He pulls at the post with his hand and it stands firm.

"He has a crush on you."

"Who?"

"The boy." Adding, "You two are closer in age anyway." Laughing at that. He takes Abbey's hand and pulls her along, notices Abbey looking back once.

"What is it?"

"Nothing."

And Dermot doesn't force it. They've circled the issue of her father one too many times; it's up to Abbey now to resolve things. Dermot had thought, at first, it was in his power to help. That if he could, he'd roll back time, make her stay with the old man, see it through. But Abbey was right to leave her father, to try to find her own life. She was no more to blame than the woman who had died giving birth to Frank, than the wife who had walked out. Matters beyond our choosing. Abbey hasn't understood this yet. People do as they will, as they must, and we can only watch them. What was it Michael had said about Eileen McGilloway? "These things happen," and even Dermot had been put off by that at the time, still reeling from the news. But now he sees the truth of it: people die or they leave us. Life stalls and then picks up and moves on. Dermot looks at Abbey standing in the field, in her skirt and his sweater, her arms crossed, gazing at the sky. Maybe when she gets back to the beginning of the story, when she realizes her place in it, maybe then she'll settle, or maybe she'll move on. *Travel a way of physically remembering the past.* From his dissertation.

When they get to the cottage, Dermot starts walking south.

"Where are we going?" Abbey catches up to him.

"The bungalow."

The black tarp over the bungalow lifts in waves, and underneath, the yellow siding is briefly revealed. The ground covered in hard soil, piles of dirt turned over for flower beds, holes dug out for hedges that have yet to arrive. Abbey walks to the north wall of the building. The light from their own porch and kitchen reaching them here although the far side of the bungalow is dark. Wind comes in gusts off the bay. Dermot trips on a stack of wood when he is close to the wall, reaches out to steady himself and feels the breath rush out of him. He stops and looks up, waits for the return of air, for his breathing to slow.

"What is it?" She's beside him, over-concerned.

"I just got winded." He smiles at her, straightens up. "Shall we?"

He holds out his arm and they lift the tarp. The doorway to the right, a piece of plywood with a hole for a handle. Dermot pushes it open and they walk in. Drywall sacks line the wall in the first room. Wood beams stretch across the ceiling, the tarp above them. In the second room an electrical box with coloured wires dangling in knots has been mounted on the wall. The floor is nothing more than wood sheets, hollow-sounding as Abbey walks over them. Dermot stares up at the crossbeams of the ceiling, just as he does in the old church, only here there is no gash of sky coming through, no rain. Above their heads, the tarp flaps like insincere thunder. Everything tainted with the smell of sawdust. Dermot looks around and around as if the walls might give him clues to the kind of people who will one day occupy this place, as if he can see in the unfixed seams of plaster whether or not they will be good neighbours.

Dermot and Abbey walk around the rooms for the better part of an hour. They talk about the hotel, about Dublin, about Dermot putting the cottage up for sale. Abbey could go back to Connor's, Dermot could go with her, or maybe, he says, "Your visa will run out and you'll go back to Canada, go back to your studies." They talk about moving on, unsure if either of them has the will to do it, if either of them even has a plan. "You're smart, Abbey. You should go to University." And he means it. Would never have left Trinity if the choice had been his. And then they just stand there, in the middle of the bungalow, holding on to everything that makes and sways them: Frank and Karen, Rory and Sophie. All of them might as well be there. Dermot eying the crossbeams along the roof, trying to take the measure of things, the underlying structures, the what-it-is that keeps the world from falling in.

IV

All and Sundry

Wending their Way up the Coast

BY EIGHT in the morning a line of cars and trucks can be seen heading up the coast towards Maam Cross. They come from all over, from every village the workmen have been through; and everyone who has met Michael in the week since he's found the hand, is tagging along. Word about the body has spread, and now the entire west of Ireland wants to see it.

Deirdre McGilloway is sitting on a chair looking out her mother's window when the procession starts. She steps onto the porch and sees people walking in groups towards the main road. There's Meehan, and Marianne Lynch's cousin, and the Flynns. Mrs. Keating, flour on her dress from the bakery, passes by with two huge wicker baskets full of steaming biscuits hanging from her arms. Roxy, the Hughes' dog, following behind her.

"Are you not bringing the babe to Maam Cross?" Keating's face is full of encouragement.

"What's at Maam Cross?"

"Have ya not heard?"

"No."

"There's a body in Maam Bog."

The first of the cars drives out the bay road, through town, over the Spiddal River, past the bungalows that line the coast. Father O'Dugain, standing outside the Church in Rossaveel, sees a few go by, then a few more, until there is almost a train of cars. Two dozen people hitch from the road in front of Hughes. Deirdre finally heads out there with the pram, waiting to catch sight of someone she knows. Cars crawl by slow enough that people wanting a lift can jump right in. Greetings called from one passenger window to another. A little girl in her yard waving a plastic doll.

In the backseat of Mrs. Joyce's car, Deirdre settles in, listens to the woman tell her cousin from Tuàm about the exorcism in Furbo. "I've not seen this many out since then."

"But sure, the 'Ros na Run' people are taking over the coast."

"Now, did you see it last week?"

"I did."

"Who'd have guessed it?"

"Indeed."

Old man Conneely walks up the road until Keating drives by and pulls over for him.

"Are we away?" she asks.

"We are," he replies. One hand on the van door, the other on the headrest as he climbs in. The smell of the biscuits fills the van. The sun comes in through the front window. Conneely considers the square of light that's landed on his lap.

"Would ya mind?" he asks, indicating the baskets behind him.

Keating narrows her eyes before turning back to the road.

"You can have *one.* "

The line of cars in front of them starts to slow. More cars are coming off the side roads.

"I say you'll do fair business today," Conneely says, breaking the biscuit, steam rising between his hands.

Fitch walks towards Spiddal with his dog Egan behind him. A few cars go by, someone honks their horn and drives on. When Fitch lifts a hand a car pulls over, brakes loudly on the gravel. A blond fellow he doesn't recognize leans over to open the door. "You're for Maam?"

"I am."

"Get in."

"Do you mind the dog?" Fitch asks.

"Not at all."

The Lab scampers into the backseat and Liam reaches his left hand out to pet him. When he's settled in, Fitch sees the Bord na Móna parking permit on the dash of the car. "Ah, you're in great shape. The rest of us will be at the gates but you'll be in."

Minding

THE MORNING of the excavation, Dermot finds himself at the O'Riordan house, on the front steps where he first met Sean. It's just past eight and already, driving over, he'd met a line of cars. He balls his hand into a fist and raps on the door. The house is silent and the front room's dark behind the veneer of curtains. Dermot thinks to turn and go, but suddenly the door opens and the wide-awake, smiling face of Eamon O'Riordan is before him.

"Dermot." Sean's father sticks out a hand, a dishtowel in the other. They shake and then Eamon, dressed in jeans and a t-shirt, holds open the door, moves aside to let Dermot in.

"How's the fence coming? I've meant to come out to see it, but Sean seems keen and says it's goin' all right."

"He's a good worker."

Eamon motions to the wing-back chair in the living room, turns on a lamp, but Dermot stays standing just inside the door. In the back of the house the kitchen lights are on.

"How's it at the ESB?" Dermot asks.

"I'm a private contractor now —" Eamon pauses when he

hears a banging noise in the kitchen. Says, "Come in," and walks to the back of the house.

Dermot follows into the bright kitchen where a baby in a high-chair is waving her spoon around. A cereal bowl is knocked over on her tray and milk drips onto the floor.

"About five years now," Eamon concludes, going to the sink for a wet towel. "It's better being your own boss." His voice hits the basin of the sink.

The last time Dermot had spoken to Eamon was when he'd come out to do some rewiring at the cottage; Eamon was still with the ESB then. Dermot's seen him some nights at Hughes but hasn't had the occasion to do more than nod. The baby lets out a laugh and slaps both hands into the puddle of milk. Eamon bends down to the floor, scoops up clumps of soggy wheat flakes.

"Did you hear about Maam Bog?" asks Dermot.

"No." Eamon goes over to the sink.

"They think they've a body out there and are digging it up today. I thought Sean —" and then it seems ridiculous to Dermot that he thought to bring the boy out. He'd thought Sean might like the education, the archeological commentary, but suddenly this seems inappropriate.

"A bog body is it?" Eamon wipes at the pool of milk on the tray, then gives up, sets the rag down, detaches the tray from the highchair. "Hold her, would you?" He goes over to the sink and Dermot puts his hand to the child's chest just as she leans forward. Dermot thinks briefly of Deirdre, in her mother's house doing similar chores.

"I don't see why he shouldn't go. I'd go myself but I'm working in Galway. Seems they're getting set to run zodiac tours out the coast."

The baby looks up at Dermot and opens her mouth, small bits of cereal all over her tongue. She spits up on her bib, on Dermot's hand.

When Eamon snaps the tray back into place, Dermot lets go.

"I'll go call Sean." Eamon starts to head out of the kitchen. Not wanting to be left with the baby, Dermot says, "Just have him by before nine if he's to go."

"Right."

And Eamon watches Dermot Fay, who, until now, had never said more than ten words to him, walk through his living room and out of his house.

Sean is at the cottage at nine on the nose, with Mary in tow. He's wearing good clothes — a white shirt and black trousers. Abbey says hello from the bathroom door, a toothbrush lathered in her mouth. Mary runs through the cottage all the way into the bedroom. Plunks herself down on the mattress. Flagon by the bookshelf, wagging her tail. Sean sits on the couch while Dermot stands at the kitchen sink and recounts the various finds in Irish bogs. A cup of tea in his hand. An old love song on the radio. When Abbey is ready, her hair pulled into a ponytail, her boots on, they stand a moment before turning, starting out the door.

By the time they get to Screeb the traffic has slowed. Mary, in the backseat, runs her fingers over the ridges of her corduroy pants. "Are we there?" she asks, sitting up straight to look out the window.

"Not yet," Sean says.

"Now?"

"No. You just asked me." Sean sits back and studies the side of Abbey's face. She has her left arm dangling out the window. When the traffic picks up speed she lifts her hand, fingers splayed in the wind.

"Are we there now?" Mary asks.

"No."

Waiting a second, finger running up and down the corduroy tread. "Now?"

"Mary!"

"What?"

Sean reaches out and taps her head with his fist. "Stop it."

Dermot takes the bay road and follows the line of cars in front of him. Abbey looks out at the countryside and is amazed again at how beautiful everything seems. The coast to her left and fields to her right. Two boys on bicycles racing each other on the roadside. Near town, a line of houses with brightly coloured doors. Abbey wonders if she'd ever grow tired of it, take it for granted. Wonders why she never saw Woodslee or Windsor as beautiful. All that dry heat, the old brick houses and apartment buildings wavering in the sun. Although there was something pleasing about the winter — the first few hours of the day when the snow came and stayed, coated everything. Abbey's father would take her to toboggan down Elsbury Hill. She remembers the two of them trudging up to the top, how he'd hold the sled until she was properly on it. And then he'd simply let go. The speed of it coursing down to the valley bottom. Abbey alone, pulling the cords to steer it.

Overhead the birds fly north and west, follow the procession. Dermot puts his foot down on the gas, hits his knee on the underside of the dashboard when he changes gears.

"Would you believe it?" he says, looking in the rearview mirror at the line of cars behind them. "You'd think someone had died."

The only funeral Abbey had been to before Frank's was her Grandpa Gowan's. They rode behind the hearse with Grandma Gowan and Abbey had laughed the whole time out of nervousness. Her mother, fed up, had told her to turn and count the number of cars behind them. Abbey got to ten, then was happy to hang over the headrest, watch the cortege that followed, wave at Jane who was driving behind them. It was 1983 and Abbey was seven. She didn't know about the Shaws then, didn't know that the Gowans weren't Frank's biological parents, that he'd been given to them. That they had kept him in the dark all those years, when they could have been honest with him about where he'd come from. Abbey had watched the cars as they drove along. Her mother pointing out how people always pulled over to let the funeral procession go by. The sunlight that day glinting off the windshields, Abbeys legs sticking to the vinyl seat. Her father saying solemnly, "All things considered, he was a good man." That's what amazes her now. The forgiveness in his words. Perhaps Frank had thought that whatever else the man had done, whatever secrets he'd kept from him, at least he'd stood by him. "All things considered." That was Frank's way of weighing a person's worth in the end, and Abbey suddenly wishes she'd said the same of him.

Starting In

MICHAEL stands near the excavation site, watching people come across the bog, mill around the fourth field. The Bord has made everyone sign waivers, stay within a cordoned-off area. Men in hardhats and white short-sleeved shirts at the gates are trying to keep everything in order. *No, you can't bring the dog on the site. No, you'll have to sell the biscuits out here. I'm afraid the toilets are for staff only.* The public relations people out in force, walking amongst the locals, talking about the conservation work they're doing, pointing out Maam Island at the end of the field. *Home to twelve distinct species of birds.*

Michael watches it all, starts to think ahead to how the excavation will proceed. He's waiting for Hopkins to come from Dublin, but all eyes are on him. Una and Gerry are still trekking back and forth, bringing equipment from the van. Around Michael a hundred people from all parts of the county move around the bog as if at a fair ground. Two men from the Museum and the paleobotanist from Clare stand just outside the pit marveling at the size of the gathering.

Three Garda stand beside them: Sergeant Joyce, Charley from Oranmore, and another one, a stout man with a pencil between his fingers, who's been holding a note pad to his chest for the better part of an hour. He's yet to write anything down. Michael looks again to the dirt road for Hopkins and the license but there's only a parked tractor and two lathered ponies tethered to an oak stump on the far side of the tracks.

He hadn't called Janey. Dermot was right. Instead he called his father in London and told him that he was finally going to dig something up. That this would be the one significant thing he'll have unearthed with his own hand. Looking across the field Michael scans the crowd for Dermot, has him listed as an assistant digger. He looks for Abbey but doesn't see her either. Jack Hopkins coming at last, walking towards the open flap of the bog.

When Hopkins, a needle of a man, arrives, it's just after ten. A hush settles over the crowd. Napkins and paper cups, a newspaper, are picked up by the wind. Keating, who has made over fifty Euros selling biscuits from her van, picks up the napkins nearest her, stuffing them in a bag. The good weather has dried most of the crumb, but as people walk over the surface of the bog the top layer of peat gets pushed down. The ground takes on a clay-like appearance.

The first twenty minutes pass uneventfully. Michael, the Museum keeper and Gerry slowly scrape the peat away. The wall with the flags remains covered while the three of them work from above. Una beside the pile of discarded soil, running the crumb through a screen. She looks up nervously every now and again, wonders if the crowd will rush the ropes when they finally uncover something. An hour goes by. The trio has trowelled down thirty centimetres. Gerry making faces the whole time that the crowd has tried to read. People come and go, wander back to their cars looking for entertainment. Liam, standing near the pit, points out the rabbit warren to a young girl inside the ropes. The crowd's focus shifts. Those who'd been holding their breath finally let it go. Later still, the congregation near the pit starts to thin. Groups of people from different villages retire back towards the trenches, stand in circles, discussing Ahern's election, the Cup, last week's episode of "Ros na Run." Here and there throughout the crowd a mobile phone rings and someone answers it, saying, "No, no, nothing yet." The sun bright, the birds circling. A breeze coming across the lough.

Michael wipes sweat from his eyes every minute or so. Works the brush over the peat, trying to expose the top of the head. That way they'll know exactly how far back they have to cut. O'Flynn from the Museum works near the area where they think they'll find the feet. After twenty minutes he looks over at Michael.

"Anything?"

"Not yet."

Michael goes back to the brush. Looks around for Dermot.

Dermot cuts through the crowd, shoulders his way closer to the front. A "guest" badge pinned to his coat pocket. Turning to make sure Abbey's following, he sees Deirdre McGilloway, the baby in a blanket against the crook of her neck. He stops and takes a few steps back through the crowd until he's standing in front of her. "Dermot!" She's happy to see him.

"How's the lad?"

"Grand. Both of us."

Abbey arrives with Sean and Mary. Deirdre sets the baby down in the pram.

"Has he a name?" Dermot asks.

"John. After my father."

"This is Abbey and Mary. Sean."

"The Canadian?" Deirdre puts her hand out. Abbey shakes it. Dermot answering, "The very one."

Michael's shirt is soaked with sweat. Both he and Gerry stop to take a break. They must be nearing the body. Hopkins takes photos very five centimeters and Una measures the cut, writing it on a slate board. The tarp hanging over the side wall of the pit. The Garda standing outside it, keeping everyone at bay. The whole of it starting to look like a giant peat step, Michael, Gerry and O'Flynn on the mount. For the next hour, word of the excavation's progress goes back and forth through the crowd.

"They're still digging."

"The Brit's gone down into the pit."

"The tarp's come off."

"The Museum man has stepped away."

By noon, tired of digging down, Michael decides to approach the body from a different angle. They start taking layers off the side of the east wall, above the hand, Michael brushing away the dry crumb. Layers of it landing at his feet. Finally he hits something hard, resistant. What he imagines must be a shoulder. The folds of skin are evident, marked by dirt creases. No bigger, Michael thinks, than a flower bulb, and the same dark brown. Wiping away the clumps of dirt, using his fingers, Michael clears off a square inch of skin.

"I've got a shoulder." He looks up for Hopkins and the camera, sees Dermot instead, standing at the edge of the pit. He's leaning forward, watching the excavation.

"Fay, give us a hand, will you?"

Jack Hopkins looks up as a wild-looking man on the other side of the rope hesitates, then steps over the boundary, climbs down the ladder, walks over to Michael.

"Professor Fay, Jack Hopkins of the National Museum. Jack, this is Dermot Fay, we taught together at Trinity. And I believe you know Una and Gerry." The two kids, covered in dirt, nod hello.

"O'Flynn, why not try for the ribs here," Michael says, indicating the cut-away he'd already been digging.

"And Dermot, go up top with Gerry and start in at this angle." He shows Dermot the direction, a sharp slant in and down. "We need to get an approximate on the head. Once we have the parameters of the body we can cut a square of turf around it. Take it out in situ."

Twenty minutes later the line of the right arm comes up from under the peat. Michael brushing the dirt away in quick strokes, scooping the pile of it away towards the corner of the pit with the cup of his hands. He sees the arm come up out of the earth, the back of the hand he'd first noticed, and it seems to him that this arm is reaching out to him, waiting for him to catch hold. The wrist thin-boned like a woman's.

Standing by the ropes Sean has one hand on the collar of Mary's shirt. She's tried to worm her way out of the crowd twice already and he isn't keen on losing her. Abbey to the right of him, watching what's going on.

"Is that the arm?" Sean asks.

Abbey leans forward and left to get a better view. "I think so."

And then, without saying anything, Sean reaches out and takes Abbey's hand. The palm soft and warm, smaller than his. He doesn't look at her. Waits for her to let go. His heart hammering away in his chest.

"Sean."

He doesn't look over. Thinks that if he ignores Abbey, she'll hold on.

Her voice is quiet. "Sean. Look at me."

He lets go of Mary's collar, turns to face Abbey.

"You're very sweet. But," she squeezes his hand, "there's nothing —" letting go of his hand, pointing back and forth between the two of them. "I'm sorry." She screws up her face as if she wishes she didn't have to say it. Sean shrugs and stares at the ground. After a minute Abbey takes his face in her hands and kisses his forehead. Feels how flushed he is before she turns away.

Dermot is aware of the thirty or so pairs of legs behind the ropes. Every now and again someone calls out to him, asks where things are at, but he doesn't look up. He'd seen Abbey somewhere behind the ropes, Sean and Mary beside her. Angus and Tomás were watching for a while before they headed back into the crowd. Earlier, he'd run into Liam in the parking lot. They'd nodded hello. Inevitably, Dermot thinks, the boy will run into Deirdre. They'll meet somewhere in the middle of the bog, or back in town, or eventually she might take up a pen as Sophie had done, and write Liam a letter. *He's yours. You have a son.* And what happens after that is up to them.

About two centimeters down, Dermot thinks he has something. The roots thicker in one spot so he has to use his fingers to gently pull them apart. He calls Jack over to take a photo. Brushes another layer away. Realizing all of a sudden that he's found the tip of the head. Rust coloured tresses come up like lost vines, the start of a braid evident.

When Michael has the arm up to the shoulder, when the top of the head is uncovered, when they realize her legs are curled up against her, that underground she is resting her chin on her chest, they stop, look up. Word is out. The crowd has come back and people jostle, trying not to fall over the perimeter ropes that surround the pit. Everyone wants to see a face, but all they can see is hair, a thin slip of her forehead. Michael makes plans to cut the wedge below her, to try to hack out the whole square of peat she's resting in. "Her knee's bent anyway. It's getting down far enough that's the concern." They guess at safe parameters, mark off what must be ten centimetres from the soles of her feet.

MICHAEL and Gerry, both of them exhausted, look at the part of the head that Dermot's uncovered. Jack, on his knees, takes three photos. Una stares down at the skin of the woman's forehead. Dermot keeps working. Pulls away another layer of peat, wants, against reason, to see her face. To see her unencumbered, come up from the ground, like a body coming up in the bath.

Abbey watches Dermot from behind the ropes, sees his right hand gripping the brush handle, swinging back and forth in an even rhythm. His eyes never leave the ground. When Abbey met Dermot at the Old Bailey, one of the first things he'd said to her was, "If I had it to do over again …" But he never finished the sentence because he knew there was no going back. And Abbey saw something wonderful in that, in him having lived a life that he could sit with. She loved how he knew it wasn't ideal, how he'd have done it differently, but how he accepted it just the same. And the fact that he didn't rally against it comforted her. But now things are different. The world has opened up and he's going in to meet it. For the first time, Abbey sees in him the possibility of moving on. That he might go back to Dublin. Find Rory. Stand up to it, after all.

When Dermot has uncovered the dead woman's eyes, brushed away the layer of peat over them, Abbey has to look away. Wonders, then, if this woman is watching — if she's standing somewhere in the crowd, if she's witnessing her own exhumation as if it were her birth. Abbey's grandmother died giving birth to Frank — that was something Frank had wanted Abbey to know. He said, once, that every woman he ever knew had left him; his mother, Stella, was simply the first.

Abbey believes that when Stella Shaw gave birth to Frank, she knew he would wrestle with her dying all his life. But even in that last instant, the baby's head just through, she probably didn't regret his birth; was ascending the stairwell, could hear the clamour of those who had gone before her in a room somewhere above. The baby suddenly apart from her — a boy, Frank, being held up for her to look at, although her eyes were already reeling. Stella standing at the far door, the same way this woman in the ground must once have done, knowing it would open for her, and without so much as a sound, going in.

Looking around, Abbey sees a clutch of familiar faces from Spiddal, a few dozen men and women from other towns, and Dermot, who is intent on the digging, who hasn't looked up to find her. The breeze is coming over from the nearby lough and Abbey, tired of being jostled in the melee of people trying to get a view, sets out towards the lake. "I was given up." That's what her father had said, time and time again, and if she listens now, if she concentrates under the din of voices, she can hear him saying it. "I was let go."

The lough is choppy and grey and the wash of waves against the shore leaves spray that settles in drops on Abbey's shoes. There's a small treed island about a quarter of a mile out in the water. A stone wall there, ruined. And a wood fence that starts out from the pier before it disappears in a copse of trees. Abbey sits on the edge of the lake contemplating the company that is her dead father, and so, when Frank sits down beside her, Abbey isn't frightened. She sees him dip his bare feet into the shallow bank of the lake. Wiggle his toes. But the water doesn't ripple. He looks over at Abbey and tries to smile. He reaches out to touch her, but his hand never arrives. Instead he just stares at her as if to say he's sorry.

"Whatever happened to Mom?" It's what Abbey has always wanted to ask. Frank shrugs as if to say maybe she's still in Ontario, standing across from the movie theatre where they left her, that maybe she's here in the space between them, that maybe she's buried in the ground. He shrugs again as if to say, *I'm dead and I have no idea.*

One night, a month before the fire, in a state of atonement, he'd told her: *This isn't what I thought my life would be. I'm sorry I wasn't a good father.* He'd spread his hands on his lap and looked up at her. Maybe all this time, since the funeral, he'd been trying to remind her of that. Trying to tell her that more than anything, he just didn't want to be left alone.

When Abbey was ten, eleven, twelve, they'd played hide and seek. Frank would hide in out-of-the-way places, in the fold-out couch, or in the storage attic that was above the trap door inside the closet. He'd leave the closet door open so that it would be easier for Abbey to find him, had even called her name to bring her closer. What Abbey remembers now is how often he'd come out before she'd given up, as if he was afraid of the moment she'd throw her hands up in the air and stop looking.

"I'm sorry." It's all she can say. But she means it. Sorry she stood on the grave, sorry he'd told her everything and she hadn't really listened, sorry she used him as a reason to run when running away had always been her inclination. And in that instant of apology, Abbey regrets everything and nothing all at once. Realizes we have no choice in it, that we are surrounded in the muck of our history whether we like it or not. Like the woman in the bog. Like Dermot, like Frank.

Abbey takes off her boots and socks and dips her feet into the lough. The water is cold. Waves lap over her toes. She looks across to the Island and its fence and then she looks behind her, hoping to see Dermot. But all she can see is the slope of the bog that leads up to the excavation. She looks over to where Frank was sitting, but he's gone. The waves crest and fall. The birds on the Island trill and go quiet.

In the cordoned-off area, Dermot sits back on his knees, his temples throbbing. The nerves up and down his left arm tingle. Looking down into the bowl he's dug out of the peat, he sees the woman's forehead, the thin needles of her eyebrows, the caved-in nose. Her hair steeling out around her.

"I've uncovered more of the face," Dermot says.

Michael climbs the ladder out of the pit. Comes over, stands beside him.

"Jesus. Jack, come here with the camera."

They stand there a minute before taking photos. The woman's eyes squeezed shut, thin traces of roots woven over them like a veil. The fine arc of her eyebrows above.

Michael is the first to speak, says, "Cover her back up with a thin layer of peat. We can't have the skin exposed."

Dermot stands up and reaches over to the pile of peat he's just wiped off her. Then he leans down, looks at the folds and creases of her skin, the protrusion of cheekbone under what looks like leather. Her forehead is smooth, fine wisps of hair still evident. Dermot wants to salute her. Instead he buries her again under the wet muck. A mediaeval woman in a bath of peat, roots grown out of her ears, out of the hole that was her nose. A leather cinch around her neck like the strap Michael'd shown him. Dermot thinking *I know what it's like. All those years.* Putting a layer over her for safe-keeping and then another. Knowing that sooner or later she'll be rid of it all. His hand over her. Over the way she is perfectly herself. The peat covering her eyes, her nose, her lips. Layer after layer until she's gone again.

Standing at the Close

DERMOT takes Abbey home and neither of them speak. Sean sits in the back of the car with Mary, and the girl puts her dirt-stained fingers to the side window. She smudges circle shapes onto the glass, laughs at what she's done. Michael is in the truck that is taking the block of peat, the body of a long dead woman, towards Dublin and the National Museum. When they finally wash the white roots of bog plants from her lips, when they pull the turf from her mouth as if it is a dark tongue, they will stand back and wait for her to speak. They will lean forward against all reason, and she will say nothing.

When Dermot begins to pack his things the afternoon after the dig, he too is silent. Abbey sits on the bed waiting for the reel of thoughts that will lead her to her father, even though she knows they are gone.

Standing at the close of the field, Sean tests the last post and kicks away the stone beside it. He watches it roll a few feet into the grass before it settles. The good weather has arrived, the days are already longer. He looks towards the cottage and decides he won't come back. Then he looks towards Spiddal and is struck by the fact that things are changing day by day. The construction still underway. The village expanding. Behind him the crows caraw, lift up from the clothesline when Dermot enters the yard.

When Dermot passes by Sean, he reaches out and pats him on the back. He keeps going then, with Flagon at his heels, the sound of a bulldozer droning on the far side of the bungalows. He walks with his boot laces undone, with dried dirt still caked on his hands; he walks, and only at the bridge does he pause long enough to look back, to see if Abbey is following.

The old church is basked in sunlight so that even the cider bottles tossed in the corner, the plastic wrappers scattered about, even the green spray-painted graffiti that's gone up, seem to have a glow about them. The stagnant pools of water have gone, the goat willow climbing the nave wall has grown, its leaves flitting about in the breeze that drops down through the ceiling holes. The walls rebuilt with small stones are holding, the chapel closed in on three sides. Dermot sits in the first pew and the wood creaks as it did when he went to mass as a boy. He sits and he closes his eyes, feels the sunlight warm his face. When he gets back he will call and have the property put up for sale. He'll pay the boy for the fence. He'll ask Abbey to go with him to Dublin although he knows she will not have him. He could tell her that he's yet to become the man he wants to be, but she will know better than to believe him. Already he has a sense that time is waning, just as he's come round to figuring things out.

Walking out of the old church, Dermot hears a hundred doors close behind him, he hears voices as if down a long hallway, he hears his own rasp of breath, the clomp of his footfall as he makes for the bridge. Abbey will be coming from the cottage, she will be crossing the field on her way to him. This is how it goes between them, this much is certain.

Twenty feet ahead of Dermot, Flagon starts barking. It's when Dermot comes through the trees that he sees Abbey, raises his hand. Abbey stops, waves back, smiling. They hold still a minute and the breeze settles down around them, the long grass standing up, the clouds out over the ocean fixed firmly in place. They walk towards each other then and the world goes back to its means. The cows swat flies with their tails, the wire is nailed to the last post, the dead watch the living. Call out, even if no one chooses to hear.

Acknowledgements

MANY THANKS to Lynn Henry, a wonderful editor, and to my agent Carolyn Swayze for finding this book a home. To George McWhirter who waded through the early drafts with great insight. To Jack Hodgins for the same. Thanks to Kerry Ohana and Angela McGoldrick. To everyone at Raincoast Books. To the National Museum in Dublin. To D for his notes and generosity. To my mother for braving the bog. And to Glenn, for his patience, humour and wisdom.

On page iv, the first epigraph is from Dermot Healy's poem "Rosses Point" in *The Ballyconnell Colours*, published by The Gallery Press. The second epigraph is from Michael Hartnett's "Anatomy of a Cliché," published in his *Selected and New Poems* by The Gallery Press.

PHOTO CREDIT: GLENN HUNTER

AISLINN HUNTER was born in Belleville, Ontario, and moved to Dublin, Ireland, for a few years before making her home in British Columbia. She currently teaches Creative Writing at the University of Victoria. She is the author of two previous books, *What's Left Us and Other Stories* (Polestar, 2001), which was shortlisted for the Danuta Gleed Award and the ReLit Award for Fiction, and *Into the Early Hours* (Polestar, 2001), which was shortlisted for the Dorothy Livesay Prize and won the Gerald Lampert Award for Best First Book of Poetry. She lives in Vancouver with her husband Glenn and their dog Fiddle.